ASYLUM

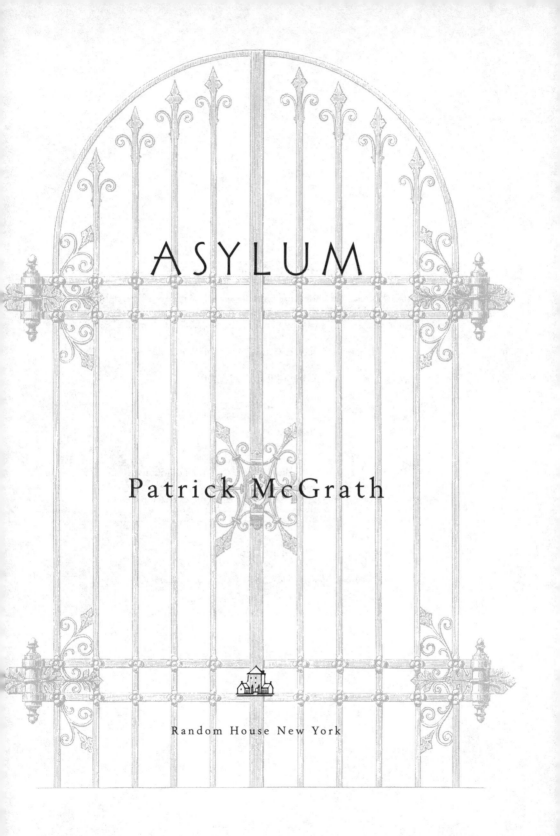

ASYLUM

Patrick McGrath

Random House New York

Copyright © 1997 by Patrick McGrath

All rights reserved under International and Pan-American Copyright
Conventions. Published in the United States by Random House, Inc., New York,
and simultaneously in Canada by Random House of Canada Limited, Toronto.

Library of Congress Cataloging-in-Publication Data
McGrath, Patrick.
Asylum / Patrick McGrath.
p.   cm.
ISBN: 0-679-45228-1
I.   Title.
PS3563.C3663A89   1997
813'.54—dc20   96-24849

Random House website address: http://www.randomhouse.com/

Printed in the United States of America on acid-free paper

2   4   6   8   9   7   5   3

First Edition

Book design by Caroline Cunningham

For Jack Davenport

ACKNOWLEDGMENTS

For all her help and support in the writing of this, my love and gratitude to my wife, Maria; and for his assistance with matters of psychiatry, my warmest thanks to Dr. Brian O'Connell.

ASYLUM

The catastrophic love affair characterized by sexual obsession has been a professional interest of mine for many years now. Such relationships vary widely in duration and intensity but tend to pass through the same stages. Recognition. Identification. Assignation. Structure. Complication. And so on. Stella Raphael's story is one of the saddest I know. A deeply frustrated woman, she suffered the predictable consequences of a long denial collapsing in the face of sudden overwhelming temptation. And she was a romantic. She translated her experience with Edgar Stark into the stuff of melodrama, she made of it a tale of outcast lovers braving the world's contempt for the sake of a great passion. Four lives were destroyed in the process, but whatever remorse she may have felt she clung to her illusions to the end. I tried to help but she deflected me from the truth until it was too late. She had to. She couldn't afford to let me see it clearly, it would have been the ruin of the few flimsy psychic structures she had left.

Stella was married to a forensic psychiatrist called Max Raphael and they had a son, Charlie, aged ten when all this happened. She was the daughter of a diplomat who'd been disgraced in a scandal years before. Both her parents were dead now. She was barely out of her teens when she married Max. He was a reserved, rather melancholy man, a competent administrator but weak; and he lacked imagination. It was obvious to me the first time I met them that he wasn't the type to satisfy a woman like Stella. They were living in London when he applied for the position of deputy superintendent. He came down for an interview, impressed the board and, more important, impressed the superintendent, Jack Straffen. Against my advice Jack offered him the job, and a few weeks later the Raphaels arrived at the hospital. It was the summer of 1959 and the Mental Health Act had just been passed into law.

This is a desolate sort of a place, though God knows it's had the best years of my life. It is maximum-security, a walled city that rises from a high ridge to dominate the surrounding country: dense pine forest to the north and west, low-lying marshland to the south. It is built on the standard Victorian linear model, with wings radiating off the main blocks so that all the wards have an unobstructed view across the terraces to the open country beyond the Wall. This is a moral architecture, it embodies regularity, discipline, and organization. All doors open outward to make them impossible to barricade. All windows are barred. Only the terraces, descending by flights of stone steps to the perimeter wall at the foot of the hill, and planted with trees, grassy banks, and flower gardens, soften and civilize the grim carceral architecture standing over them.

The deputy superintendent's house is just a hundred yards from the Main Gate. It is a large dark house of the same gray stone as the hospital, set back from the estate road and hidden by pine trees. It was much too big for the Raphaels, having been built at a time when doctors came with large families and at least two servants. For several years before their arrival it had stood empty, and the garden was neglected and wild. To my surprise Max took an immediate interest in its rehabilitation. He had the goldfish pond at the back of the house cleaned out and restocked, and the rhododendron bushes around the edge of the lawn cut back and made to flower.

The project that most interested him however was the restoration of an old conservatory at the far end of the vegetable garden. This was a large ornate glasshouse built in the last century for the cultivation of orchids and lilies and other delicate tropical plants. In its time it had been an imposing, airy structure, but when Max and Stella arrived it was in a state of such disrepair there was talk of pulling it down. Much of the glass was broken and what panes remained were thick with dust and cobwebs. The paintwork had flaked off and the woodwork in places was rotted and splitting. Birds had nested inside it, mice and spiders had made their home there, weeds had sprouted through the cracks in the stone floor.

But Max Raphael had an affection for all things Victorian, and the exotic architecture of this garden conservatory, with its intricate glazing and joinery, and the graceful Romanesque arches of its windows, all this gave him peculiar delight. He was fortunate that among the hospital's parole patients was a man confident that he could do the work of restoring the conservatory. This was the sculptor Edgar Stark.

Edgar was one of mine. I have always been fascinated by the artistic personality, I think because the creative impulse is so vital a quality in psychiatry; certainly it is in my own clinical work. Edgar Stark was already influential in the art world when he came to us, though what we first saw was a confused and very shaky man who shuffled into the hospital like a wounded bear and sat hunched on a bench for hours with his head in his hands. He intrigued me from the start, and once I'd settled him down and got him talking I discovered him to be a forceful individual with an original mind, and I also realized that he was possessed of considerable charm, when he chose to use it. He and I quickly came to enjoy a warmly combative relationship, which I encouraged, up to a point; I wanted him to feel he had a special relationship with his doctor.

At the same time I was wary of him, for his was a restless,

devious intelligence. He was quick to grasp the workings of the hospital and always alert to his own interest. I knew I could rely on him to exploit any situation to his own advantage.

Oddly enough I saw him with Stella only once, and that was at a hospital dance, a year after the Raphaels arrived here and just three weeks after he began working for Max in his garden, around the beginning of June. Dances are important events in the hospital calendar and there is always much excitement beforehand. They take place in the Central Hall, a spacious high-ceilinged room in the Administration Block with a stage at one end, a line of pillars down the middle, and casement windows opening onto the top terrace. Soft drinks and sandwiches are spread on long trestle tables at the back, and the band sets up onstage. Parole patients from both the male and female wings of the hospital may attend, and for this one evening they and the staff become an extended family without distinction of rank or status.

This at least is the idea. The truth is, the mentally ill are not at their best at a dance. Our patients dress eccentrically and move awkwardly, handicapped as much by the medication they take as by the illnesses that make the medication necessary. Despite the energetic efforts of the hospital band, and the contrived high spirits of the staff, I have always found it a poignant affair, and attend out of duty rather than in anticipation of any pleasure. That night, as I watched the proceedings from the shadow of a pillar at the rear of the Hall, I was not surprised to see Edgar Stark approach the deputy superintendent's wife, nor to see her step out onto the floor with him. The band went into something quick and Latin and she darted away in his arms.

Until recently I didn't learn precisely what happened next. Perhaps I should have guessed that something was wrong, for I noticed her becoming slightly flushed. I watched them move briskly across the floor, passing directly in front of the superintendent's table, and it is only now that I recognize just how bold, and bald, and reckless was the insult Edgar flung in our faces that night.

The dance ended promptly at ten and the patients filed out

noisily. Jack asked those of his senior staff remaining in the Hall to come back for a drink. I strolled along the top terrace with Max, both of us in dinner jackets and both smoking good cigars as we chatted about various of our patients. The sky was clear, the breeze warm, and the world spread beneath us, the terraces, the Wall, the marsh beyond, all was dim and still in the moonlight.

Stella's voice drifted clearly back to us on the warm night air. Oh, I have known many elegant and lovely women, but none matched Stella that night. She was in a low-cut black evening dress of coarse ribbed silk, an exquisite grosgrain I had never seen before. The neckline was square and showed the curve of her breasts. It clung to her body then belled from the waist, scooped in a fold over each knee like a tulip, with a split between. She was wearing very high heels and a wrap thrown loosely about her shoulders. She was asking Jack about her last dance partner, and as I heard my patient's name I glimpsed again in my mind's eye the shuffling men and women in their ill-fitting clothes, something subtly askew about all of them except him.

Jack was standing at the end of the terrace, holding open the gate for Max and me. Stella was clearly amused at the sight of two consultant psychiatrists in dinner jackets hurrying so as not to keep their superintendent waiting. A minute or two later we were in the Straffens' drawing room and the phone was ringing. It was the chief attendant, to tell the super that everyone was present and accounted for and the hospital was safely locked up for the night.

I am not a gregarious man, and at social gatherings I tend to stay in the background. I let others come to me, it is a privilege of seniority. I stood by the window in the Straffens' drawing room and murmured small talk to the wives of my colleagues as they each in turn drifted over. I watched Stella listening to Jack tell a story about something that had happened at a hospital dance twenty years before. Jack liked Stella for the same reasons I did, for her wit, her composure, and her striking looks. I know she was considered beautiful: her eyes were much remarked on, and she had a pale, almost translucent complexion and thick blond hair, almost white, cut rather short, which she brushed straight back off her forehead. She was rather a fleshy, full-breasted woman, taller than the average, and that night she was wearing a single string of pearls that nicely set off the whiteness of her neck and shoulders and bosom. In those days I considered her a friend, and often wondered about her unconscious life. I asked myself was there peace and order beneath that demure exterior, or did she simply control her neuroses better than other women? A stranger, I reflected, would take her self-possession for aloofness, or even indifference, and in fact when she first arrived at the hospital she encountered resistance and hostility for this very reason.

But most of the women accepted her now. She had made an effort to join several of the hospital committees and generally to pull her weight as senior staff wives are supposed to. As for Max, he stood there with his glass of dry sherry, listening with a half-smile of slightly distracted indulgence as various horror stories were told by the women about their misadventures on the dance floor with patients of such clumsiness that they put last year's plodders and stampers to shame.

Stella did talk about Edgar Stark that night, but not to the company at large, and certainly without any mention of what he'd done in the Hall. It was when she reached my side that she told me the man danced like a dream—wasn't he a patient of mine?

Oh yes, he was one of mine all right. I suppose it was with a sort of affectionate cynicism that I said this, for I seem to remember that she peered at me closely as though it were important.

"He works in the garden," she said. "I often see him. I won't ask you what you think of him, because I know you won't tell me."

"As you saw yourself," I protested. "An extroverted man, well liked, and possessed of a certain, oh, animal vitality."

"Animal vitality," said Stella. "Yes, he has that all right. Is he very sick?"

"Pretty sick," I said.

"You wouldn't know it," she said, "from talking to him."

She turned and glanced at the party, the little clusters of those old familiars, each one distinct and idiosyncratic as tends to be the case in psychiatric communities. "We *are* more eccentric than the general population, aren't we?" she murmured, her eyes on the crowd.

"Undoubtedly."

"Max says psychiatry attracts people with high anxiety about going mad."

"Max must speak for himself."

This elicited a sidelong glance from those large sleepy eyes.

"I noticed you didn't dance once," she said.

"You know I'm hopeless at this sort of thing."

"But the ladies enjoy it so. You should, for their sake."

"How saintly you're becoming, my dear."

At this she turned and gazed at me. She hitched up the strap of her dress, which had slipped off her shoulder. "Saintly?" she said, and I saw Max looking in our direction, absently polishing his spectacles, his mournful demeanor faltering not a jot. She noticed him too and, turning away, murmured, "And my reward, I suppose, will be in heaven."

Later that evening I returned to my office to write up my observations. I had been impressed with Edgar's behavior. Watching him dance with Stella it was hard to believe that he suffered a disorder involving severe disturbance in his relationships with women. He had been a working sculptor for some years before he came to us, and was, as such, subject to the unique pressures that a life in art imposes. About a year before his admission he became obsessed with the idea that his wife, Ruth, was having an affair with another man. By all accounts Ruth Stark was a quiet, sensible woman; she modeled for Edgar and supported him financially much of the time. But as a result of his wild and violent accusations the marriage became severely strained and she threatened to leave him.

One night after they'd been drinking there was a terrible quarrel and he bludgeoned her to death with a hammer. What he did to her *after* that indicated to us how very disturbed he was. No one came to help Ruth Stark though her screams were heard the length of the street. Edgar was in a profound state of shock when he reached us. I tidied him up and then prepared to see him through the inevitable reaction of grief and guilt. But to my concern there was no grief or guilt; he regained his equilibrium after a few weeks and was soon involved in a variety of hospital activities.

We were worried about him. Although he functioned at a high level of intelligence he never showed any insight into why he had killed his wife. What troubled me was not just the persistence of his delusions, it was their intrinsic absurdity. He claimed to have a wealth of evidence of Ruth's infidelity, but when asked for it he produced only trivial everyday occurrences, into which he read bizarre, extravagant meanings. A flushing toilet, a stain on the floor, the placement of a box of washing powder on a windowsill, these were the sorts of things that signified. He had otherwise fully recovered his sanity and was ready to be released, but he remained on this one point unshakable, that the murder was justified. Oh, he agreed it shouldn't have happened, and he regretted drinking so much, but he insisted that he'd been driven to it by her taunts and insults. I didn't feel we should let him out yet, and nor did anyone else. He'd been with us for five years, and it looked to me as though he'd be with us another five at least. This was how things stood when he was given the job of restoring Max Raphael's conservatory.

Every morning that summer several parties of parole patients, each under the supervision of an attendant, and all dressed in baggy yellow corduroy trousers and blue shirts, with white canvas jackets slung over their shoulders, emerged from the Main Gate to maintain the grounds of the estate. Edgar was one of the group assigned to the deputy superintendent's garden. Stella often saw him when she went out to pick vegetables or flowers, and if there was no sign of the attendant, a senior man called John Archer, she would sit for a few minutes and they would talk. She admitted she was attracted to him almost from the start. For obvious reasons she tried to ignore the feeling, but his presence out there every day made it easy for her to invent pretexts for seeing him. Though what harm was there in befriending a patient? This is what she said to herself, in justification of her behavior.

How had it happened?

On this point she couldn't at first give me any sort of satisfactory answer. She avoided my eyes, she became vague. Perhaps it was just a case of household lust, easily enough aroused, just as easily crushed out, but when I suggested this the dreamy abstraction vanished and for a moment I felt a flare of spirited hostility from her. Then it faded. She was already deeply depressed; she could not sustain affect. She mentioned something he'd done one day that expressed, oh, strength, tenderness . . .

Perhaps. I let it pass.

Then in a later conversation she described it more fully, what it was he'd done that had so charmed and attracted her at the beginning. She'd gone into the vegetable garden one warm afternoon to pick some lettuce, and saw Charlie down at the far end with a patient, the big black-haired man she had been aware of simply as the one working on Max's conservatory, she didn't even know his name; this was a couple of weeks before the dance. Curious to see what the boy was up to, she wandered down the path and he shouted to her that he'd invented a test of strength, and that she should come and see. Charlie Raphael was an overweight little boy with pale skin like his mother's, which in the summer became lightly freckled. He had dark brown hair that fell over his forehead in a thick fringe, and when he grinned you could see the gap between his two rabbity front teeth. That summer he invariably wore a short-sleeved cotton shirt, baggy shorts, and sandals, and his legs were always scratched and muddy from his various outdoor projects.

Stella sat on the bench by the wall, in the shade, and watched as Charlie made the patient stand there on the path holding a spade horizontally with a hand at either end of the shaft, then, with his knees bent, ducked underneath and grasped the middle of the shaft.

"Lift!" he cried.

The patient glanced at Stella and lifted, and Charlie rose slowly off the ground, his face screwed up with concentration and his knees drawn up beneath him as he clung with both hands to the spade. "I'm counting!" he shouted. "One, two, three, four . . ."

He hung from the spade to a count of twenty, at which point Stella, laughing, begged him please to allow the poor man to put him down. "Down!" shouted Charlie, and was gently lowered onto the path. "You're a strong man," he said, gazing with admiration at Edgar, who seemed not at all strained by the ordeal. Stella told me that it was while Charlie was clinging like a monkey to the shaft of the spade that she felt the first stirring of interest in the man. He had good hands, she noticed, long, slender, delicate hands, and she wondered what his work was, on the outside.

The next day she again went down to the conservatory to see what he was doing. She freely chose to do so, nothing can excuse or obscure this fact. She found him up a ladder, removing broken glass from the frame of the structure, carefully working it free of the crumbling putty. He was dropping it into a dustbin beside the ladder, and every few moments the drowsy stillness of the afternoon was shattered by breaking glass. When he saw her approaching he came down the ladder and pulled off his heavy gloves.

"Mrs. Raphael," he said, standing squarely in front of her, panting slightly and pushing his hair off his forehead. He produced a red bandanna from his trouser pocket and wiped the sweat from his face and then from his hands, watching her throughout with an expression that she described as affable but at the same time mocking, somehow, or rather challenging, as though he wanted to provoke her to show him who she was.

"You didn't have to stop working," she said, quite at ease with this sort of jousting, and liking the man immediately. "I only wanted to see what you were doing."

"Edgar Stark."

They shook hands. Stella shielded her eyes as she turned away and gazed up at the conservatory. "Is it worth saving?" she said.

"Oh, it's a lovely thing. They built them to last back then. Like that place."

He grinned at her, indicating the Wall, visible through the pine trees on the far side of the garden by the road.

"This won't be quite so grim, I hope."

"It'll be a nice little summerhouse when I'm finished. Settling in all right?"

"We've been here a year."

"Is it that long?"

He took out his tobacco tin and began to roll a cigarette. It smacked of independence, this gesture, and she approved of it. He didn't behave like a patient.

"How long have you been here?" she said.

"Five years now, but I'll be out soon. I killed my wife."

When I heard this I thought, vintage Edgar. But Stella could match his candor.

"Why?"

"She betrayed me."

"I'm sorry."

He was no fool. Here there was tragedy, and she was sympathetic. The wife of a forensic psychiatrist was hardly likely to shrink in horror from such a confession.

"Were you a carpenter on the outside?" she said.

"Artist. Sculptor. Figurative mostly. You like art, Mrs. Raphael?"

"I have so little opportunity down here. In London, yes."

He wasn't at all obsequious, she said, this was her first impression, nor did he condescend to her. She said there was something solid and mature about him, and I couldn't help thinking of all the wildly delusional talk I'd heard on the subject

13

of his late wife. She wouldn't have thought him so solid and mature had she heard any of that, I thought. But she hadn't, and so, the next day, after gathering what she needed from the vegetable garden, she again went down to the conservatory.

He was up his ladder and this time he wasn't wearing a shirt. Charlie was on the garden wall, and Edgar was talking to the boy about football. He was a big man with broad shoulders and a heavy build, well fleshed out on the chest and hips and belly, with soft white skin. There was no hair on his body, and she thought he might be the sort of man who grew fat later in life. She suggested they might like a cold drink.

When she came back out with a jug of lemonade Edgar had his shirt on. She asked would he mind if she sat on the bench in the shade for a while. She enjoyed watching him work, she said, and I thought of Max, cerebral Max, as tall as Edgar but stooped, and pale, and forever polishing his spectacles; Max may have conceived the idea of restoring the conservatory, but it was another man's labor that carried it through. And already his efforts were apparent. Much of the old glass had gone, and the structure was beginning to assume a skeletal appearance. It was strangely beautiful, she said, and when she returned to the house this was the image she carried with her, of that big confident man up a ladder with his shirt off, carefully picking broken glass from the frame of the Victorian conservatory.

She went back the next day, and the day after. He told her about his son, the boy he'd deprived of a mother; Leonard, his name was, he'd be Charlie's age now, though Edgar hadn't seen him for more than five years. His late wife's family were looking after the boy and they were determined, he said, that he should never know who his father was. It was a story guaranteed to arouse a mother's sympathy.

All lies. Edgar had no son.

One day he asked her if he could call her by her first name, and she said yes, but not in front of John Archer or Charlie.

Another time, as he was sketching the design of an iron finial that had rusted badly and would have to be recast, he asked her if he could do her head. She said he could. He had her sit on the bench while he worked, and in a few minutes had produced a strange sketch, all smudged lines, not at all naturalistic, with none of the roundedness and monumentality I saw in Stella, but a curious likeness all the same. She asked if she could keep it and without a word he tore it from the pad and gave it to her.

"But you must sign it," she said.

She kept it in a locked drawer and showed it to nobody, for reasons she was reluctant to look at too closely. Nothing improper was occurring, on the surface, but she hadn't said a word about her new friend to Max; and by consistently failing to mention an event of significance in her day she was practicing a form of duplicity. She rationalized it. She should have known that deception eventually eats away all that is wholesome in a marriage, and she should have faced this, but she didn't. She chose not to. From this evasion all else followed.

Oh, but it was so trivial, she told herself, it was absurd to think that talking to a patient in the vegetable garden could amount to anything. But if it was all so trivial, why did she have to conduct this argument with herself? Because of her growing sexual warmth for the man, which she foolishly indulged in this oblique manner, seeking his company, allowing him into her imagination.

It was not easy at first for her to talk about any of this. I know she was tempted to blame fate, or the vagaries of the human heart, for what happened, the tragic outcome of it all. She had a natural impulse to displace responsibility, we all do, but she disliked the idea of making excuses or hiding behind abstractions. Edgar, the one person she might have blamed, instead she defended to the end. Not once did I hear her hold him responsible for what happened.

The first I knew of their growing intimacy was the day Charlie fell off the garden wall. There was an old apple tree beside the conservatory and when Edgar was up his ladder Charlie would scramble onto the wall, and from there climb into the tree. He was a fearless tree-climber but, being plump, not too agile, and one day as he was stepping out of the tree back onto the wall the branch broke—he lost his balance—and with a shout he tumbled onto the path and knocked himself out for a second or two.

Stella was upstairs when Edgar came striding in through the back door with the dazed boy in his arms. Mrs. Bain, the woman who helped with the housework, was sitting at the kitchen table shelling peas. She was the wife of a senior attendant, a man called Alec Bain, and it was he who told me later of his wife's reaction to a patient who came into the house without knocking, shouting for Mrs. Raphael and using her first name. He wanted to lay the boy down on a bed or a couch but Mrs. Bain lacked the presence of mind to direct him to the drawing room, so he pushed past her out through the kitchen and into the hall. She began to shout at him just as Stella came running down the stairs. She cried out in horror.

Charlie was all right. He recovered in a matter of minutes, and Stella didn't feel it necessary to phone Max at the hospital. She held him while Mrs. Bain went for a damp facecloth, showing by the shape of her back what she thought of patients who came barging into the house without being asked and called the doctor's wife by her first name. Charlie tried to get up but Stella told him he must lie still a little longer. She turned to Edgar, who stood there pushing his hands through his hair.

"Thank you for bringing him in," she said. She saw how relieved he was that the boy wasn't hurt. He clearly felt responsible.

"No harm done," he said.

"I don't imagine so. But we'll keep him inside for the rest of the day."

"No!" said Charlie.

"Oh yes," said Stella.

Edgar went out through the kitchen door. Stella knew she should try and explain to Mrs. Bain why he behaved toward her with such familiarity, but her old proud carelessness welled up and she didn't say a word, because she didn't see why she should.

.   .   .

Nothing physical had happened yet, but this incident helped establish a sort of bond between them. It should of course have been severed at this point, as soon as Stella saw that to behave so informally with a patient was bound to cause trouble sooner or later. But it didn't occur to her. At the time she didn't properly analyze why she was amused rather than alarmed by the incident, but later she said she thought it was because she found Mrs. Bain's attitude so ridiculous, as though patients belonged to a lower order.

He began to tell her about life in the hospital, and she was surprised that she had never understood before what went on other than from Max's point of view, the psychiatric perspective. Now she glimpsed a new perspective, she began to see how it was to live, eat, and sleep in an overcrowded ward, sixty men in a dormitory meant for thirty, and to put up with plumbing that dated back to the last century and rarely functioned properly. One story horrified her particularly, about a patient in Block 1 who washed his face in his own urine, then dried himself with the communal towel.

She became involved. Identification, hazy at first, hedged around with friendly detachment, quickened. The idea that this man, this *artist*, should suffer the indignities of primitive plumbing, lack of privacy, bullying, boredom, and utter uncertainty about his future, all this aroused her indignation. He was in Block 3 now, a parole patient with a room of his own, but he still had to tolerate much that, to Stella's sense of justice, was incompatible with the care and treatment of the mentally ill. Though she was starting to doubt that he *was* mentally ill. She thought he was guilty of a crime of passion; and passion, in essence, was good, surely?

He didn't push too hard. He was never serious for long. He made her laugh with stories about the Cambridge mathematician who spent his days sitting in a corner of the dayroom doing higher calculus on a sheet of toilet paper. He told her about games of bridge played with such intensity that a patient almost

17

lost an eye once when a dispute turned ugly. He told her that at times he felt he'd joined a superior gentlemen's club, for he knew bankers, solicitors, army officers, and stockbrokers; old Etonians as well as men from the lower depths.

"But we all have one thing in common," he said.

"What's that?"

"We're all mad."

She remembers the moment distinctly. She was sitting on the bench in the shade of the garden wall, and Edgar was up his ladder, bare-chested, looking down at her and grinning at his own joke. She wasn't amused.

"I don't think you're mad," she said.

His mood instantly shifted into accord with hers.

"Neither do I."

"Then you shouldn't be here."

You shouldn't be here. Wasn't that exactly what he'd been angling for? That the wife of the deputy superintendent agreed with him that he shouldn't be here, this was real progress.

Then came the dance.

Stella describes how, the morning after the dance, she was sitting at the kitchen table with a cup of tea, idly turning the pages of the newspaper. She was uneasy. She had spent much of the night thinking about what had happened. The essence of it, she told me, was that while they were dancing she became aware that what was pressing against her groin, through his trousers, was, in fact, his penis, and it was getting hard. She said she kept remembering, first, her incomprehension when she felt it, and then, an instant later, her realization that it was, yes, what she thought it was; but even as she recoiled from him, even as she opened her mouth to cry out her outrage, she recognized something in his expression that changed her mind, a sort of mute abashed helplessness—he couldn't control it! It was funny, and it was sad, too; she was moved by the need she at once perceived behind it. So she'd returned his pressure, and this is how they'd danced around the Central Hall, clinging together with his erection pressed between them, Edgar now beaming broadly and she gazing off into the middle distance with a demure and inscrutable expression on her face. At no point then or later did her composure fail her. She was almost sorry when the music stopped and he turned abruptly and went back to the other side of the room.

I was not shocked by any of this. I was surprised, however, surprised and annoyed, not so much by the nature of their collusion—Edgar's libido was strong, as was Stella's, and both, clearly, were excited by the public nature of the situation—but rather that he would put in jeopardy *our* work together, his and mine, in such cavalier fashion. For he said nothing to me about what had happened at the dance; and how could I hope to help him, when I was being deceived?

The day after the dance was one of the hottest of the summer. She took three or four baths at various times, and each time, as she undressed, she remembered the sensation of the erection pressed into her groin. To this point her sexual interest in Edgar had been a strictly private indulgence and she hadn't considered that it might be reciprocated; apparently it was. This made his presence in the vegetable garden a problem for her.

It was irritating. There were things she needed: chives, radishes, lettuce. She was not a timid woman, but she had no desire to resume her relationship with him. She realized, quite rightly, that it was impossible for her to in effect acquiesce a second time. She decided that since she would have to go down there and deal with him sooner or later, it might as well be sooner. The next morning she cleared away the breakfast things, brushed her hair, put on some lipstick, then went out through the back door and across the yard. She was in a light summer frock and white sandals and her legs were bare.

The sun was already hot. The wall that enclosed the vegetable garden was shaggy with large-leaved ivy and furred with moss between the bricks. The wooden door, with its round Moorish arch, had recently been given a coat of green paint. She paused in front of it, apprehensive. The latch was hot to the touch. She went through. The path wound through a profusion of flowers and vegetables, with clumps of catmint spilling onto the gravel. The day was still and shimmering, and insects murmured among the roses. Flowerpots glowed in the sunlight. When she was halfway along the path she saw John Archer at the far end, sitting on the bench in the shade of the wall in his shirtsleeves, leaning forward with his elbows on his knees and rolling a cigarette. She had no wish to talk to him but it was too late to turn back. He heard her on the gravel and immediately stood up. "Mrs. Raphael," he said.

"Good morning, Mr. Archer."

Panes of glass were stacked against the wall. Edgar was on his knees chipping away at the crumbling mortar in the brickwork at the base of the conservatory. Shading his eyes with his hand, he squatted on his heels and gazed up at Stella where she'd stopped some yards back along the path. He said nothing, just gazed at her, waiting, unsmiling, his hair pushed back off his forehead and his expression one of deadly seriousness. She was aware of the delicacy of the situation. John Archer owed her deference because she was a doctor's wife. Edgar was a patient and therefore technically of lower caste than either of them. Yet what obliquely had drawn her into the vegetable garden was the direct physical overture he had made to her, his mute sexual gesture, man to woman. He had risen to his feet now. Still he said nothing, just stood there, silently defying her to betray him.

"Mr. Archer," she said, "would it be all right if Charlie helped the men with the bonfire?"

John Archer said it would.

"You know what boys are like. But you must send him away if he's a nuisance."

Picking her way back along the path in the sunlight she could imagine the glances being exchanged between the two men behind her back. She'd felt excitement when she saw him squinting mutely up at her, but she had resisted it, she had no further wish to be sympathetic. He is a crafty, unpleasant fellow,

20

she thought, and he believes he has me at a disadvantage because I let him get away with that thing at the dance.

She dismissed the entire sordid experience from her mind.

Despite the fact that we were friends, or perhaps because of it, Stella was inhibited with me at first by what I assumed to be a sense of shame. I tried to show her that she need hide nothing from me, as I had no intention of sitting in judgment on her. I realized a little later that it wasn't shame that made her reluctant to talk to me, but uncertainty about my attitude to Edgar. She didn't know if she could trust me to understand what she had done or, more important, why. She suspected I would condemn him. As soon as I grasped this I made it clear I had no intention of judging him either. I told her that as a psychiatrist I wasn't in the business of moral judgments. She seemed to need this reassurance.

She began to talk then, and it felt as though a valve had been opened, for out it all came in a flood of detail. She was in the back garden with Charlie. She was reading a novel, but every few moments she glanced up with some unease, for he was kneeling on the edge of the goldfish pond, gazing into the water. The pond was deep and she disliked seeing him there on the edge but she was trying not to be too protective. All summer he had been busy with amphibians of one sort or another that he kept in glass tanks in the backyard. Max had said that he'd be delighted if Charlie decided to become a zoologist.

Stella disliked amphibians and she disliked Charlie poking about in the pond like this. She was about to tell him to come away when she heard the telephone ringing in the house. "Get back from the edge!" she shouted as she crossed the lawn and went in through the French windows.

Edgar had a room in the ground-floor ward in Block 3. At one end of the ward was the dayroom. At the other end were the attendants' office and two small interview rooms, in one of which there was a telephone. How he found the means of using

21

this telephone I have never been able to establish. Certainly it was at great personal risk, for had he been discovered he would instantly have lost his parole status. All internal calls go through the hospital switchboard, so I presume he impersonated an attendant and told the operator he was looking for Dr. Raphael.

When she came back out a few minutes later she was not sure exactly what had happened. He had apologized for his behavior, and been so funny, and, oh, just so grown-up about it, she said, that she found herself liking him after all. He had reminded her of their friendship and told her how important it was to him, and mentioned that he hadn't really known a woman for five years. He was a clever one, my Edgar; what he had done was inexcusable, he said, but he appreciated that she'd said nothing. It didn't occur to Stella, then or later, that she should tell Max about the call, just as it had never occurred to her that she should tell him what Edgar had done to her at the dance.

Charlie was still at the edge of the pond when she came back out. He shouted to her that he thought there were snakes. She sat down and opened her novel. She did not tell him to come away, though he was still bending close to the water, one hand gripping the edge while with the other he groped about at the bottom of the pond. Her mind drifted almost at once, and she gazed unseeing at the back of the house, the open French windows of the drawing room, the door giving onto the hall, and at the end of the hall, on the other side of the house, but visible from where she sat in the shade of the old ash tree, the front door. Beyond the front door lay the drive, the trees, and the Wall. She felt relieved, she felt at ease, as though the disturbance in the order of things effected by that unruly penis had now been quelled, and her friendship restored.

2

At this stage Stella had no real idea how disturbed Edgar Stark
was. She had never regularly listened to him spinning out his
morbid delusions, as I had, and though she knew by his own
admission what he'd done, she'd excused him by thinking of it
as a simple crime of passion, which of course permitted her to
romanticize him. When Edgar realized this he changed his tac-
tics, but in the beginning I believe he simply wanted her to
influence Max to look favorably on his efforts to secure his
release. In this he displayed his naïveté, for things simply don't
work like that. Much more pertinent from my point of view was
that he was behaving manipulatively and, at the outset at least,
attempting to use his considerable sexual attraction as a means
of control. The fact that the one he wanted to control was a
doctor's wife was a mark of the extravagant grandiosity of his
designs.

Early in our relationship I had discussed with Edgar my

strategy for the psychotherapy. I told him that what I wanted to do was break down his defenses: strip away the façades, the pretenses, all the false structures of his disordered personality, and then start again, rebuild him from the ground up, as it were. Because this would be such a difficult, long-drawn-out process he would need all the support I could give him. For almost four years we had been working together. This clandestine relationship with Stella, however, this suggested that he was behaving toward me in bad faith. Far from attempting to examine the pathological manner in which he related to women, he was setting in motion the process that had led to murder once already, and had been the cause of his coming to us in the first place.

Then something happened that I don't think either of them consciously anticipated. They didn't realize—and who does, in these sorts of affairs?—that the violence of feeling he had aroused in her would shatter the constraints of caution and common sense, and overwhelm their fragile status quo.

It has not been easy to talk to Stella about the sex. She naturally finds it distasteful to be explicit. But she has described to me in detail how it began. It was another clear, bright, hot summer day, and she padded about the house in bare feet throughout the early afternoon, going from room to room, unable to be still. The sunshine streamed in through the windows of the big rooms downstairs, bringing up the burnish on the wood floors to a glare. She paused in front of the mirror over the fireplace and frowned at her reflection.

She touched her hair. She went upstairs and changed into a loose summer frock with a low neck, then sat in front of her dressing-table mirror and put on fresh lipstick. She went back downstairs and stood at the French windows in the drawing room and gazed out across the back lawn. She poured herself a drink. That morning he had bluntly suggested she come into the conservatory with him. It had flustered her badly. It had sent her running down the path and back to the house. Sex with the

man: the idea of it, long active in her imagination, frankly artic-
ulated had a terrible power.

She left the house by the front door and crossed the drive to
the gate in the high hedge opposite, which opened onto what
had once been the front lawn but now, through neglect, had
become a meadow of thick grass and wildflowers. She crossed
the meadow to an arched opening in the garden wall close to
the conservatory. She stood in the rounded archway with her
back against the bricks and waited.

She could hear him working. She could hear glass smashing
in the dustbin. She knew he would soon become aware of her
presence in the arch, for her shadow fell across the path. She
wasn't sure she could sustain herself there for very long. She felt
that at any moment she would find her behavior ridiculous and
abruptly go back inside.

Silence. Then he was standing in front of her. Without a word
she pulled him into the conservatory. She took his head in her
hands and with her fingers spread across his cheeks she kissed
him fiercely on the lips. They got down onto the floor, hidden
from view by the low stone wall at the base of the frame. She
rapidly arranged herself on the ground as he knelt over her
unbuttoning his trousers.

I probed her gently. I could not challenge directly her reluc-
tance to talk about what happened next. We would return to it.
I imagine it was urgent and primitive, a thing of hunger and
instinct. I imagine he took her at once, without finesse, and that
she wanted this, she was as avid as he was, no coyness now, no
hesitation at all. And I imagine it was over rather quickly, and
that afterward, flushed, burning, she ran back into the house
and straight upstairs to the bathroom. I know that bathroom.
The original fittings are all intact. The big tub with its tarnished
brass taps stands on clawed feet on a floor of discolored tiles. A
fern that flourishes in the steamy atmosphere of that large
damp room overflows its terra-cotta pot by the door, and beside
it there's a large wicker laundry basket.

Water gushed from the taps. She flung off her clothes and

stepped into the bath. The fever subsided. She lay in the bath for an hour with her eyes closed and her mind empty, though not properly empty, for beneath the surface moved the knowledge of what she had just done. It was not to be looked at, it was not to be acknowledged at all; but there are forms of mental experience that exist outside the machinery of repression, and in those obscure regions of her psyche arose the question whether, having done this once, she would do it again, and though she did not actually think this thought, and would have denied it vehemently had it flickered into consciousness, she was aware, as one is aware of all such things that don't bear thinking about, that the answer was yes.

Some hours later she was sitting on the back lawn, with a drink, in a white wicker chair, in the shade of the ash tree, her novel in her lap, when she heard Max at the front door. She came into the house, went down the hall and let him in; he seemed to be having trouble with his keys. He was in his dark suit, his tie was loosened, he was hot and tired, and more than anything he wanted a drink.

"Bloody day," he said.

Behind him on the far side of the drive the pines rose in a dark mass against the evening sky. She embraced him with a warmth unusual for her, and as she did so an ironic thought sprang into her mind, that it's the guilt of the adulterous woman that drives her into her husband's arms.

"Hello," he said as she clung to him like a woman adrift, a woman drowning, "what's all this?"

She moved away to the mirror over the empty fireplace and patted at her hair, and tried to find some sign of sin on her face.

"Nothing. I missed you today, that's all."

"Why did you miss me?"

She turned to face him. There was real curiosity in his voice, and she felt the psychiatrist in the man, or rather, the man receded and the psychiatrist emerged as the wheels turned and she saw him examine this fragment of her psychic life and fish around for its meaning. In that moment he became her enemy. She knew then that any openness between them was dangerous, and that her explosive secret must be hidden with especial skill from the eyes of this sudden stranger with his desperately acute powers of mental intrusion and perception.

She poured them each a drink and thought, How easily he will find out, unless I am on perpetual alert. Not through any carelessness of the obvious kind but through *reading my mind*—reading me like a book, finding it written in fragments of behavior, fleeting nuances of expression, certain absences of response of which I would not be aware. Oh, I must be vigilant, from this point on I must be vigilant. This was her thought. But she didn't have to put this policy of dissimulation into immediate effect, for Charlie came running in and began breathlessly telling his father about a bone he'd found in the marsh.

"I think it's *human*," he said.

"I rather doubt that," said Max, smiling slightly.

"I think," said Charlie darkly, "there may have been a murder."

Stella drifted over to the French windows and gazed out at the setting sun and allowed herself to think about her lover.

She thought about him intermittently for the next three days without once going down to the vegetable garden. Max startled her at dinner one night by mentioning him by name.

Did she disguise the shock it gave her, to hear his name on Max's lips?

She thinks so, though perhaps Max wasn't paying attention, often his mind was elsewhere. He said that Edgar Stark was needed for a few days in the chaplain's garden. Thank God, she thought; now I don't have to imagine him out there all the time.

A horribly anxious few days, then she started to feel calmer. She thought it was the relief that came of running a risk and getting away with it. She was surprised to discover a fresh affection for Max, and realized she was grateful to him for suspecting nothing, for unwittingly allowing her to bury her guilty secret. And so the first sharp shock of horror at the appalling transgression she'd committed—having sex with a *patient*, not fifty yards from the house—began to subside, and she told herself it had been a moment of madness, no more than that; never, of course, to be repeated. Though it worried her that Edgar would return to the garden, and that when he did, she would be able to find him, if she wanted to.

Now, predictably, as they moved toward assignation and structure, Stella began to create a sort of arabesque in her mind, a pattern of thought and feeling whose function it was to lead her back to him. She told me how one hot July morning she put on her wide-brimmed straw hat and took her tea out onto the terrace on the north side of the house and watched the patients feeding a bonfire with barrowloads of the dead wood and other debris strewn about this neglected part of the garden. It had been overgrown for years, a long, shallow, wooded slope that gradually flattened out and then beyond the back fence climbed into a stand of deciduous trees that crowned the far ridge and formed the outskirts of the forest.

Max's plan was to clear this slope and plant it with new turf. He envisioned a rolling pasture here, an idea that disturbed Stella, for it suggested that their tenure of the house would be longer than she'd been led to believe. It had occurred to her that his ambition was to tame and cultivate both the hospital and the estate, make them over as his twin gardens.

The patients worked on steadily. The wood was dry and caught quickly, sending up showers of sparks as it burned white and gold in the sunshine. Onto the blaze they forked heaps of dried grass, the mowings of the back lawn, and the grass damped the blaze and produced clouds of black smoke. She saw them step back from the smoke and lean on their forks. One man turned and, shielding his eyes from the sun, gazed up the slope to where she stood in her straw hat, holding her cup of tea. She held his gaze.

Her own behavior puzzled her. She asked me what it meant. She made no gesture of any kind, merely stood there staring at the man. He took the handles of his wheelbarrow and started to push it up the slope, coming not straight in her direction but by the path that led to the gate in the back fence. He was wearing the baggy yellow corduroys of the outside work parties, and the blue institution shirt with no collar. The cuffs were unbuttoned and they flapped at his wrists. He paused and pushed a strand of hair off his forehead and wiped the sweat away with a red-and-white-spotted bandanna that was certainly familiar to her, for Edgar had one. Her eyes were still on him and he knew it. She began to fan herself gently with her hat. Then, annoyed, she turned and went in.

I did not tell her that as a function of her relationship with Edgar not only had she begun to identify with the patients, she had eroticized them. She had eroticized the patient body.

Edgar spent all that week working in the chaplain's garden. Then on the Monday he was back on the conservatory. Stella knew he was out there, she could hear him working. She waited until Max had left for the hospital and Charlie had gone off on his bike. She had decided that when she met him she would be cool. They would behave toward each other in a manner appropriate to their respective situations. She was sure he would see that this was the proper course. She crossed the yard and went into the vegetable garden. He was there, and her heart sang at the sight of him.

With Stella it was always the heart, the language of the heart.

He was standing at his workbench, an old potting table where he did his carpentry, and he had his back to her; and though he must have heard her on the path he didn't turn until she had almost reached him. Then he swung around. They stood face to face. She was trembling. He touched her cheek, smiling slightly at her agitation.

"Thank God."

She leaned against the wall and felt its soft warmth through her blouse. There was no question of resisting temptation. She was lost. His large hands were splayed on the wall on either side of her head and he was leaning forward, his face close to hers.

She gazed coolly into his eyes, though her thoughts were far from cool. She took hold of his shirt and gripped it tight.

"Have you been thinking about me?"

He nodded. She pulled his face to hers and as they kissed his hand moved from her breast to her hip to her groin.

"Not here," she whispered.

He stepped back as she pushed herself off the wall. She paused beneath the arch in the wall and turned to him where he stood in front of the conservatory, wiping his fingers on a rag and watching her intently. She crossed the meadow to the copse of pines on the far side. She saw no one. She wandered among the trees and then lay down in the ferns. The sun streamed through the branches and she lifted her hand to shade her face.

She was waiting for him, her blouse unbuttoned, when she heard the voices. She sat up. She couldn't make out what they were saying but they were men's voices and they were coming from the meadow. She held her breath. She realized what was happening. He had met John Archer coming across the meadow. They were talking in the meadow while twenty yards away she sat hidden in the trees. After a few moments she was seized by a bizarre impulse, she wanted to laugh, to shout out with wild joy at the sheer comic indignity of her position, for she couldn't help imagining Max's reaction, what he would say at seeing his wife hiding in the woods, half undressed, denied her furtive few moments of pleasure with Edgar Stark because an attendant had unwittingly intercepted the man on his way to their tryst.

The voices died away soon after. She slipped out of the woods and ran across the drive to the house. She went upstairs and ran a bath. She was still a little giddy when she came back down to the drawing room and poured herself a drink. She sat in an armchair with a book, her drink in hand, and lit a rare cigarette.

Her reaction astonished her. That she should want to *laugh*—what did this mean? In the full knowledge of the consequences of discovery, to laugh was to say she didn't care what happened to her! This was her interpretation. I suggested that instead it might be connected with anger.

What anger?

Anger with Max. It seemed clear to me, I said, that her behavior was linked to a desire to hurt Max.

She shook her head. I don't think so, Peter, she said. But there was, as I suspected, a massive reservoir of resentment in her. She was not ready to talk about it yet, and I didn't force her. It would come.

Assignation, this was the next stage. Establishing the times and places, giving the thing a structure. What made it so difficult, of course, was the fact that Edgar enjoyed such limited freedom of movement. But despite the constraints they did find the times and places, one always does; they had their assignations.

The day after Edgar was intercepted by John Archer they met by the conservatory and she told him they ought to get organized.

He was at his workbench. There was a long pause.

"You want to go on with it then?" he said at last.

She was sitting on the bench in the shade of the wall. She was wearing her straw hat and sunglasses. She lifted her head and nodded. He seemed to sway slightly, and then turned back to his work. "Archer," he murmured.

She had a basket with her and had tossed some flowers into it. She stood up and set off back down the path toward the house. John Archer came toward her, his boots crunching on the gravel. She made a conscious effort to behave naturally.

"Good morning, Mr. Archer. Lovely tomatoes you're giving us. Nice and sweet."

He nodded affably and said something about summer salads. Stella wondered what there was in that steady gaze that put her on her guard. Perhaps nothing. Perhaps only her own guilty conscience. He had a way of waiting for one to speak, of creating a silence that must be filled, and such men made her uneasy at the best of times.

She was right to be uneasy. John Archer reported to me, and he had sharp eyes and a devious mind, every bit as devious as Edgar's; he soon let me know about this budding friendship. Perhaps I was wrong, but I decided to do nothing about it. I was curious. Edgar had had no contact with a woman for five years.

The staff cricket field is a broad stretch of level ground fringed with pines and bordered on one side by the estate road where it passes the Raphaels' garden on its way up to the Main Gate. Beyond the trees on the hospital side a back road runs down the hill close to the Wall, winding past the chaplain's house, then out across the marsh. Just above this road, looking out over the cricket field and shaded by the pines, stands the pavilion. It is a graceful old wooden building with a shingled roof and a weathercock. It has a shady veranda at the front, where we sit to watch the cricket, and inside, a cool and gloomy club room with a bar.

That summer there was always a party of patients at work in the garden of the chaplain's house, for like Max the chaplain had embarked on a number of projects including the construction of a greenhouse. Edgar was the best carpenter we had on an outside work party, and was often needed. He moved unescorted between the two gardens, and the cricket pavilion lay close to the path he took down the hill. Stella had keys to the building, being a member of the cricket committee.

So they had their place of assignation.

She did have moments of sanity when she looked dispassionately at what she was doing. She describes how she drifted out onto the back lawn one evening and wandered in the moonlight over to the goldfish pond. She sat on the edge and watched the fat vague silvery shapes gliding among the lilies in the black water, and thought with a smile of Charlie's water snakes. She gazed at the light from the drawing room as it spilled out through the French windows onto the lawn, and above it, in darkness, the open windows of Charlie's room, the curtains stirring slightly in the breeze. She was moved suddenly by the idea of the security of her family life, its comfort and meaning and order, all of which rested squarely on Charlie and his welfare. Then she thought about this dawning adventure of hers, and it was suddenly vividly apparent to her that by indulging it she was putting that order in jeopardy. She felt then a powerful tremor of apprehension.

The feeling stayed with her for several days and precluded any further developments. But she could not be still. One morning she went down the drive and across the road to the cricket field. It was another clear hot day; two patients in floppy white hats, and with their shirts tied around their waists, were sweating in the sunshine out in the middle of the field as they pushed the big roller back and forth. Unseen, she hoped, deep in the pines at the edge of the field, she walked around the side to the pavilion. There was an empty shed at the back where the big roller was garaged, and in the darkness she smelled fresh-cut grass and soil. She found what she was looking for, a narrow window at the back of the pavilion that could be reached from the roof of the shed.

She came around to the front and darted up the wooden steps to the veranda. The two patients were hazy in the sunlight and there was no attendant in sight. She turned to the door of the pavilion and unlocked it.

Inside, deck chairs were stacked against the wall. A single shaft of sunshine penetrated the gloom, lighting a patch of floorboards marked with hundreds of tiny dimpled indentations where over the years cricketers in their studded boots had stamped out from the changing room at the back. She found cushions and blankets in the storeroom and spread them on the floor. It was as she stood there gazing down at this crude bed that she felt a sudden astonishment at what she was doing: she was planning to bring a man here for sex. And not just any man, a patient. Your patient, Peter. She fled the place, locking the door behind her, and returned to the house, where she found Mrs. Bain at work in the kitchen.

That day and the next she didn't go near the vegetable

garden, though she could hear him out there hammering and sawing. At last a reaction had set in, a slow, horrified recoil, first aroused, she said, the night she'd sat at the edge of the goldfish pond and was affected by the warmth and security the house had seemed to offer. This reaction was slow to appear because drawn from deep in her psyche, so that by the time it rose to consciousness it had grown massive and was experienced not as apprehension but as horror. Horror at the very thought of endangering not only her own security but Charlie's too; it seemed then cruelly irresponsible to put at risk the boy's happiness.

How quiet he could be at times, she remembers thinking when he came home that afternoon. She was eager to be with him, guilty for the thoughts she'd been thinking in the pavilion that morning, as though, she said, she'd been unfaithful to *him*. Perhaps that's the whole point about infidelity, I suggested, not that one has sex but that by doing so one puts at risk someone else's happiness? It's not the blunt fact of the thing, it's all in the effect it would have if known. The thing itself is insignificant. She agreed with me, in principle. But none of that was relevant anymore. Now the point was to guarantee utter secrecy. This was what preoccupied her as she sat on the back lawn in the shade of the ash tree, and Charlie lay on his front on the grass in the sunshine nearby, propped on his elbows and frowning at a book with his hair flopping over his eyes. As though he sensed her thoughts he suddenly looked up.

"Mummy."

"Yes, darling!"

He then produced an extraordinary physical contortion, as though he were thinking with his whole body and the thought was a complicated one. He rolled half over onto his side and stared up at the sky, one plump arm pulled around the back of his neck, his hand clutching his chin, the other lifted straight up, fingers splayed against the sun.

"I've thought of a joke," he said.

"Well?"

"Ask me why I fell out of the apple tree that day."

"Why did you fall out of the apple tree that day?"

"Because I was ripe!"

"Very funny."

She couldn't stay away from him. She tried. She had had her moment of horror when she confronted the implications of what she was doing, but the effects were short-lived. Knowing how close he was she couldn't control the constant restless excitability of her imagination. The next morning, after Max had gone up to the hospital, she crossed the backyard to the gate in the wall.

It happened again, that extraordinary feeling she could only think of as intoxication. He was at the far end, down by the conservatory, where he had set up a sawhorse on trestles beside his workbench, and he was hard at it, pushing the saw with a strong, easy stroke. He heard her when she was halfway along the path, and he turned and watched her approach.

"Go on with your work," she called quietly as she came closer. "Don't stop for me."

But he didn't go on with his work. He fished his tobacco tin out of his trouser pocket, sat down on the bench by the wall, and rolled a cigarette. She sat down beside him.

"I've been over to the pavilion," she said.

"I know." His tone was sardonic.

"How do you know?"

"One of the men saw you."

She should have been alarmed by this but she wasn't.

"Can you come this afternoon?" she said.

He paused a moment, faintly smiling as he licked the edge of the cigarette paper. He enjoyed the urgency he had aroused in this pale passionate woman. She saw it, and touched his face.

"Can you?" she murmured.

"Yes."

She tried not to show him how the excitement mounted

within her as this conversation went forward. She felt the fabric of his corduroy trousers against her bare leg. It was stupid to take risks in the vegetable garden but she kissed him anyway.

That afternoon they met in the cricket pavilion. They undressed each other, they lay down together, but all she would say about the sex was that it was effortless, and mutually intense; she had never known anything like it, this vigorous physical struggle their bodies took to with such immediacy and force. Afterward he took some whisky, and this worried her slightly, it seemed an unnecessary risk. He had a flat metal flask in his pocket and he filled it from a bottle behind the bar.

"Suppose they miss it?"

He crossed the room and knelt down beside her where she sat soft and flushed and disheveled on their makeshift bed. He took her face in his hands and kissed her.

She saw him as her charming rogue. She couldn't argue with him. She couldn't oppose him at all, it wasn't possible, for she had begun to surrender herself and no longer felt distinct and separate from him, rather that she was incomplete without him. She understood what was happening, she was falling in love, and she didn't want to stop it. She said she couldn't stop it. She acquiesced in his stealing from the pavilion; she assumed his own attitude of disregard of risk, and rationalized it. A few days later, when he asked her for money, she gave him everything in her purse.

No control. You don't control falling in love, she said, you can't. At the time it had amused her that it should happen like this, with this man. A patient. A patient working in the vegetable garden. Stella, I said, you could not have chosen more unwisely had you tried. But the truth is, she said, I didn't choose.

She functioned as normally as she could at home but she was never properly there. Her day became focused on that one point in time when she waited with rising excitement in the gloom of the cricket pavilion, waited to hear his boots on the wall as he clambered onto the roof of the shed, then heaved himself over the windowsill and dropped to the floor inside. He would come toward her, grinning, where she waited, ready for him, on the blankets, and sink down with her, and she lost herself completely when she reached for him and felt his strong hands on her body. Oh, she loved him.

Perhaps.

3

I believe now that the visit that summer of Max's mother, Brenda Raphael, in a curious way accelerated the progress of the thing. One Friday afternoon in early August, five or six weeks after the dance, she arrived at the deputy medical superintendent's house while I was there. I had left the hospital early and dropped in on Stella on my way home. I had recently heard from John Archer about her budding friendship with Edgar, and naturally I wanted to talk to her. I had no chance to bring it up, however, for she at once told me her mother-in-law was expected.

"I offered to meet her at the station," she said as she led me down the hall and into the drawing room, "but oh no, she didn't want to put me to any trouble. She makes it sound as though I'm so stagnant it would be dangerous to move me."

We had a drink in the garden, and she was distant, distracted. At the time I did not associate her mood with the faint sounds of shattering glass and hammering that drifted in the still air from the direction of the vegetable garden. Five minutes later we heard a car in the drive. Together we went down the hall to the open front door just as the taxi driver brought up the first of Brenda's numerous suitcases; she herself was just emerging from the back of the car. She was an urbane, autocratic woman, and she was also wealthy. I happened to know she was helping Max and Stella maintain their standard of living here, and that their car—a white Jaguar, of all things—had been her gift when Max was appointed deputy superintendent. She and I often spoke on the telephone. We understood each other. She relied on me for reports about her son.

She handed the driver his fare and tip with all the graciousness of royalty. "Peter," she then said, "how nice to see you. Stella, my dear. You seem well." They kissed, and Brenda advanced along the hall. She was, as always, fashionably dressed, and I knew this caused Stella a pang of envy not to be living in London still, not to be generating this same aura of chic.

"Would you like to go upstairs," said Stella, "or shall we have a drink and take it into the garden?"

"That would be lovely," said Brenda. "Now, Peter, don't run away just because I've come. Where is Charlie?"

"I expect he's out in the marsh," said Stella, "or down by the conservatory."

Brenda lifted a thin, plucked eyebrow. "He might have been here to say hello to his grandmother, but that's a boy for you. I don't think Max was very different. How is Max?"

As she said this she sank into one of the armchairs, crossing her elegant legs, and took her cigarettes out of her handbag.

"Busy," said Stella. "Happy, I think. He likes it here."

"I was rather afraid he would. Max is a cautious man, I'm sure I don't need to tell either of you that. He'd be drawn to the security of a job here."

"I think he wants to be medical superintendent. Don't you agree, Peter?"

I was pouring the drinks, with my back to the women. I

stiffened slightly at this unpleasant suggestion and murmured some demurral.

"You don't want to stay here, of course," said Brenda, and as I handed them their drinks I saw again how things were with them: Brenda was not a woman's woman, but she and Stella had worked out certain unspoken compromises over the years. Now, it seemed, at least on this issue, they were allies. Neither of them wanted to see Max bury himself in this provincial institution.

"Oh, I could tolerate it for a couple of years," said Stella, giving me a private smile as I handed her a gin and tonic, "but I'm afraid it's more than a couple of years Max wants. Shall we go into the garden?

"It's the attention he gives the garden that worries me," she went on, when we were settled in wicker chairs in the shade, and again I was struck by how distracted she was. We gazed out over the back lawn. The goldfish pond sparkled in the sunlight.

"A garden takes years to do properly and Max is working on this one as though he'll be at it for the rest of his life."

"How worrying." Brenda glanced at me, but I was sustaining a studious neutrality here.

"He's having the old conservatory fixed up now."

It was the second time she'd mentioned the conservatory.

"I do hope you're wrong about this," said Brenda. "But tell me, my dear, how are you? You certainly look well. In the pink, I'd say."

I glanced at her. In the pink. I rather whimsically reflected that it sounded like a euphemism, something to do with sex; and it was then that it occurred to me that something *was* happening to Stella, sexually. I regarded her with care.

"I'm having a lazy summer," she said in an offhand manner. "I don't really have a great deal to do, even though it's such a big house. Mrs. Bain comes in in the mornings and I can usually leave it all to her." She brushed at a wasp that was buzzing around her glass.

Brenda then began to talk about her social life in London,

and this litany of lunches and cocktail parties and formal dinners was accompanied by the usual weary complaints at how much in demand one was, and how tired one got, and how few people appreciated how precious one's time was. As Stella listened to this, murmuring that a smart, busy London social life was about the closest thing to heaven she could imagine, I wondered idly with whom she might be having sex, but could think of no likely candidates on the estate.

"You must come up to town more often," Brenda was saying. "Everybody asks how you both are. Spend the night. We'll go to the theater and have supper afterward."

"We will, soon."

They talked about Charlie then, and a little later Brenda went in to wash her face and have a rest before Max came home from the hospital.

I made my own departure shortly afterward, but not before Stella had told me in a fierce whisper that she could expect nothing but torment like this for the next few days, and how was she going to cope without going mad? I was sympathetic. I managed to make her laugh. She slipped her arm in mine as we walked around the side of the house to where I'd left the car at the end of the drive. "Peter," she said.

Her tone was casual, dreamy even. "Yes, my dear?"

"When is Edgar Stark getting out?"

It wasn't so unusual a question, but it gave me a shock. I told her it would be a long time if it had anything to do with me. "Why do you ask?" I said as we reached my car.

"No reason. He's the one doing Max's conservatory. Will we see you on Tuesday night?"

"Yes, you will," I said, as I kissed her cheek.

My Edgar?

When the professional staff leave the hospital at the end of the day the place assumes a different atmosphere, rather like a town by the sea when the season is over and the tourists go home. I like it then. Over the years it has become my practice to return to my office in the stillness of the evening and reflect in tranquillity on the events of the day.

"Back again, Dr. Cleave," says the attendant at the Main Gate as I collect my keys.

"Back again," I say. With the custodial staff I have always projected a sort of patrician affability. They like it. They like structure and hierarchy. They know me well. I have been here longer than any of them.

My office had a good view of the country beyond the Wall. It was particularly lovely on summer evenings, when the last of the light brought a soft, hazy glow to the marsh, and over to the west the setting sun turned the sky all shades of red. One day some months after Edgar was admitted to the hospital I returned to my office at this quiet hour. I poured myself a drink—I keep a small stock of alcohol in my desk, under lock and key—and stood a few moments gazing out of the window. I remember it so well because it was in the course of a session with Edgar earlier in the day that he first began to reveal the full extent of his delusions, and dropped all pretense that the murder had been as impulsive as he'd first maintained.

I had been to see him during the afternoon in the dayroom of his ward in Block 3. This is a large, sunny room with a well-waxed floor and a snooker table in the middle. There were couches and armchairs upholstered in a tough dark-green vinyl, and a large table at one end where men played cards or read the newspaper. A television set had recently been installed at the other end. He was playing snooker, bent over his cue, about to take his shot, when someone whispered to him that Dr. Cleave was here. He made his shot.

"Oh yes?" he said, straightening up. He turned, grinning, toward the door.

I mouthed the word "Come."

We had spent almost an hour in the interview room, and I had taped our conversation. He'd told me first about his promotion to the downstairs ward in Block 3. I had been instrumental in arranging this, of course, but he needed to take the credit and have me applaud him, as a child might. This is not uncommon, the projection by the patient onto his psychiatrist of the feelings of a child toward its father. Such transference of affect can be useful, as it was in Edgar's case, for bringing to the surface repressed material.

When he settled down I turned the machine on. At this point my understanding of his personality was not extensive. He had told me something of his reasons for killing his wife, and what I'd heard was quite fantastic. There is often a ghostly resemblance to logic in the thinking of delusional patients, and it was apparent here. Driven by morbid unconscious processes to suppose that his wife was betraying him with another man, he had reasoned, first, that they must have ways of signaling their arrangements, and second, that their activities must leave traces. He had then manufactured evidence of such signals and traces from incidents as banal as her opening a window just as a motorbike was going past in the street below, and from phenomena as insignificant as a crease in a pillow or a stain on a skirt.

I asked him, as I did at the beginning of every interview, if he still believed he had been sexually betrayed.

"Oh yes."

This was said with utter assurance. He was rolling a cigarette, his eyes on his fingers. He nodded several times.

"How long had it been going on?"

He looked up and glanced out of the window, gathering his thoughts. A slight frown as he touched the edge of the cigarette paper with his tongue. He looked eminently reasonable and sane. I saw him come to the decision to be frank with me at last.

"Eight or nine years."

His expression said, Now you understand everything.

"But that's how long you'd been married!"

He nodded, genuine sadness in his face.

"When did you first suspect it was going on?"

"I knew from the beginning."

"Are you saying that throughout your marriage you knew your wife was being unfaithful to you?"

"Yes."

"With the same man?"

"No. There were others."

"How many?"

His face came suddenly to life. He was bitterly amused.

"How many? Hundreds. I lost count."

"And you did nothing about it?"

"I pleaded with her. Threatened her. I don't think it was her fault. She wasn't responsible."

He began pushing his hands through his hair.

"It did no good?"

"She laughed at me."

"I see."

I allowed a silence. The reports I'd read indicated that the marriage had been relatively stable until a year before the murder. Were they wrong? Was Ruth Stark promiscuous? Had he been plaguing her with accusations all along?

"Did anyone know about your unhappiness?"

He nodded. He gave off the air of a man forced to make a difficult admission, one harmful not to himself but to another.

"Who knew?"

"Various people."

"Friends? Family?"

He nodded again. I now knew that what I was hearing was all a product of the delusional structure.

"So she was sleeping around with a lot of men from the start of the marriage. You knew this, you talked to her about it, but she paid no attention."

His eyes flared with a sort of astonished incredulity.

"She laughed at me!"

"She laughed at you. And others knew what was going on."

"I didn't have to tell them. They could see for themselves."

"And she didn't care."

"It was her *work*," he said. "She was a whore."

This was new. "Go on."

"She brought them to the studio while I was out. I'd see them waiting in the street, hanging about till I was out of the way. She could do ten or twelve a day. She couldn't help it."

He paused there. He gazed at me with such a pathetic expression, begging me to believe him, that I was moved to get out of my chair and come around and put my hand on his shoulder.

"And you knew," I said quietly. "All those years you knew."

There hadn't been anything more after that. I sat at my desk and listened to the tape recorder humming in the silence and then clicking off. I stood up and gazed out into the evening as it stole across the marsh. Morbid jealousy. The delusion of infidelity. Freud thought it a form of acidulated homosexuality, the projection of repressed homosexual desire onto the partner: *I* didn't love him, *she* does. But I considered this unlikely in Edgar's case. For despite his confidence, and his apparent maturity, I suspected that there was in him a deep and childish need to elevate, and idealize, the love object. This is not uncommon in artists. The very nature of their work, the long periods of isolation followed by public self-display, and the associated risk of rejection all conspire to create unnaturally intense relationships with their sexual partners. Then, when disillusion occurs, as of course it must, the sense of betrayal is profound, and will in some individuals translate into a pathological conviction of the other's duplicity.

But what particularly impressed me in Edgar was this retroactive adjustment of the memory so as to bring the early years of the marriage into line with the delusions that so tragically dominated it at the end, to the point that they now involved hundreds of men and a bizarre set of false memories. Insight, I realized, this is what we must work toward, a moment of insight when the inherent absurdities in his thinking undermined the foundations of the delusional structure and brought it crashing down. Only then could we begin to rebuild his psyche.

But now, this affair with Stella, this would set us back months; for in deceiving me he blocked the flow of candid confidences essential to our reaching our goal, and rendered the psychotherapeutic process a travesty.

They had the French windows wide open for the dinner party, and a warm breeze drifted in from the back lawn, carrying with it the scents of the garden. It was all for Brenda. The visiting dignitary expected to be honored by the psychiatric aristocracy of the estate, and Max would not disappoint her. Dinner was seven-thirty. I was the first to arrive, and found Stella composed and in control. My attitude to her had naturally undergone a profound revision since my discovery of the previous week, or rather, since my intuition that there was more between her and Edgar than simple friendship; but I showed nothing of this.

She had had two and a half hours in the kitchen by herself, she told me quietly as she took me out into the garden, Her Majesty leaves me alone if I appear to be actually working. Max had been sent to the pub for brandy. Stella saw me as an ally; she was unaware of course of the suspicion I now harbored toward her. I was sorry in a way that we couldn't talk about it, about Edgar's sexuality. She asked me to entertain Brenda, who was sitting in the back garden, so I went out and settled down beside the matriarch, and Stella stayed in the kitchen.

"It is all rather pastoral," Brenda said with a sigh, as we gazed across the lawn at the back of the house and the trees beyond. "Peter, do *you* have the impression Max is happy? Stella worries that he'll never want to leave."

I understood of course that it was Brenda who was worried.

"It's ideal," I said carefully, "for a certain sort of psychiatrist. Fascinating population, a few truly glorious specimens, all in an institution large enough to simulate the outside world."

"But do you suppose he wants to be superintendent?"

I was diplomatic.

"It is tempting," I allowed, "to run one of these large closed hospitals. To exercise Victorian paternalism on the grand scale . . ."

I trailed off. There was a silence.

"You sound as though you're tempted yourself."

I laughed with light self-deprecation. "Oh no," I said, "not me. No, it's a young man's game, running the big bins. I'm much too long in the tooth."

She turned toward me and fastened on me a gimlet eye. "Hm," she said skeptically.

Max joined us soon afterward; a little later the Straffens arrived, and the party was complete. We stayed out in the garden, all except Stella, who was still in the kitchen, and Bridie Straffen, who went upstairs to see Charlie. Brenda guided the conversation, and we three psychiatrists found ourselves directing all our remarks to her, in deference to her matronly authority. Max made sure all glasses were filled and then went back inside, and ten minutes later we were called in to the dining room. Stella had been selfish about the table, and put me at her end, and Brenda down at Max's, with Jack Straffen between herself and her mother-in-law, and Bridie between me and Max.

We were eating the salmon when the subject of marriage came up, I forget exactly how. But with a table of only six, all can take part in the same conversation. Brenda, I believe, said something about her first husband, Charles, whom she had divorced when Max was a child, and spoke of him in such a way that Max then asked Bridie Straffen why she thought some marriages survived and others did not. Bridie was decisive. She was a large clever woman from Dublin who'd spent the last twenty years successfully playing the role of superintendent's wife here on the estate. She was boisterous and popular, and her capacity for alcohol was equaled only by her husband's.

"I made him take the Oath." She looked at Jack, who lifted his hands.

"What oath?"

I thought she meant the Pledge.

"The Hippocratic Oath," she said. " 'Do no harm.' Think of me as a patient, I told him, and we'll survive. And we have."

There was a murmur of amusement around the table. Everyone wanted to add to this. Stella's voice was the clearest.

" 'Do no harm'?" she said. "Most of us are dying of chronic neglect!"

There was a silence. We were all embarrassed. There was too much in the remark, it was too private, it smacked of a bitter truth. She had gone too far. Bridie came to the rescue.

"Dear Stella, you take me much too literally. The point is not that they do harm but that they do as little as possible. They are human, after all. Even Max is human."

Max had no choice but to agree, and within a few moments the conversation was back on the rails. But in that tiny ghastly silence I glanced down the table and saw Brenda fixing on Stella a bright gaze charged with hungry curiosity.

After dinner we wandered out through the French windows onto the back lawn, and there was talk about the extraordinarily warm weather, the continental summer we were having that made possible our being outside, in the moonlight, at eleven at night, with the air still as warm and fragrant as it had been during the day. Max told Jack what he'd been doing with the garden and the pair of them went off to have a look at the conservatory. In light of what Stella had said about Max's ambitions I was not surprised to see him attending to the superintendent so assiduously. Jack was due to retire in the next year or so, and would appoint his own successor.

I settled down in a garden chair and listened to Brenda and Bridie talk about houses in general, which led them on to the great houses of Ireland, and from there to their mutual acquaintance the Earl of Dunraven.

When Max and Jack returned from the vegetable garden we all began the preparatory movements of departure. I noticed that Stella again seemed to be finding it difficult to maintain her composure. Her unease grew stronger as she listened to the conversation that followed.

Jack was telling Bridie and Brenda about the decrepitude into which the garden had sunk before Max and Stella came to the hospital. He was delighted, he said, that Max was bringing it back.

Max said, "With help. No one knows more about these big hospital gardens than John Archer. Nothing would have happened without John."

"And Edgar Stark," said Stella quietly, almost to herself, I thought.

Jack, Max, and I, we all turned toward her.

"I hear him hammering away all day," she said, trying to deflect what she later called our terrible psychiatric gazes. "The man works like a demon."

"A demon indeed."

"What are you going to do about him?"

This last question was put by Max to Jack. Stella told me she had the familiar impression of an exclusive professional knowledge, something to do with Edgar in this case.

"Do tell," said Brenda. "I'm intrigued."

"All very tiresome," said Jack in that slightly weary tone of voice he employed when something happened in the hospital that was annoying rather than alarming, one of the petty problems that interfered with the practice of forensic psychiatric medicine; though one might argue that these sorts of problems were precisely the stuff of the practice of forensic psychiatric medicine, institutional forensic psychiatric medicine, that is.

"Someone's been bringing in alcohol. We think it might be Edgar Stark."

"That's rather serious, I should have thought. Why do you think it's this man?"

Jack was vague. Stella thought bitterly, They're all so damn vague when it comes to their suspicions. Their power is absolute, and suspicion alone is quite enough to seal a man's fate; they can stall him indefinitely on the basis of suspicion. Now Jack was vague. He had no evidence, but on the grounds that it must be a patient who was bringing it in (though why not a crooked attendant? she wondered), and therefore a parole patient on an outside working party, and therefore one of three or four obvious suspects, including Edgar, then Edgar was under a very dark cloud indeed. Perhaps he was the only suspect? That would be quite enough to get him pulled off the working party, stripped of his parole status, and set back, in terms of his discharge, months or even years. It was the raw bare face of institutional power she was seeing on the back lawn that night, she was hearing the voice of the master. It hurt her cruelly, hurt her as though her child were being taken from her, and what was worse was that that voice would not be contradicted, because Edgar *had* no voice; he was silent, just as she was now silent on his behalf, unable, although here in the inner council of hospital authority, to speak for him because to do so would not help him. So in her silence she grieved for their lost voices.

What are you going to do about him? Pull him off the working party, keep him inside? Jack didn't want to discuss it in front of the women, he said as much. The evening was over, it was time to go home. For a fleeting moment institutional realities had intruded upon a purely social occasion. Such things cannot be avoided; wives and mothers, after all, are closely involved in the work of their husbands in a maximum-security setting such as this one. But there are always the deeper secrets, Stella reflected, the layers of knowledge from which the women are excluded. Her lover's fate would be decided not by an affable wine-warmed medical superintendent in the moonlight of a warm summer evening. No, it would be decided in the cold clear light of day, at a desk in an office at the heart of a complex of old large buildings with bars on every window.

Max and Stella lay awake in their bedroom, side by side in the darkness. As she silently worried at her lover's predicament, her husband worried at what she'd said that provoked that awful silence.

"They all knew you were attacking me," he said.

"Don't be so paranoid."

"Don't use psychiatric jargon to me."

They fell silent. When Brenda was in the house they spoke in whispers, when they spoke privately, despite the thickness of the walls.

"Why did you want to humiliate me?"

"That's an absurd exaggeration. It was a silly conversation, no one took it seriously."

"You were drunk. Why did you drink so much more than anybody else?"

Silence then, a brooding, angry silence, a silence thick with resentment. This was Max's silence. She had said too much, and his punishment was to create this monstrous silence that filled the room with hurt and anger. She turned away from him and flooded her mind with images of Edgar. But she couldn't suppress the dread she felt that Jack Straffen would revoke his parole, and she wept softly in the darkness. Max made no sort of attempt to comfort her, nor would she have allowed it had he tried.

She had a premonition that everything was about to shatter.

The day was hot and cloudless, and the insects murmured among the old roses as she made her way toward her lover, whom she could see indistinctly at his workbench by the conservatory. Charlie was with him. Edgar put his tools down when he saw her coming and wiped his hands on his corduroys. She had her basket, and in it gardening gloves and secateurs. He had picked broad beans and chard for her, and pulled a bunch of young carrots. She sat on the bench as he filled the basket.

"Mrs. Bain's left something for you in the kitchen," she said to Charlie.

"I'm too busy," he said.

"In you go, darling. She made it specially."

He frowned at her and she frowned back. "I'll be back out in a minute," he said to Edgar, and plodded off along the path.

"What's wrong? Something's happened. You're upset." He said it quietly, without looking at her.

She told him he was suspected of bringing alcohol into the hospital. She didn't reproach him in any way, it didn't occur to her.

"Don't worry."

"I do worry."

She wandered to the apple tree. Through its branches she could see the perimeter wall. Wherever you stood on this side of the garden your view was defined by the Wall.

"What would I do if you were kept inside?"

She sat down beside him again. He took her fingers and brought them to his lips, turned her hand over and kissed the palm. But she wouldn't be comforted.

"What would I do? I'd come down one morning and there'd be some other patient working here. I'd ask where you were and they'd say you weren't on the working party anymore. That would be it, cut off, just severed, no chance to say anything at all. I'd never see you again."

"It won't happen," he said, and continued kissing her palm, but she pulled her hand away.

"You don't know them."

"Oh yes I do."

"Then you know they can do anything they want and nobody can tell them otherwise. You can't. I can't. That would just be it."

"Will you come to the pavilion today?"

"I don't know."

She walked back and forth on the path. Edgar set his elbows on his knees, leaned forward, and gazed at the ground. I believe I know what he was thinking. He was coming to a decision. Stella stood with her back to him, again staring up through the apple tree to the Wall beyond. She heard him abruptly get to his feet and murmur, "Charlie." She picked up her basket and set off down the path toward the house.

She left the basket on the kitchen table and went upstairs. The house was empty. Brenda had taken the car to do some shopping. She threw herself onto the bed and lay there staring at the ceiling.

Ten minutes later she sat up. She was feeling under the bed for her shoes when she heard footsteps coming rapidly up the stairs.

"Charlie, is that you?"

It wasn't Charlie. To her utter astonishment Edgar was standing in the doorway.

"What are you doing!" she whispered. "My mother-in-law is staying with us!"

She began to laugh. She imagined Brenda confronting Edgar in the middle of the morning on the upstairs landing as he emerged from the master bedroom, buttoning his trousers. Still laughing, she crossed the bedroom and closed the door.

She was *amused* that he came to her bedroom?

She was amused, horrified, excited. Risk excited her, I realized, situations of risk. He wasted no time, stripping his clothes off, the blue shirt and yellow corduroys, the patient's uniform. She quickly slipped out of her own clothes. Just the thought of it: here he was in her home, in her bedroom, she was defiling the bed with him, though I don't believe she was aware of the spike of aggression that drove the sex: she was dealing with Max that morning, as well as Edgar.

She lay there in his arms, their clothes in a heap on the floor at the end of the bed. By the clock on her bedside table it was ten to eleven. How desperately I must want to be caught, she thought, to do this, but the thought was not accompanied by any feeling of alarm, it was the calm and tranquil voice of truth. She said she realized that regardless of the cost there is an impulse in us that cries out to declare our truth. Or destroy ourselves. She certainly felt it then; what pleasure it would give her to announce to Max, to me, to all of us that she loved Edgar Stark and found it intolerable to have to conceal it! Though she was not so abandoned as to allow this feeling to surface for more than a few seconds; pragmatic concerns are never far from the thoughts of the secret lover. Then she heard a car in the drive and all her vague ideas of exposure vanished: It must be Brenda returning from her shopping expedition, hours before she was expected. Edgar sat up and she told him they had to get dressed, she'd heard the car. They stared at each other for a second then scrambled out of bed, laughing like a pair of wicked school-children.

Brenda was coming in through the front door as Stella came downstairs.

"Too hot, my dear," she called, "I simply cannot function in this heat. Oh, and there was nowhere to park, and some dreadful little man kept honking his horn at me, so I thought I'd just forget the whole thing, come home and get cool and relax."

"What a good idea. Shall I put the kettle on?"

"A cup of tea would be heaven."

She went upstairs. Stella paused at the kitchen door. She heard the bedroom door close. Then Edgar was coming down with his boots in his hand like a character in a farce, and she ran ahead of him across the kitchen and opened the back door to make sure no one was in the yard.

She turned to him and saw that under his arm he had a bundle of Max's clothes.

"What are you taking those for?" she whispered.

He put a finger to her lips, then walked boldly across the yard. She went back upstairs. The cupboard door was open, and clothes were missing from several hangers on Max's side. She heard Brenda coming out of her room. She was making the bed for the second time that morning, this time with clean sheets, when Brenda spoke from the doorway.

"Would you mind if I ran a bath? One gets so sticky."

"Of course not," she said, not turning.

She went downstairs and sat at the kitchen table. Why had he taken Max's clothes? What could he possibly want with Max's clothes? What on earth was he up to?

Max came home from the hospital just after one, so there were four for lunch. Stella became more animated when she felt under pressure, and she most certainly felt under pressure that day. Even a couple of large gins could not reduce the magnitude in her mind of the risk they'd run. She couldn't begin to imagine the consequences if they'd been caught. So she gaily served cold meat and new potatoes with butter and chives, and a tomato salad with a garlic dressing, and energetically pursued a semblance of normality. Max was quiet and preoccupied throughout, and when it was over he asked her to bring his coffee to the study.

He was at his desk. He turned toward her as she came in, and his expression provoked a fresh flare of anxiety in her. She was very much on the defensive, and her response was to assume a blithe unconcern; but she was afraid they'd been seen and reported, and this seemed confirmed when he said: "What dealings do you have with Edgar Stark?"

"I see him in the vegetable garden most days," she said, frowning slightly as though attempting to fathom the source of this unusual inquiry. "Why?"

"Has he ever come into the house?"

Has he ever come into the house! The bed was still warm with the impress of his body, the sheets in the laundry basket stained and damp!

"Only the time he brought Charlie in."

Max sighed. He took off his spectacles and rubbed his eyes.

"There's no doubt now that alcohol's being smuggled into the hospital. The nuisance of it is, the attendants get so badly rattled. We have to be seen to be taking it very seriously indeed."

"Is it out of the question that an attendant brought it in?"

She was unsure of the wisdom of putting this to him. If she was under any suspicion it would look like a diversionary tactic. If on the other hand she was not suspected it would be a perfectly logical question. She watched him closely. He did not lift his head. She knew she was safe. For now.

"It's not out of the question but it's not an idea Jack's eager to pursue just at the moment. It's all so bloody political."

"Are you looking for a scapegoat?" She was deliberately pressing her advantage. "That's not very fair."

"Of course we don't want a scapegoat. Nor do we want to accuse anyone until we're certain."

"It hasn't come from this house."

"It might have come from the cricket pavilion, I suppose."

"It might," said Stella. There was a pause.

"Walk over there with me," he said. "I'll get my keys."

His keys. Upstairs, on his dressing table. Or perhaps in the pocket of his linen jacket. In the cupboard. She sat there in the study and waited for him to come down. His desk was neat, only the morning's mail and a couple of files on top, all his pens and pencils and papers sorted and consigned to their various drawers. The study window looked out onto a patch of lawn bordered by flower beds, and beyond it the pine trees that hid the house from the road. On the bookshelves, stacks of psychiatric journals and textbooks.

"Stella."

She came out into the hall. He was on the upstairs landing, leaning over the top banister.

"Did it go to the cleaners?"

"What?"

"My linen jacket."

Think fast, Stella. Get it right. Save the situation. "No. Can't you find it?"

He went back into the bedroom. She climbed the stairs. He had his back to her as she came in. He was going through his suits and jackets on their hangers. He didn't turn around.

"This is very odd. I'm missing a shirt and a pair of trousers too."

"Nothing's gone to the cleaners this week."

"I had my estate keys in the pocket. Where's Charlie?"

"I don't think he would take your clothes."

"Nor do I."

He sat on the side of the bed frowning at his fingernails. Stella leaned against the door frame. The sunlight streamed in across her dressing table. She knew she was about to lose everything, and in a way she didn't care. She was curious to see how it worked itself out. His accusation was imminent and she had no idea what she was going to say.

"He must have got in here."

"Who?"

"Edgar Stark."

"That's impossible. How could he, with me and Brenda here? Let me see if Charlie's in the garden."

He was sitting with his hands in his lap, frowning. A man as organized as he was, a man so much in control of his world: such a man did not lose a shirt and a pair of trousers and a linen jacket with the estate keys in the pocket.

Stella darted downstairs and out through the front door. They weren't back from lunch yet. She ran through the vegetable garden and into the conservatory, where Edgar's white jacket hung from a nail by the door. She tore open an empty seed packet and with a stub of pencil scrawled him a note. She stuffed the note into the pocket of the jacket and left it sticking out so he wouldn't miss it.

As she crossed back to the house she saw the working party appear at the end of the drive. There was no more she could do except pray that Edgar would see her note and find an opportunity to get rid of the clothes. She met Max in the hall. She told him that Charlie wasn't in the garden and probably wouldn't be back for hours now.

"I don't think Charlie would touch my clothes," he said again, and went back into the study.

She stood there in the doorway. "What are you going to do?"

He was beside his desk, the phone in his hand, facing her. "Put me through to Block Three." This he said into the receiver as they stood there gazing at each other.

The news came that evening. Brenda came down at five and Stella told her about the missing keys and clothes, and they went into the living room and each had a large gin. Stella couldn't keep still. Her anxiety was of course explicable in terms of sympathetic concern for her husband.

"Max will cope, my dear," said Brenda.

"Of course he will. But one does worry."

They'd both had another large drink by the time Max came home from the hospital. Brenda was still in the living room and

Stella was in the kitchen making dinner. She heard the front door open and came out into the hall. His face was closed and angry. She went down the hall to him.

"What is it?"

He didn't look at her properly, his eyes merely flickered to hers, then slid away. In the living room he stood in front of the empty fireplace and delivered his news.

"Edgar Stark has absconded."

And at that moment the siren began its awful singsong wail.

4

This is what we think must have happened: Edgar told John Archer after lunch that they wanted him in the chaplain's garden, and went off by himself. He retrieved Max's clothes from where he'd hidden them in the woods at the end of the Raphaels' garden. Wearing Max's clothes he had then made his escape, keeping well away from the road until he was clear of the estate, and then, by thumb or bus or train, he found his way to London. I was not at all happy to hear how lax security was on the outside work parties, but the question that most disturbed me—and Jack too—was what Max had been doing in the hours between the discovery of the missing clothes and the discovery of Edgar's absence, close to five?

This was an interval of *almost three hours*. The search of Edgar's room and a subsequent search of the entire ward had yielded nothing, but Max hadn't told Jack what was going on. If he had looked for Edgar in the chaplain's garden immediately, and discovered his absence, the alarm would have been raised very much sooner and we'd have quickly picked him up.

But Max was apparently so determined to get to the bottom of it all before he saw Jack that he made mistakes, and the most significant was this failure to establish Edgar's whereabouts during the afternoon. After returning to the hospital and checking with the staff in Block 3 that nothing had turned up in his absence, he went to his office. He then, apparently for no good reason, waited *another half hour* before calling Jack. By that time the working parties were due back in, and John Archer had already discovered that his patient was missing. I was told at once, and without delay I went to Jack's office. When Max telephoned, I was with Jack, and he already knew that Edgar had gone. What Jack did not know, and what it must have galled and humiliated Max to have to tell him—and this of course accounts for much of Max's behavior that afternoon—was that the escaped patient was wearing his, Max's, clothes. I certainly had no sympathy for him; he had allowed my patient to escape. And Edgar, for all his sexual bravado, still needed me. He was a sick man.

Jack and I decided not to use the siren immediately, reluctant to arouse the countryside to the escape of a patient until we had to. Better to organize a search party and mount a quick sweep of the estate, try and pick him up before he got too far. We were both aware there were two things a patient needed to abscond successfully, clothing and money, and one of those at least he had secured. For two hours attendants fanned out across the estate. They searched the farm and the marsh, and they penetrated some way into the forest. Dusk was coming on. They didn't know how much of a lead Edgar had. No more than three hours, they believed, but three hours was enough for a resourceful man with clothes and money. Nobody knew whether he had money; nobody but Stella, of course, who had more than once given him cash, enough certainly to get him to London. In the meantime we could only hope that he was still out there somewhere, stumbling blindly cross-country, and as such an easy quarry for the local police, who were informed of the escape when after two hours he had not been found.

Brenda and Stella responded to the announcement of these dramatic events with exclamations of surprise and concern. But it was Brenda who thought of Charlie, who had not come home yet. Stella promptly simulated extreme anxiety; she channeled the emotional impact of Edgar's escape into anxiety for Charlie. She hoped that Max didn't notice that the boy's welfare was his grandmother's rather than her own first thought.

Max's curt response was that Edgar Stark had no interest in boys. "He wants to get as far away from here as he can."

Shortly afterward Charlie came running into the house in a state of high excitement at hearing the siren, and eager to know everything.

Stella went back into the kitchen to finish cooking dinner. He wants to get as far away from here as he can. She stood at the stove with the tears coursing down her face. She heard Brenda come in. She wiped her eyes with her apron and lit the gas under the potatoes. She had to maintain a façade that suggested nothing other than reasonable distress that the hospital would now undergo gross disruptions, to the detriment of patients, staff, and staff families alike. She murmured something of this to Brenda.

"It is a terrible nuisance," Brenda said. "Very tiresome of the man indeed. And he worked in the garden?"

"He was restoring the conservatory."

"It's shocking to think he came into this house. What would have happened if one of us had been here at the time? I understand he's committed violence against women in the past."

"I suppose he made sure the house was empty first."

"What if Charlie had surprised him upstairs in your bedroom? In your *bedroom*, Stella! Don't you feel violated? That he came into your bedroom?"

"It's a shock. I haven't altogether assimilated it."

"Of course not."

Brenda conducted this interrogation without once taking her

eyes off Stella. Something in the younger woman's reaction to the escape puzzled her, and Stella was aware of it. What had she given away? Was it her failure to think of Charlie, when told that an escaped patient was at large in the countryside? Or had she failed to show sufficient surprise; as though she'd *known*? She prayed she could get through the evening without further scrutiny.

But worse was to come. Halfway through supper the telephone in the study began ringing, the hospital telephone, and Max left the room. When he returned he told Stella that Jack wanted to see them both at his house.

"He wants to see you both?" said Brenda.

"Yes, Mother," said Max with uncharacteristic firmness. "He wants to see us both."

They drove up past the Main Gate just as it was getting dark. Long strips of cloud, pink, blue, and mauve, were strung across the fading sky, and against the thickening evening light reared the Main Gate with its two square towers and the double gates between. As they'd got into the car Max had asked her why she thought Jack wanted to see her as well, and she'd told him she had no idea. He said nothing more, and they drove in silence until they reached the superintendent's house, up beside the female wing.

Bridie opened the door to them, looking suitably grave. With a pang of distaste Stella recognized how deeply over a long marriage she had insinuated herself into the fabric of Jack's working life, and it occurred to her that she would never be in Bridie's position now. Previously she had thought it hers for the taking, the role of medical superintendent's wife, and she had mentally spurned it. Now she saw she would never be offered it; the superintendency was lost. She wondered had Max grasped this yet.

Bridie showed them into Jack's study, a large book-lined room, comfortably furnished, and Jack, his broad back to them, fussed at the whisky decanter and asked them without turning if they would have a drink. Stella said yes with some alacrity. Bridie closed the door and left the three of them alone.

"Make yourselves at home," murmured Jack, and there was a gruffness and a detachment in him that she had never heard before.

"Bloody business," he said, when they were settled. "This is my fifth escape. Always hell, even if we get him fast. Edgar Stark."

He fell silent, frowning at his whisky, and the name of Stella's lover hung there in the gloom as the evening died and the last of the birdsong drifted in from the garden.

"This is difficult. I'll come straight to the point. I haven't told you this, Max. I saw no reason to distress you both by passing on wild rumors. But in view of this afternoon's events I must bring this thing into the open."

He paused again. This "thing"—what "thing"? The way Jack pronounced the word, to Stella it was a disgusting thing, decaying, bad. Why did she need to be present for the bringing into the open of something decaying and bad?

"What rumors?" said Max.

The superintendent sighed. He turned to Stella. "It's been suggested," he began, "that your relationship with Edgar Stark went beyond what's proper for a doctor's wife."

"Where has this come from?" said Max sharply. "Why wasn't I informed?"

"It doesn't matter where it came from. I don't need to tell you how these things work. The patients talk among themselves, an attendant overhears, the attendants talk, it soon gets back to me."

"I'm astonished you take it seriously!"

Stella said both she and Jack were surprised by Max's vehemence.

"Max. Please listen to me. Of course I am skeptical of rumor. I hear a great deal in the course of the day, little of it with any basis in reality. But this is a large institution, and people talk. Of course I give it no credence. However. I need to know why such a rumor might have arisen."

"Stella talked to him in the garden, but there's nothing beyond that."

"Stella?"

They both turned toward her. Max was angry, and while on the face of it his anger was in reaction to Jack's accusing Stella of impropriety, she understood that the fact that this interview should even be necessary, plus, of course, his sickening awareness that he'd mishandled the theft of his clothes and in effect allowed Edgar to get away, all this complicated the situation, and his defense of her was not as gallant as it appeared.

"Of course not, Jack," she said, a tone of disbelief softening the outrage in her voice. "I chat with him sometimes when I go into the vegetable garden. Or I did. I chat to all the patients, I think it's important."

"Did you see him every day? I'm sorry, Stella, I have to know where this came from."

A pause here. She assumed an expression of dignity in the face of insult. She was a respectable married woman whose virtue had been questioned. She allowed that expression then gradually to give way to a pained acceptance of the realities.

"We eat a salad from the garden every day. If I see Edgar I say good morning to him, and sometimes we talk."

Jack allowed a small pause while he frowned and nodded and watched Stella carefully.

"Thank you, Stella," he said at last. "I thought it must be something like that. I do apologize. But you understand. I pity the psychiatrist's wife, it's a thankless task you perform. We're the only ones who know the cost." This was addressed to Max, who also nodded absently and frowned.

"Let me give you another drink."

"No thanks, Jack," said Max, rising, "we must go."

Jack didn't apologize further. He knew it had to be done, and he'd done it. It would take a good deal to convince him that a doctor's wife could commit any sort of impropriety with a patient. He was satisfied. This at least was what I imagine Max made of the interview.

I was with Bridie in the drawing room when Jack joined us. I'd been there for the last hour, bringing them up to date on what little I knew about Stella's relationship with my patient.

"Well?" I said.

He nodded. "I'm afraid it's true."

"Oh God."

"What will you do?"

Jack sighed. "That depends."

"Max doesn't see she's lying?" said Bridie.

Jack opened his hands. He said nothing.

"I suspect," I said, "that he does. But he would rather *not* see it. Which is why he let him get away."

Jack gazed into his whisky. I suddenly saw that he was out of his depth. He was genuinely shocked to think that Stella might be guilty of what I'd suggested. He didn't want to believe it.

Bridie had no such qualms. "To think of it," she murmured, "to think that a doctor's wife—"

She fell silent. It was too much for her too.

"Perhaps," I said, "I should have a word with Max."

It seemed, said Stella, that the evening would never end; it seemed as if every permutation, every ripple of this stone dropped into the still pool of their lives must wash through before she could take a pill and go to bed and properly be alone with the misery walled up behind the façade she had erected against the world. As they drove past the Main Gate she had said to Max: "What will you say to Brenda?"

"I hadn't thought."

Their voices seemed now to be operating in two registers, a front register that functioned as a screen behind which seethed unspoken reservoirs of feeling. Max's front was one of weariness and preoccupation; behind it she felt the storm system of his anger, directed both at himself and at her. Though why he should be angry with her was unclear. Hadn't she explained herself, and hadn't that explanation been accepted by Jack Straffen? But there was no point in going into any of this now.

Max went into his study and without a word closed the door behind him. Brenda's avidity to know everything was barely veiled.

"I sent Charlie up to bed," she said. "He wasn't very happy to be missing all the excitement." They were standing in the hall. Stella put her bag on the table under the mirror and gazed at her reflection. Brenda waited.

"Well?"

"There have been rumors," said Stella. "About me."

Brenda followed her into the drawing room and stood by the fireplace while Stella poured herself a drink. She would have to be told, but Stella was damned if she'd hand it to her on a plate.

"About you?"

She moved to the window with her drink. She gazed out into the garden. The curtains were still open though night had fallen. There was a full moon.

"It's a lovely night," she said. Where is Edgar now? In a ditch or a barn or a haystack, huddled in the darkness, dressed in Max's clothes, eking out his tobacco? Or had he disappeared into some world she knew nothing of? She turned away from the window.

"Yes, about me."

"Stella, please tell me what happened. Or don't, if you don't want to. But I am concerned, you know. I would like to help."

"Someone told Jack there was impropriety in my relationship with Edgar Stark."

"Was there?"

"Of course not. Need you ask?"

"I'm sorry."

She gazed at her calmly. Oh, Brenda was ready to cast her as the scarlet woman and see all of Max's troubles laid at her door, but Stella wouldn't allow her to do it.

I had meanwhile left the Straffens' and driven down past the Main Gate to the deputy superintendent's house. Already I felt a different atmosphere on the estate: there were men about despite the lateness of the hour, there was urgency in the air. This was a delicate interview I had to conduct with Max, and the point of it was to prevent him adopting, psychologically, a posture of isolation. Unfortunately we needed him with us. About Stella I was less certain, but what I predicted was that she would now see that she'd been betrayed, and would become angry not so much at Edgar as at herself. Which might in turn trigger a depressive episode. We would have to be vigilant.

I rang the doorbell. On her way down the hall Stella again paused briefly at the mirror. There was no sound from the study. She opened the front door.

"Peter, come in. Max is in the study."

"Let me talk to you first."

"We're in the drawing room."

I followed her down the hall. She moved with an exaggerated ease, her body denying its tension. Brenda greeted me warmly. I sank into an armchair.

"Bloody for all of you," I said, as Stella gave me a gin.

"Peter, tell us what's going on," said Brenda.

"All the usual procedures. Jack carries the worst of it of course. He'll be crucified in the press, questions in the House, the whole parole system will be condemned. As escape like this sets the hospital back five years." I was trying to project a sort of weary languor, to cast the whole thing as a nuisance merely and mask the true seriousness of the crisis. Brenda had assumed her woman-out-of-her-depth stance, designed to appeal to my gallantry and prompt confidences.

"But surely he'll be caught quickly?"

I sipped my gin and allowed a hand to fall over the arm of the chair. "Perhaps. Though we think he may have friends in London."

"I didn't know he had friends in London," said Stella.

"How would you?" I gazed at her rather dreamily.

"Max said nothing about him having friends in London. Who might be involved, I mean."

"He has friends from the old days. Soho. That crowd."

Stella says she suddenly saw the three of us as though she were on the other side of the window, as though she were standing in the garden, in the darkness, watching a man in an armchair talking to two women, each in a state of rapt attention.

Brenda's expression was one of naked curiosity mingled with fascination and horror. Her mask had slipped.

After a few minutes I rose to my feet. "I'd better have a word with Max," I said. "Please don't get up, Stella."

But she did. She stood at the door of the drawing room and watched me go down the hallway and tap lightly on Max's door, then go into the study and close the door behind me.

She doesn't know when Max came to bed. She went upstairs soon after. She took a pill and lay there waiting for sleep. The moonlight filtered through the curtains. The house was quiet. She pressed her face into her pillow and wept until the pillowcase was sodden. She changed the pillowcase and lay on her back staring at the ceiling, having discharged the most immediate weight of her misery. She pondered this new information. It meant one thing only: if he had friends he was probably safe. Holding tightly to this thought she fell asleep.

I am satisfied this is the truth. I don't believe they planned it together. I don't think she was actively working against us.

It happened much as I said it would. The press resurrected Edgar's case, and Stella was forced into an unwilling recognition of what had brought him here. He had killed his wife with a hammer, and he had mutilated her corpse. Two psychiatrists testified at the trial that he suffered from a paranoid psychosis, and the insanity defense was accepted by the court. I admitted him the following day. Now the press wanted to know why such a man was allowed to leave the hospital on a daily basis and work in the gardens of the estate.

They were dreadful days for all of us. In the deputy superintendent's house Brenda took charge of Charlie, leaving Stella and Max to handle the crisis undistracted. Stella feels she succeeded in concealing her feelings, which were concentrated, of course, on her absent lover. The deception she practiced during these days cost her dearly; she was after all in the heart of the camp of the hunters. Max came home from the hospital most days at lunchtime, and Brenda and Stella tried to create out of thin air a warm, womanly flurry of domesticity around him to give him some sense of his home as a haven, a safe place insulated from the appalling pressures he faced in the hospital at this time.

Everyone was under such scrutiny! There were reporters all over the estate, asking questions of anyone who would talk to them. In a summer devoid of major news Edgar Stark effortlessly dominated the front pages. We felt besieged. Charlie was forbidden to leave the garden. On the one occasion that he disobeyed this order a reporter approached him in a friendly way and, on learning who he was, asked him embarrassing questions about his father, such as what Daddy talked about at lunch. Poor Charlie came home confused and tearful, afraid that he'd done something very wrong in talking to the man but too polite not to.

No working party appeared on the estate. Stella wandered about the garden and the stillness was alive with his absence. She went into the vegetable garden to pick lettuce and gooseberries. Amid all that greenness, all that summer growth, there was no glimpse of yellow corduroy by the conservatory at the far end. The trees hanging over the garden walls seemed weighted with a peculiar dull heaviness, and cast deep pools of shadow. It was all so full-blown, the grass in the meadow thick and high and the climbing roses blowsy in their second flush, but in the ripeness there was no lover. She wandered down the gravel path, her basket on her arm, and paused by the phlox she'd transplanted from old clumps in the spring. She inhaled the fragrance. A fat bumblebee crawled up a thistle head then lifted into the drowsy air and sailed away. She sat on the bench and picked with her fingernail at a spot of lichen furring the soft gray wood. Then she went into the conservatory.

Even the conservatory seemed desolate, abandoned, forlorn. Like her. He had begun to replace the rotten woodwork, and the new struts and sashes were notched into the sound wood of the original with a clean exactitude of fit. The pattern of old wood and new was pleasing to the eye. She lay down on the cracked stones, among the weeds, where they had first lain together. Against her will the tears came. She brushed them away and rose to her feet, left the conservatory and moved purposefully along the path, stooping to pull slim sticks of rhubarb from the soil. The garden missed him as much as she did. Here and there clumps of flowers were drooping; the hydrangeas had collapsed for want of water. Everything needed deadheading, and the path through the rough grass of the meadow was sprinkled with dandelions gone to seed. The hosepipe hung unused and neglected on its post by the tap in the hedge. The freshness of the garden was lost.

She mentioned this to Brenda when they were getting lunch ready. "I shall have to do it myself, I suppose."

"What a nuisance. And here I was thinking you were the only woman I knew who'd properly solved the servant problem."

Stella glanced at her. A slight movement of Brenda's lips indicated that she was being facetious.

Stella didn't know what, if anything, Jack or I had said to Max about his failure to report the theft of his clothes immediately. It was hard for her to get anything out of him at all, beyond the fact that the search was now concentrated on London and that there were no leads.

"He's gone to ground," said Max.

"Someone's sheltering him," said Brenda.

He was safe, this was what Stella heard. He was safe, and he was thinking of her; whatever little room he was holed up in, he was keeping his head down and thinking of her. But as the days passed, and September came, there were times when she was filled with despair, when she faced the possibility that she would never see him again. It upset her so badly however that she pushed the thought away and remembered instead the conversations they'd had and the understandings they'd arrived at. He would not abandon her, she was certain of this. She did not lose faith. She told herself to be patient, and to take comfort in the fact of his safety, wherever he was. She felt she was in a state of suspension; nothing had ended, but it was changing. She did not try to imagine what would happen next, for such thoughts made her miserable, they strayed into practical questions that were for the moment unanswerable. She simply asked herself what he would want her to do, and answered that he would want her to be, yes, patient, silent, and relieved that he was safe.

She drank constantly, it seemed essential if she were to maintain any sort of equilibrium at all. She avoided practical thinking and remained as much as possible buoyed by a sort of blind faith; that, and gin. There were moments—moments of practical thinking—when she understood that blind faith and gin couldn't remain her sole spiritual nourishment forever; but while she could manage it she would. Everyone else was so utterly distracted by the crisis, by the eyes of the world, that none of them noticed that she drifted through her days in a state of detachment and abstraction, functioning as she was expected to but not ever, really, totally there. None of them noticed but me. I was watching her.

She had one bad shock during this period. She was in the vegetable garden with the hosepipe one morning. The hot weather continued. There had been no rain for weeks. The soil was slightly sandy and needed lots to drink, and to thirst she was particularly sympathetic just then. So she hooked up the hosepipe to the tap in the hedge and set about giving everything in the garden a drink of water. She moved steadily along with the hose, in Wellington boots, light summer frock, sunglasses, and wide-brimmed straw hat, and there was a pleasantly mindless quality to the experience, a quality she sought in all her activity during these strained days. The sound of footsteps on the gravel behind her was unwelcome. She turned, the hose in her hand still gushing into the soil, and less welcome still was the sight of Jack Straffen advancing along the path toward her. Vigilance. Vigilance. She called to him to wait while she turned off the water. She came tramping out of the lettuce patch, the hose on the ground still gushing, and went to the tap and turned it off.

"Max is up at the hospital," she said.

Jack was in a black suit and a Panama hat and looked hot and uncomfortable and very much alien to the greenery all about him.

"I wanted to talk to you. Can we sit down?"

She took him to the bench beside the conservatory and they sat in the shade. Jack took off his hat and set it on the bench.

"Smoke?"

"No thank you."

"A man like Edgar Stark," he said, and then stopped. He tapped the ash from his cigarette with deliberation onto the gravel at their feet and stared at it. He sighed. "We have a number of patients diagnosed as paranoids. Now, these patients, Stella, are every bit as dangerous as our schizophrenics who've killed. The peculiar thing is, in many of them there's not a flicker of psychosis, not a flicker. We don't medicate them. We try and treat them, but not I'm afraid with any great success. We can manage them, we can contain them, but we don't really know how to treat them. Because we don't really understand what they are."

Is he talking about his patients, she wondered, or women?

"Appearances to the contrary, Edgar Stark is a deeply disturbed individual."

"I know this, Jack."

"I wonder if you do. Do you know what he did to that woman after he killed her?"

She said nothing.

"He decapitated her. Then he enucleated her. He cut her head off, and then he took her eyes out."

She gazed from their shady seat down the length of the garden, and found it remarkable how the plants she'd watered looked more alive already than their neighbors. Beside the bench at either end, in the shade, was set a half-barrel that Edgar had filled with soil and planted with winter cyclamen. She remembered him sawing the barrel in half. She'd held it steady for him. They needed water too.

"Shall we have a drink?"

"It's not ten yet, Stella."

"The garden will be ruined without the working party. Look at it."

"Are you listening to what I'm saying?"

She turned toward him. "I don't know what it is you want," she said. "You think I'm hiding something. I'm not."

"Did he ever touch you?"

"No!"

"Did he ever ask you for money?"

"No. Don't you think I'd have told Max if anything like that had happened?"

Jack took his spectacles off. He rubbed his eyes with a thumb and forefinger. He sat up straight and leaned against the bench and stared out into the sunlit garden. He was a big, worried man in his sixties with shrewd eyes and a gray, cropped skull. He was close to retirement. He didn't want this problem. The gold band on his ring finger gleamed in the sunlight filtering through the ivy over their heads.

"I don't believe you're telling me the whole truth," he said.

She didn't protest. She made a shrugging motion and shook her head slightly, as though at a loss how to convince him.

"Stella, if you're in some sort of trouble, if he's persuaded you into something—"

"What?"

"I know Edgar Stark. I understand how he operates. There is no shame in admitting that he has involved you in his case, won your sympathy, set you against Max and Peter and myself. He would have identified you immediately as someone he could use. Did he tell you we were going to discharge him shortly? None of it is true. But I can't help you unless you tell me what happened."

"Nothing happened."

Jack sighed. "Nothing happened."

"No."

"You won't tell me."

"I am telling you."

He picked up his Panama. "Perhaps it's as well for you that he's gone. Come and talk to me soon. Will you?"

She nodded.

She watched him walk heavily back down the path. Her heart was beating very fast and her hands were trembling.

Vigilance. There was nothing Jack had said that Edgar hadn't already told her he'd say. She made her way slowly back along the path. She was uncomfortably aware of how persuasive the superintendent was, of how easy it would be to succumb to the warm, paternal tone he employed as he offered her his understanding and support. It required vigilance, and more than vigilance, it required a deliberate act of will to keep in the foreground of consciousness that it was Jack Straffen who was attempting to manipulate her, not Edgar.

Oh, he was cunning, my Edgar. He had prepared her for something like this, and shown her how she should react. He had secured her silence, and his own security, in advance; and without even telling her he intended to escape.

During the period immediately after the escape Stella and Max kept a curious distance from each other. She had good reason to avoid him, but why, she wondered, was he so wary of her? Because he was afraid that the rumors were true. He knew her well enough to entertain a doubt. She admitted to me at the end of a long, emotional session that a year before any of this happened she'd told Max that she was not prepared to be buried alive in a cold marriage, a white marriage, because his own sexual drive was weak, or because he lacked the moral or physical imagination to continue to find her attractive, or because he channeled all his libido into his work, or because of whatever explanation he cared to offer. She thought he had probably discounted the threat implicit in this ultimatum, but now he was faced with the possibility not only that she'd carried it out but that she'd done so with a patient. This was something that must be pushed away, for to see it as feasible was to accept responsibility for the failure of the marriage, at least at the physical level, and perhaps for Stella's disastrously ill-judged choice of a lover as well. Max was not prepared to talk to her about any of this. As far as he was concerned, the best medicine was denial.

So they moved around that large sad house during the last hot days of summer like ghosts, drifting past each other, saying nothing that mattered, barely acknowledging each other. What substance there was, it came from Brenda, whose concern for the rituals of civilized life acted as a sort of adhesive and bonded them into a semblance of a family, which was important for Charlie, whose sense of excitement at this unfolding drama was tempered by the strain of living in a house of ghosts. Brenda held them together and Stella, meanwhile, sustained herself as best she could.

Eventually Edgar slipped off the front pages and then, with no fresh reports of him, the papers lost interest altogether. Gradually the hospital adjusted to his absence and the crisis softened into something approaching normal routine. The weather broke at last, and after weeks of hot dry sunshine it started to rain.

5

She stood at the drawing-room window watching a sudden shower of rain. After several minutes it turned to a light drizzle, which then gave way to a clearing of the clouds and the tentative reappearance of the sun. The garden glistened and shone. Everything seemed suddenly greener, more vigorous; but not for long. The clouds came back, the sky darkened, and again it rained. This changeable weather persisted for a few days, and we were soon talking about the summer in tones that said, Despite everything it had been glorious but it was over now and England could expect no better. Brenda went back to London, and Stella began to think about getting Charlie ready for school.

She says she never gave up hope. At no point did she turn from him in her mind. She never lost the feeling that he was with her. She had learned to trust him. There was no good reason why she should trust him, and that in a way was why she did; trust, and faith, and love, it seemed, were what they were because they were aroused and sustained regardless of reason, because they lay *deeper* than reason. She had no idea what was happening to him. My own guess was that he'd slipped into some shadowy London underworld of artists and criminals, but I couldn't be more precise than that; I had quietly talked to everyone I knew who might have information, and to my frustration drawn a complete blank. I knew he would turn up eventually; my concern, of course, was that without treatment, without my guiding hand, he would form a relationship with a woman and his illness would blossom anew.

In an odd way my own intense preoccupation with Edgar's whereabouts and welfare was mirrored in Stella: her sexual and romantic infatuation with him I later saw as a reflection, primitive and distorted, yes, but a reflection all the same, of my own solicitude for a sick man going untreated in what must have been a situation of great tension and uncertainty. She told me about those days, and I recognized in her experience something of my own. The evenings were the hardest, she said. Max would go to his study after dinner and she'd drift into the drawing room. When he went up to bed an hour or so later she didn't go with him, she told him she wanted to read for a bit longer. She'd hear the bedroom door close, and that was her signal to put aside her novel and seriously fortify her drink.

The hours that followed were Edgar's hours. She gave herself over to memories of their summer. She referred to her diary; she had not kept a written account, but by means of cryptic markings on particular days she could remember each meeting, and each act of love, as she called it. There was a way she found of holding an image in her mind as though it were cigarette smoke until she had entirely absorbed it, all the substance and meaning and feeling that were in it, and some images, she said, were more potent in this regard than others. In the cricket pavilion once, a few seconds after sex, he laid his head on her shoulder, and she listened to his breathing subside. Then he lifted his face, and she had no words for the expression in his eyes, no means of describing what it was they silently said to each other during those seconds before their thoughts turned again to practicalities, to haste and concealment. In the stillness, only this wordless recognition, and it seemed to her there was a breakdown of their separate egos, a falling away of personality, a sense of identity, a sense that they were essence to essence, fused—

I listened patiently to all this and did not ask the question, What of him? What of Edgar? Did he, too, feel that they had been essence to essence, fused? At the time I believed he had deliberately aroused these feelings in her in order to use her, and that once he was clear away from the hospital she would never hear from him again. I was wrong.

One evening around this time Max invited me to dinner. It was just the three of us. We had a drink in the drawing room and the conversation inevitably turned to Edgar. Max was saying that the escape was carefully planned. He kept worrying at it. He had become rather a bore on the subject.

"All he needed was street clothes. He waited until the house was empty. Once he was sure nobody was in the house he didn't waste a second."

"Fortunate," I murmured, glancing at Stella, "that you and he are the same size."

"Fortunate for him," said Max, frowning. He disliked this aspect of the thing, this identification, however indirect, between himself and Edgar Stark. He sat forward in his chair, his glass and his spectacles between his fingers, the spectacles dangling. Since the escape he had been unable to shake off the guilty awareness that after discovering the theft of his clothes he had delayed, and allowed Edgar to get away. He was too experienced a psychiatrist not to have analyzed, as I had, why he'd delayed, and by this time Stella, too, had realized that it was because he'd reached the conclusion that Edgar had entered the bedroom at her invitation. Better let him run than face that.

"Something I've never properly understood," I said, rather maliciously, I'm afraid, "is this business of drink being taken from the pavilion. Presumably he only got your keys the day he took your clothes, which was the day he escaped."

Max shook his head. "I don't think it came from the pavilion," he said.

"How odd," said Stella. I was watching her, she said, in that rather dreamy way I had, when it occurred to her that there was nothing in the least dreamy about the busy, intelligent mind behind those lazy eyes. She suddenly wondered how much I knew about what had gone on in the cricket pavilion. At that moment the telephone rang and she put her glass down.

"It'll be on the table in five minutes," she said. She went out into the hall and closed the door behind her, and I heard her pick up the telephone.

I learned only later it was him.

At the dinner table I remarked that I'd been right about Edgar still having friends in London. "They knew he was coming," I said. "There was a place ready for him. We won't get him now, not unless he does something stupid."

"They always do something stupid," Max muttered, picking at his curry. Stella glanced from Max to me with the bright, interested look of the good psychiatrist's wife. She was alert, elated even, but it didn't occur to me to wonder why. It should have, considering how grim this talk must have sounded to a woman in love.

"Really, Peter?"

"I don't think so. I doubt we'll see Edgar Stark again."

The conversation moved on. Stella cleared the table and took the plates out to the kitchen. She stood at the sink, staring across the yard, her heart on fire. You can imagine what it meant to me, that call, she said.

Yes, I said, I could.

But I couldn't imagine why, after successfully escaping from the hospital, Edgar was risking everything to see her again. What I have since realized is that it was connected to his art. After making no work for almost five years, he sent for Stella because he needed a new head. And because of what she was, and who she was—but most of all because she loved him—it had to be hers.

The days now dragged with a terrible slowness. Even at this late stage she was not immune to panic. Am I mad? she asked herself. How can I jeopardize everything, how can I be so irresponsible, a grown-up woman, a *mother*? But the idea of seeing him again dispelled all doubt and hesitation.

On the Sunday night she told Max she was going up to London the next day. He asked her if she would need the car to get to the station and she said she'd take it if he didn't want it; otherwise she'd call a taxi. How polite they were to each other. When she went to bed that night Max was still awake. His voice came out of the darkness.

"Darling?"

She made a sleepy noise.

"This bloody business has blighted everything. I'm sorry."

He turned onto his side, facing her. His hand came stealing under the sheet.

"I'm very tired, Max."

"We haven't for weeks."

She turned away from him. He fitted his body around the curve of her spine so his legs were pressed against the backs of hers. Why tonight?

"Go to sleep," she murmured. She could feel him getting hard.

"I've lost you," he whispered.

"Don't be silly. Go to sleep."

I found it all too easy to imagine Stella's experience now: the feverish anticipation, the almost intolerable tension as she counted the hours till she saw him again. She had decided to take an early train. She could do enough shopping in an hour to justify the journey and still leave the rest of the day free. From

Victoria she took a cab to Knightsbridge and made some hurried purchases. Then she returned to the station and sat in the cafeteria with a cup of coffee. The great glass roof made her think of the conservatory. She waited. She was wearing a white suit and white high heels. She sat at the back, where she could watch the entrance, and at ten past twelve she saw him come in. He stood at the counter with his back to her and bought a cup of tea; she was both exhilarated and terrified, she said. But then when he turned she had to cover her embarrassment by lighting a cigarette, for it wasn't him, it was nothing like him! He saw her staring at him and she looked away, she frantically signaled indifference, and to her relief he did not come over. A woman alone in the cafeteria of a large railway station to many men looks like prey.

He didn't come. At two o'clock she gave up. She hadn't the heart to do any more shopping. She caught the next train back and drove home from the station without incident. Nobody was in the house. She lay in a hot bath with a large gin and tonic and told herself that something beyond his control had prevented him meeting her.

She went back the next day. It was easier the second time. Like having sex with him the second time. The transit was made the first time, that was what put her on the other side, that's what shifted her beyond the law, not just the criminal law but the law of her marriage, her family, and her society, which of course was the hospital. Again she was exhilarated, and again she was terrified. Being out there, beyond the law, she told me, was always the most intense experience, this was why it intoxicated her. Romantic women, I reflected: they never think of the damage they do in their blind pursuit of intense experience. Their infatuation with freedom.

Once again she sat in the cafeteria in Victoria. She wore sunglasses and a hat with a low brim so that she could maintain surveillance of the entrance but without drawing attention to herself. Close to noon a tall thin young man slipped into the chair opposite, keeping his eyes on the table. He had hair the color of straw and a patchy beard. He was wearing an old stained tweed jacket and no tie, and the collar of his shirt was grimy. There were spatters of paint all over his clothes. He spooned sugar into his tea and as he stirred it, still without looking up, he said, "Stella?"

She froze. She thought that despite his appearance he was a policeman. It hadn't occurred to her that Edgar wouldn't come to Victoria himself. She began to gather her bag to leave.

"You're Stella Raphael," said the shabby man as his lowered eyes darted to right and left. She recognized at once that his accent was public-school. He was leaning across the table toward her. "Edgar said I was to bring you to him. Well, aren't you?"

Still she saw no reason to trust the man. Her affair with Edgar had been so utterly exclusive, she was shocked at encountering a third party with knowledge of them. She assumed he must be an enemy rather than otherwise.

"You've made a mistake," she said coldly. "I don't know you and I don't know any Edgar."

She made as if to rise from her seat. The man threw another quick anxious glance around the crowded cafeteria. "You are Stella," he hissed. "He told me what you look like. I'm the one who's been looking after him."

He thrust his face forward as if to challenge her to deny it. She read his fear and desperation. She allowed a silence and didn't get up from the table. He waited for her to respond, his nervous fingers drumming on his cigarette packet. He again glanced around, and it was this that convinced her. It was precisely the glance she had been casting at the door for the last hour; apparently casual, it was a glance with a specific object, and it missed nothing.

"All right," she said. She took out a cigarette, and he leaned forward with a match. His relief was palpable.

"I saw you up here yesterday," he said. "We had to be sure no one followed you."

" 'We'?"

"Edgar and me."

"What's your name?"

"Nick."

She said later it felt as though everything had been turned upside down. Instead of her emerging from her full world and reaching out to a solitary, fugitive man, it was he who from the security of his world drew her in. She was the solitary, not he, she was now at home nowhere. The melodramatic behavior of this lanky young man in the shabby clothes only made the situation that much more disconcerting.

What followed had the quality of a dream. The man called Nick led her out to an old Vauxhall parked behind the station, a dirty car with ripped upholstery and litter on the seats and floors and dashboard. They crossed the river at Westminster and then drove east. It was an unseasonably warm, smoggy day, and though the sunshine sparkled on the Thames the air felt stale and dusty and oppressive. There was no wind. It was not a part of London she was familiar with. Narrow streets ran between derelict warehouses built in the last century or the one before. Little light penetrated between the buildings, and all the windows were bricked up or smashed or thick with dust. They passed a bomb site behind a chain-link fence, and Stella glimpsed a small black cat picking its way across the rubble in the sunshine. Grass and weeds covered neglected heaps of broken brick and lumber. There were very few people about, despite the time of day. They had only one brief exchange during the journey, when a question occurred to her.

"What did he tell you I looked like?"

He smiled but he wouldn't say.

"Tell me."

"Rubens."

"Oh, Rubens."

It was a joke they had. Now Nick was in on it. She thought

about this. Curiously, she didn't mind. Eventually she saw him glance in the rearview mirror and the car came to an abrupt halt on a deserted street near the river. He threw it into reverse and backed rapidly up an alley that opened into an empty yard at the rear of a warehouse. There were buildings on three sides, and on the fourth, facing them, a railway viaduct whose arches housed a wholesale fruit and vegetable market. It too was deserted. Padlocks hung from the gates and fences.

"Here you are," said Nick.

Stella got out of the car. The air smelled of ripe oranges. The windows of the buildings around the yard seemed to peer down at her like so many blind eyes. Old lorry tires were stacked against a wall, baking in the sun. A scrap of newspaper lifted slightly in the still air. Nick left her standing by the car in the middle of the yard and disappeared back out into the street. When he returned a few seconds later he took her to a passage at the rear of one of the buildings. It was dark and smelled of urine. It occurred to Stella that she might be murdered.

He pushed open a door at the end of the passage. A steep, narrow staircase climbed into shadows. The air was damp and chill. There was a smell of mildew and shit now.

"Go on up, then," he urged her.

"Where is he?"

"He's on the top floor. Go on."

He gazed at her with faint amusement and she felt she was being mocked, but was she being mocked because she had accompanied him so willingly to this place, or because she hesitated now, a fine lady out of her element and losing her frail resolve? He was no longer comic, he was sinister, but she started up the stairs, what else was she to do? They sagged and creaked under her feet. The air was clammy. A wooden rail, smooth to the touch, was loosely screwed into the plaster. She realized he was not following her and she paused, one hand on the rail, and looked back over her shoulder. He stood at the foot of the staircase, his face turned up toward her. He gestured upward with a long forefinger, keep going up, all the way up.

She passed several landings on her way up. At the top a dusty window looked down onto the yard below. She saw Nick opening the door of the Vauxhall and she drew back, knocking over a length of metal pipe that clattered onto the floorboards and raised a small cloud of dust. There was a door on the landing and she hesitantly pushed it open. She was desperately frightened. She was looking into a room so large that the light from its row of windows didn't penetrate beyond the beams down the middle of the floor. Her eyes grew accustomed to the gloom. There were doors at the far end, doors in walls from which much of the plaster had crumbled away, exposing the studs and laths beneath.

"Edgar?"

She came a few steps into the room. Her high heels seemed deafening on the floorboards. She was wearing a head scarf and a light tan raincoat with the belt not buckled but tied in a knot, and she had a large bag slung over her shoulder. A bearded figure stood in the shadows watching her. The sudden sight of him caused her to cry out. He moved toward her, grinning, and she ran to him.

She got back shortly after six, and when she came down from her bath she found Max home from the hospital. He was in a good mood, a rare event these days. He wanted to know had her shopping been successful. His interest was feigned, and it was simple for her to give him the impression of annoyances and frustrations that would necessitate yet another trip to London on Friday. He suggested a walk around the garden before dinner and she thought it politic to agree.

They went first to the vegetable garden, and she found it ironic that, technically at least, this was Max's territory, for she sensed her lover's presence everywhere. He had grown a beard! On a warm evening in early September the air was still and sultry. Summer's growth had exhausted the soil, and all that would remain after this brief interlude of ripeness and maturity was decay. There was a din of birds from the trees beyond the garden wall.

"Did you see Brenda?" said Max as they wandered along the path, pausing here and there to inspect this plant or that.

"I didn't have time."

"No, why would you go and see her? You've had quite enough of my mother this summer. All this other business, of course . . ."

His voice trailed off.

"Brenda and I get along if we have to. Actually, I was glad she was here. She was a help with Charlie."

They had reached the conservatory. No further work had been done and it seemed a ruin in its skeletal incompletion, the great white frame glowing feebly in the fading light. Max sighed. Inexorably the conversation had turned to the days after Edgar's escape. Stella could never properly talk to Max about the events of those days, and how they had affected his position in the hospital. If they had. Perhaps they hadn't? They sat on the bench by the wall and smoked. Max asked her again about her day in London and it cost her an effort to shift him back to his more usual themes, which revolved around his work. She asked herself why she was getting all this attention, and remembered him saying in bed a few nights before that he had lost her. It occurred to her then that if she was to see Edgar regularly in London she must get her marriage back to the way it had been. She now required Max to find her invisible again.

He reached for her hand. "I love it here in the evening," he said. "Are you getting cold?"

"I'm a little chilly," she said. "I should have brought my cardigan."

"We'll go in."

They walked back along the path in the twilight, holding hands.

I didn't learn until some days later of this trip to London, or of the one she took later in the week. Stella's position at this time was precarious. In the early days of the affair, desperate though they were, the pressure, oddly, was less acute. Then she had feared that it might be the very constraints of their situation that were driving the passion, and that without those constraints and the tension they bred she might find herself limply, blankly wondering what it was that had provoked her to take such risks. There were times, she confessed, when she had even hoped, in some corner of her mind, some small place where prudence, safety, and security were priorities, in that place she had faintly hoped to see the thing defused and herself set free of this compulsion over which she seemed to have no control whatsoever—

Not now. Now all the structures that had previously sustained daily life—her responsibilities, the family, appearances, routines—all had become shells merely. She sustained them, but only for reasons of cold pragmatism: she wished to attract no attention and no interference, otherwise, she said, she could not go to him.

So what happened?

She wept a little as she described how she'd gone up the stairs and into the loft that day, and there he was, waiting for her. They wasted no time. They hurried down to the far end of the loft, to a room he called his studio, and climbed a staircase to a sort of sleeping platform, where they lay down together on the mattress. Again I probed her, curious to learn if this sex differed from the sex she'd had with him on the hospital estate, but all she would say was that for the first time they didn't have to be quiet about it. Primitive, urgent—and loud, this was my surmise. Later, sprawled naked on top of the blankets, they talked about the days following his escape, about how, after he'd reached London, Nick had come for him and brought him here to his loft and given him his studio. She said she'd never been in a room like this before. It was raw industrial space, with grimy brick walls and high ceilings hung with pipes. There were three large dusty windows facing onto a shuttered warehouse on the far side of the street. A huge trestle table pushed up against the wall was littered with drawing paper and other materials. She liked it, she said, this artist's room, it made her feel, oh, bold, and original, and free. She went down and wandered about in her open raincoat, a drink in her hand, picking up objects, examining everything. A little later, back in bed, she told him about living on blind faith and gin while she waited for his call.

"So you didn't doubt me."

She turned to him and shook her head.

"I would have."

"You're not me."

"Who am I then?"

She pressed herself against him, her hand playing across his body, tracing its form, and then his face, rubbing her fingers in his damp beard. They had sex again, the time fled by, and it wasn't until she sat up and said she must leave that the one sour, ominous note was sounded. He stirred on the bed behind her.

"Back to Max," he said.

"Back to Max."

"Does he know about us?"

"He doesn't want to know."

Suddenly his voice was full of contempt.

"He's a spineless man. What about the others? Cleave must be climbing the bloody wall!"

She was startled by this outburst. From sleepy indolence he had suddenly reared up fiery with resentment and scorn. She knelt beside him, kissing his face and his neck, stroking his head, murmuring words of comfort. He shook his head, shook off his irritation, and calmed down. He was suddenly unwilling to let her go. He had to know when she'd be back. He said he needed her. She lay down beside him and took him in her arms. She had never known him like this before, she had seen him almost from the start as the outlaw, the artist, grinning, fearless, passionate, free. Now she understood the shape her life must take: frequent trips to London on pretexts that would arouse no suspicion. She didn't care how difficult this was going to be.

I was not surprised by this sudden vulnerability. Jealous men are inherently weak. They are terrified of being abandoned. Despite her protests he came with her when she left. He had regained his good temper and there was no more drama. Clinging tightly to each other they walked up to the nearest busy street, where he waited smoking in the doorway of a pub while she flagged a cab. The heat was less oppressive now. She watched him through the rear window of the cab as he emerged from the doorway, threw away his cigarette, and turned in toward the river again. He was wearing Max's linen jacket, she realized, and also his trousers, cinched tight around his waist with a narrow leather belt. It made her smile whenever she thought of it.

The next Friday Nick met her again and now she saw him as her ally, her go-between. He drove her to the warehouse, and this time she noticed the name of the street, it was Horsey Street. As she climbed the staircase to the loft she was barely aware of the gloom, the creak and sag, the sharp foul smell of a neglected building that now housed only outcasts and vermin. She clattered quickly up the last flight, opening her coat, and went straight in. He came loping toward her, like a great wolf, she said, and again they spent the afternoon in bed, and again the time slipped by absurdly fast. She'd brought him clothes, soap, and whisky, and they'd drunk a fair bit of it. When she came down the staircase into the studio she was unsteady, and she stumbled pulling her skirt on. All that alcohol on an empty stomach; she had a strong head, but not without any lunch inside her. When they walked up Horsey Street to look for a taxi, and she had some slight trouble moving in a perfectly straight line, she realized she must get control of herself before she arrived home. The object after all was to resume her invisibility; this would hardly happen if she came home sloshed from shopping.

She had a black coffee and a sandwich in Victoria then walked up and down the platform until the train was due to leave. She sat by an open window inhaling deeply, then found the whole thing ridiculous and shut the window and lit a cigarette instead. Of course she was not drunk.

She got off the train and made her way to the car park. She started the car and let out the clutch, and it leapt backward like a startled gazelle and promptly stalled. She restarted it and carefully backed out, this time without mishap. She drove home slowly and with fierce concentration.

She came straight into the kitchen and stood at the sink drinking cold water. Fortunately Max was not back from the hospital. She must go upstairs and have a bath before she saw him. She turned from the sink and was startled to find Charlie sitting at the table, swinging his legs and watching her. His gaze was clinical.

"Darling! How long have you been here?"

"Not very long. Where have you been?"

"I had to go up to London again. Why?"

He continued to watch her carefully as she drained her glass of water.

"Are you drunk?" he said.

"Of course not! Why on earth did you say that?"

"Your eyes look funny."

She was in the bath when Max got home from work. She heard him downstairs talking to Charlie. When she emerged she was feeling entirely presentable. She was bathed and powdered, she'd brushed her teeth and scrutinized her eyes for any sign of the drunkenness that Charlie had apparently detected in them, and could find no evidence at all. She would dress, go downstairs, and start preparing dinner, and all would be just as usual, a typical night at home, *en famille*, in the deputy medical superintendent's house. She was after all the invisible woman.

Not altogether invisible. She wandered from the bathroom into the bedroom, her light dressing gown open over her bare skin, and found Max there. He was in his black suit, and he was standing at the window by her dressing table, gazing into the garden. He turned as he heard her coming in, and she pulled her dressing gown closed and knotted the sash.

"Here you are," she murmured. She went to him and kissed his cheek, then sat at the dressing table and began to apply a cleansing cream to her face. As she did so she glanced up and met his eye. He was frowning.

"Sit down, darling," she said. "Talk to me. Tell me about your day." She didn't like his manner. She felt a prickle of alarm.

"Where have you been?" he said.

She put down the pot of cream. "Where have I been? You know where I've been, I've been shopping in town. What is it, Max?"

"Tell me the truth."

"I am telling you the truth. Why on earth wouldn't I? I'm sorry, I don't understand. Tell me why you're interrogating me like this."

"Show me what you bought."

A long pause here. She sat at the dressing table, half turned toward him where he had settled on the bed. They stared at each other and there was a sort of nakedness, she said, in the moment. She said nothing. She was as strong as he was at these naked moments; all his insight, all his psychiatric expertise, none of it could penetrate her womanly shield. Still without a word she turned back to her mirror and resumed applying cold cream to her face. It was a mirror with a movable wing on either side; she adjusted them so that she could watch him. He did not move from the edge of the bed. By giving him her back she intended to tell him she would try and ignore what he'd said. She would assume he didn't intend to insult her. She was offering him the chance to apologize. He did not apologize, however. His face remained as cold as steel.

"Show me what you bought," he said again.

Without a word she wiped her fingers on a tissue and rose to her feet. She crossed the end of the bed to the cupboard that ran the length of the wall by the door. She opened it at her end and stood on her toes to reach a box on the shelf above the dress rack. The box was wrapped in gift paper. As she came back to the dressing table she tossed it onto the bed.

"What's this?"

Still she said nothing. She went on applying cream. There was a hint of uncertainty in his voice now, but she was silent.

"I'm going to tear the wrapping," he said. Her face was close to the mirror, but not so close she couldn't see him take the wrapping off. He managed not to tear it. Inside he found a long cardboard box.

"Harrods," he murmured. He opened the box. He folded back the leaves of tissue paper. He lifted from the box a pair of silk pajamas. He turned from the pajamas to the dressing table.

"Are these for me?"

All the anger had drained from him. She swept out of the bedroom, pausing at the door to say: "Who the hell do you think they're for?"

She slammed the bathroom door and locked it. She waited. After a minute or two she heard him go downstairs; he didn't attempt to apologize through the locked bathroom door. She went back into the bedroom and dressed.

When she got downstairs Max was in the drawing room. She made straight for the drinks table and poured herself a gin; she was certainly sober by this point, and in need of a large one. He crossed to the door and closed it.

"I am a fool," he said. "I'll tell you what happened. Charlie said you came home drunk and I constructed a fantastic scenario. A scenario of infidelity. An apology's in order."

She sat in an armchair and drew out his discomfort for a few more moments. At last she spoke. "Charlie told you I came home drunk?"

"Yes."

"I will have to talk to him. No, on second thought, you will. How dare he, Max? And how dare you? How dare you come upstairs and accuse me of infidelity because that child has a malicious imagination?"

"I feel very foolish. I'm sorry."

As she sipped her drink she watched him. "I don't think that's enough. This worries me. This summer has been a terrible strain. You didn't notice it, but while all the fuss was going on this house was kept clean and meals appeared on time. Who do you think managed all that? Not your mother."

"I know."

"You may know now, but it's the first time you've acknowledged it. I saw how difficult it was for you. I don't think you thought for one moment about what I had to do. *And* with your mother in the house."

"The timing was unfortunate."

She snorted. "It certainly was."

She was angry now, and enjoying herself. Max paced back and forth, frowning. He had once told her he always learned something from their arguments.

"Why did you buy me pajamas?"

"Peace offering. Consolation prize. New beginnings. I don't know, why does a wife buy her husband a present after they've been through a difficult time? You're the bloody psychiatrist."

He sat on the sofa with his elbows on his knees, gazing at the carpet, twiddling his spectacles in his clasped hands. "I feel horrible about this. How coarse you must think me."

"Don't overdo it."

He looked up. He smiled. "You don't give an inch, do you?"

"I will not tolerate being taken for granted, nor will I have that boy telling tales on me and you taking them seriously. It's outrageous. How dare he? More to the point, how dare you let him?"

"I will talk to him. Stella, for the third time, I apologize. And I'm pleased with my pajamas. Thank you." He crossed the room and she permitted him to kiss her cheek. "Would the drunkard care for another drink?"

"Yes," she said, "she would."

He made love to her that night and she had to allow it, in fact she had to do more than allow it, she had to feign enthusiasm, all in the cause of invisibility. Max was pleased with himself when it was all over. He smoked a cigarette in his silk pajamas, sitting propped against the headboard as the shadows of the branches outside the window stirred against the upper walls and ceiling. She let him revel in his small postcoital glory. She wanted to see him content, she wanted him to feel that all was well in his marriage, that he was a good husband and she was a good wife.

She made one more visit to London and that visit tells us much about the tensions and contradictions of the double life she was attempting to lead during this period. She took a cab from Victoria to the end of Horsey Street, went up the alley and straight upstairs to the loft. She was picking Charlie up from school later in the afternoon and she only had an hour. They were in bed when Edgar said: "Don't let him touch you."

It should have sounded a loud alarm but it didn't.

"Don't let who touch me, my darling?"

"Max."

"You don't have to worry about Max, it's dead between us. It has been for a long time."

"Do you have to sleep in the same bed as him?"

She realized that he had no real understanding of her marriage, or of the difficulties of her situation generally.

"He'd find it odd if I didn't."

"Do you like it?"

"Of course not, but what can I do? My darling, I couldn't stand anyone touching me but you. Of course I won't let him touch me. He doesn't, anyway."

"No?"

"Not for years."

That seemed to relieve him. She took him in her arms again, and then, to his distress and her own, she had to leave him, and wash and dress, and find a cab to take her to the station. She had left it all dangerously late.

They descended to the yard and made their way to the usual place, where they clung together a few moments in the doorway of the pub, and then he turned his collar up and slipped away and Stella stood looking for a cab. There weren't any, and as the minutes passed she realized she would miss her train, and that Charlie would not be met from school as he'd been promised. For a few seconds this filled her with panic, and she ran as well as she could in her high heels to the nearest corner, where the traffic was heavier.

Then she discovered she didn't care. She didn't care if she missed her train. She didn't care if she was late. Charlie could go home on the bus and she would tell him some story, and it wouldn't matter. She was alert enough to recognize the hostility in the thought, and to understand that she hadn't forgiven him for betraying her to Max. She caught the train with a minute to spare. She sat by the window and gazed at the narrow back gardens of the terraced houses with their high back walls and the sheets on the washing lines flapping in the wind. She saw the railway cuttings, the backs of the factories, the allotments, then fields and open country. She thought about Edgar. She was moved by his insistence that she not let Max touch her. She was aware, she said, of just how monstrous jealousy could become in the wrong conditions. Was their situation, with all its difficulties and frustrations, a breeding ground for sexual jealousy? It would be, she thought, unless she maintained a strict vigilance. Edgar was so isolated, she was his only harbor, his only safe place, and she left him each time to return to the house and the bed of a man he hated. Such a situation could easily provoke sexual jealousy. She would go to any lengths to prevent that happening. They had quite enough enemies at the gates of their city.

I was frankly astonished at this display of naïveté. Was she really so blind to the danger she had placed herself in? Had she learned nothing from living among psychiatrists?

6

She was in the vegetable garden. She told me later that she went
there when she wanted to indulge her nostalgia for the early
days of the affair. The first signs of autumn were on it now, the
afternoon light casting its long shadows, the colors of things
starting to deepen and glow. There was a faint hint of crispness
in the air that spoke to her of dead leaves and cold nights and
heavy dew shining in the cobwebs in the trees at dawn. The outside party of parole patients was back at work, supervised as
before by John Archer. They were sweeping, clearing, burning,
cutting back the spent season's growth, putting the garden to
bed for the winter. She sat on the bench by the conservatory and
watched a patient she didn't know push a loaded wheelbarrow
to the bonfire that was smoldering on cleared ground at the far
end. Smoke rose from the malodorous heap and hazed the light
of the afternoon. She had a feeling of closure, of ending. The
apple orchard was heavily laden, and fallen fruit was starting to
rot in the grass; she should be collecting it for canning. But she

preferred to sit and remember the events of the high summer, how blindly they had behaved given how little they knew. Now that she had the first stirrings of a perspective on what had happened, she saw how unthinkable it would have been to hold back, though she was still astonished at her own recklessness. Their love was stronger now, she thought, more robust, more resilient than she could have dared to hope in the summer. The garden was dying, it was being put to sleep for the winter, but what had sprung to life here was still young.

With these pleasant, faintly elegiac thoughts running through her mind, their passage eased by the couple of gins she'd had before lunch, she considered going back into the house. Another five minutes, she said to herself, just as the door in the wall at the far end opened.

I came along the path, picking my way carefully between the dead grass and flowers heaped on the gravel, and trying not to inhale bonfire smoke. I had guessed, after Edgar's escape, that she was hiding knowledge of him; and I had sensed that she knew that I had guessed it, for she had begun to avoid me. My policy had been to wait and watch and do nothing; until, that is, I learned of her trips to London. Then I knew that I had to act with some urgency. My intrusion alarmed her. As she watched me coming through the haze of smoke she remembered Jack Straffen making his way along the same path a few weeks earlier. Why was she so irresistible to the psychiatrists? We couldn't keep away from her.

"Peter, what a nice surprise. Sit down. I was just enjoying the last of the summer."

"And what a summer. I think I should rather like to go to sleep until next spring. How are you, my dear?"

"I'm all right. I think Max is up at the hospital."

"Can't I sit here and enjoy the last of the summer too? I've seen so little of you recently. You look very well. Are you?"

Oh, and then I turned my dreamy gaze upon her, and Be careful, Stella, she told herself; though at the same time she was conscious of an almost overwhelming urge to confide in me as she used to, before our friendship was compromised. How strongly a great passion wants to declare itself, to tell its story, and how logical a listener I was, a wise, gentle friend. And how relentless must be her effort to keep it from me.

"I have more time to myself with Charlie back at school. The summer was a strain, having him at home, and Brenda here, of course. I don't think Max understands what his mother does to a household."

She told me later she set this hare running to see if I might go after it.

"Your dear mother-in-law. How priceless she is. Do you know, she asked me to dissuade Max from applying for Jack's job."

"I don't believe it."

"Drew me aside, told me how much she respected my judgment, then asked me not to encourage him, the reverse if possible."

"I must say I'm with her on this."

"You want to get back to London of course."

I let this pregnant phrase hang in the air before going on.

"But does Max want the job? I haven't spoken to him about it."

"I think he does, I'm afraid."

"I see."

I took my flat silver cigarette case from my inside breast pocket and we smoked. An idea formed in her mind, something that had never occurred to her before.

"Peter, do you want Jack's job?"

I was vague and pensive, but not surprised.

"I wonder sometimes. But no, I think not. It's a young man's game, and I should have to work much too hard. And all so political nowadays."

I fell silent. I allowed her to think of my life, my handsome house a few miles away with its fine paintings, its fine furniture, and its fine library, and no, she didn't see the administration of a large, complicated institution as having any place in my measured existence, with its balanced commitments to forensic psychiatry and aesthetic indulgence. She probably wondered

was there a sex life too? She would have heard people specu-
late, but her intuition told her that whatever I may have done
as a young man, it was all the stuff of memory now. And frank
as we were with each other, or as we had been until recently,
this she had never asked me. She presumed my sexual drive was
not strong, and tried to imagine how it would be to live as I
lived. She couldn't.

All this I sensed going through her mind.

"Dear Peter," she murmured.

"You're still seeing Edgar Stark then?" I said.

Vigilance! I was dangerous. She must not underestimate me.
Could she buy safety with a partial disclosure? No. It had to be
denial. And it had to be convincing. She wheeled around slowly.
A small incredulous smile, eyes wide.

"However did I give you that impression?" A calm tone; no
straining after outrage.

I brushed at imaginary specks of dust on my trousers. I was
in a black suit that day, the familiar psychiatric black, fine dark
cloth impeccably cut.

"Your reaction to his escape."

She realized I would not have concerned myself with cir-
cumstantial evidence: the hours she'd spent alone with Edgar
here in the garden (though John Archer had kept me fully
abreast of all that), her presence on the cricket field around
the time that he was suspected of stealing drink from the
pavilion. No, I had practiced my psychiatric arts, I had observed
and penetrated her emotional reaction to his escape.

"I don't understand."

"He didn't tell you he was going, that's clear."

"Why would he?"

I said nothing.

"Why would he, Peter? Why would a patient tell a doctor's
wife he intended to escape?"

"Why indeed."

Outrage now. "This is hurtful and insulting. You may not
speak to me like this!"

She stood up and stormed off through the bonfire smoke and

out of the vegetable garden and across the yard to the house. She went into the kitchen and stood at the sink. She could feel our hot breath on the back of her neck.

She was not free of me yet. As she stood there trembling I followed her across the yard, glancing in at her through the window as I came. She had never seen me look as I looked then. The habitual expression of amused detachment had given way to something frighteningly serious. A moment later I was with her in the kitchen.

"You will hear what I have to say to you. I want to warn you as emphatically as I can that Edgar Stark is a dangerous man. Do you understand that?"

She noticed I had brought her basket in with me and was still holding it. It made her smile slightly. She took it from me and put the cooking apples on the cutting board beside the sink. She opened the cutlery drawer and took out a coring knife and went to work on the apples. I had no time for her displacement activities now. I set my hands on her shoulders. Gently I turned her from the sink so she faced me. I took the knife and slipped it into my pocket.

"Do you imagine I'm going to stab you?" she said.

"Listen to me carefully."

She saw I was not to be put off. She sat down at the kitchen table and told me she didn't know why she must hear this. I sat down too. I told her that Ruth Stark had been Edgar's wife but she had been his model first. He had structured his art around her until disillusion somehow set in. His idealization of her collapsed and he began to develop morbid delusions about her. These spiraled out of control and eventually he murdered her. He then cut her head off and mutilated it. He had shown no insight into why he had done any of this, and no real remorse.

She heard me out in abstracted silence, refusing to look at me. Then she insisted it was all irrelevant as she had no idea where he was, and she had no reason to go and see him, and if that was all I had to say then would I please go now. I told her again that my purpose was to warn her, and would she please take it seriously, whatever else she did; and then I left. She told me later she ran straight upstairs and fell on her bed and wept. She hated me for what I'd just done to her.

She didn't know how long she lay there weeping. She let it all come flooding out of her, all the anxiety of the last weeks, and now this, the realization that we knew about her. If we knew about her, then she and Edgar were finished: this brought on a fresh wave of despair, and she wept until she was exhausted and empty. Then she started to think. She turned onto her side and told herself it need not be the end after all.

She went to the bathroom and washed her face, then sat at her dressing table and set about repairing the damage. As she did so she told herself again that it need not be the end. If she gave up now, if she didn't go back to London, then Edgar would be safe but that would be the end. If she waited and did nothing, when she did go back he would be gone. But if she acted now, if she went to him now, then what could we do? Nothing, we could do nothing, if she acted now.

If she acted now. She came back downstairs and went into the drawing room. The house was empty. Max was having lunch in the hospital and Mrs. Bain had gone home. Charlie was at school. She had a drink. If she acted now. She paced the drawing room. The day was cool and there was a light mist on the garden. She could smell the bonfire. If she acted now she would go back upstairs and pack a suitcase and call a car to take her to the station. Then she would go to Horsey Street and not come back.

She had another drink and then she called the car. For a moment or two she stood rooted to the spot as she thought of what would happen to Charlie, and she almost changed her mind. But she didn't, she pushed the thought away. The car came, and she told the driver to take her to the station. On the way she made him stop at the bank. She withdrew in cash everything in the joint account, a few hundred pounds. At Victoria she felt overwhelmed by the crowd and made her way with some trepidation across the station hall to the cafeteria. She couldn't get a drink yet so she sat at the back with a cup of coffee and smoked. She was terrified. Then she found herself leaving a coin by the saucer and rising from her chair and gathering her handbag and her suitcase, and in a state of detachment she watched herself make her way out of the cafeteria like any other middle-class lady up from the provinces for an afternoon of shopping, and perhaps the theater later, hence the suitcase, and out of the station to the taxi rank. She told the driver Horsey Street then settled down in the backseat and lit another cigarette and gazed out of the window. Almost immediately the sense of detachment was replaced by exhilaration: there were no further decisions to be made. She had done it, and she felt now what she always felt when a meeting with Edgar was imminent, she felt giddy and glorious and nothing else mattered but that the few minutes separating them cease to drag and start to fly until she was with him again.

Now every traffic light and street obstruction was her enemy. Off to the left she caught a glimpse of the river shining in the sunlight, the mist of the morning burnt off, and on the other side the dome of St. Paul's. Then they were among the warehouses. Then she was standing at the top of the street with her suitcase and the cab was pulling away.

She walked toward the river, her high heels tapping on the stones. Two boys at the other end of the street were kicking a football against a wall where they'd chalked a target in the outline of a man. She turned up the alley. In the yard a freak wind was blowing, and a few sheets of newspaper were gusting around and around in tight circles just above the ground. A train suddenly rumbled by on the viaduct over the fruit market and startled her.

She went quickly up the stairs to the top floor. The door was locked. She put her suitcase down and knocked. Nobody answered. She called through the door as loudly as she dared. Still nobody came. Now she was alarmed. It hadn't occurred to her that he might not be here. She knocked again, calling his name more loudly now, and then she sat on her suitcase to wait. Twenty minutes later she heard someone coming up the stairs. There was nowhere to hide. She stood at the top of the staircase. The steps grew louder, a figure appeared on the landing below. To her enormous relief it was Nick.

"Thank God," she said. "Where is he?"

"You weren't expected."

"I didn't know I'd be coming. Is he in there?"

Nick hammered on the door and shouted to Edgar to open up. Eventually the door was unlocked from the inside and there he was, staring at her. She picked up the suitcase.

"Can I come in?"

His eyes flickered to Nick, then back to her. "You've come to stay?"

"Yes."

"You've left him?"

She nodded.

"You're with us now?"

"I'm with you."

He produced his big grin, his big wolfy grin, and then he boisterously flung an arm around her neck and together they lurched into the loft and stood there hugging each other in the middle of the floor.

It had of course occurred to me that she might do something like this, but I'd rather thought she would listen to me. I didn't rightly gauge her level of desperation, nor, I suppose, the extent to which he had ensnared her. So I lose sight of Stella at this point, and have only her own account, offered to me in conversation tentatively and disjointedly, and sometimes emotionally, of the days that followed. One of the first things I asked her was how she imagined *we* had reacted to her departure. On this point she was both lucid and precise. Max, she said, would have come home from the hospital and not known where she was. Poor Charlie would be back from school by that time of course, though she was trying not to think about the effect on him of all this. Phone calls would be made. Bewilderment would turn to concern, which would then turn to anxiety. At some point in the evening Jack and Max and I would meet and work out what had happened. Max would be unwilling to accept it at first, but as the hours passed and still she didn't appear he would realize what she'd done to him. She said she didn't want to think about his state of mind, nor did she want to think about Charlie and how her absence would be explained to him. She had deliberately not considered him when she was packing her suitcase and ordering the car and failing to leave a note. She had tried to blur him into Max, she said, to make him part of the man she was leaving. To think about Charlie's reaction to her disappearance was clearly much too dangerous. In the morning, awakening to the awareness of what she'd done, she again pushed it away. All that remained of her guilt was a shadowy presence moving behind her lover's light. She would not look at it, she must ignore it, her happiness depended on that.

What was that first night like?

It was perfect, more than perfect, it was the happiest night of her life. Nick went out for fish and chips and drink and they sat at the table in his kitchen for hours. It felt, she said, as if they'd *stolen* their happiness, or rather, that they'd come upon it by chance and made off with it, for it really belonged to someone else and they had no right to it. They drank till late and she was elated at the prospect of spending all night there and never having to go back to the hospital again. Nick was part of it, part of their charmed circle; hadn't he been their friend and helper from the beginning? And it was his loft, he was sheltering them both now. She liked Nick and he liked her and it was clear that the bleak life the two artists had been leading was about to change for the better. As for Edgar, I could well imagine his satisfaction at this development. He had lured her away from us, he had persuaded her to leave behind all safety and security and follow him underground, where she expected to find freedom. Freedom!

As usual he wasted no time. He knew what he wanted, I believe it was what he had wanted since before the escape, it was what had impelled him to call her so recklessly from London: he wanted to do her head. For he was an artist again, and he was impatient to translate his relationship with Stella, the complex of strong emotion she had aroused in him, into some form of expression. He sketched her for an hour in the studio, and she was fascinated, watching his eyes lifting from the paper, feeling his gaze on her, his impersonal gaze, and hearing the darting pencil scratching at the pad, the grunts and sighs that suggested he was performing a delicate surgical operation rather than making a drawing. She had never seen him properly at work before. She felt she didn't know him.

Later she looked at what he'd done, and what she saw bewildered her. There were multiple lines, smudged outlines, crosshatching, whorl marks. She sensed rather than saw herself there. It all seemed so tentative and indefinite, so *soft*, somehow. She asked him had he always drawn like this. Nick was in the studio, sitting over on the windowsill.

"Have I always drawn like this?"

He glanced across at Nick.

Stella stood at the table, gazing down at the paper, frowning.

"I mean," she said, "why?"

He came and stood beside her. "Why what?"

"Why don't you want to do an outline? Am I being very stupid? It's as if you don't know who I am."

"That's the point," said Nick.

"What I don't want," said Edgar, "is to see you—"

He rubbed his face, irritated at having to put it into words. His hands were smudged with graphite. Some of it came off on his forehead as he pushed his hair, now grown long and shaggy, out of his eyes. He had only the most obscure understanding of why he worked as he did. Curiously, he denied his emotion.

"To see me how?"

"As you see you. As others see you. As a desirable woman, a beautiful woman, I'm not interested in any of that. I don't want certainty. I just want to get a likeness."

She didn't understand.

"As a stranger, then?"

Now he too was frowning at the drawing and impatiently tapping his pencil on the table.

"Not even as a stranger."

"As an object?"

She rubbed at the smudge on his forehead.

"Inanimate? Unfeeling?"

"No, not inanimate. Just what I see."

She began to glimpse a meaning here.

"Not what you feel."

"Not what I feel."

"And that's what you call a likeness."

"That's what you call the truth," said Nick.

Edgar looked up sharply. "That's what you call bollocks," he said, and the two men shouted with laughter. Edgar stood there grinning at Nick then crossed the room and took his face in his hands and kissed him on the forehead. Nick was absurdly embarrassed and pleased at this display of affection.

This was the pattern of her first days with him. They spent their mornings in bed. Then they'd dress and go down into the loft. She abandoned cosmetics, she wore a head scarf and an old shirt loose over a plain black skirt or slacks. She'd make a meal and they'd eat with Nick in the kitchen. After lunch Edgar would work, and she would sit for him, sometimes for three or four hours at a time. He worked with intense concentration. He told her he wanted to draw her before he modeled her in clay. On the third day he posed her nude from the waist up. He had her stand on a sheet in front of the wall. He was quite matter-of-fact about her nakedness and she affected an equal frankness. Nick wandered in from the other end of the loft and stood there gazing dispassionately at her. It didn't matter, she supposed. Edgar didn't notice him until he said something, and then he quietly told him to fuck off. She was strongly aroused by the experience.

When he was finished with her she would sit by herself in the kitchen with her compact mirror, trying to see what he saw. If she wandered back into the studio, either he ignored her and carried on working, or they went to bed.

At night she cooked for them again, or Nick went for fish and chips, and they got drunk together and talked. They talked about everything, but mostly about art.

·   ·   ·

After four or five days she became susceptible to sudden gusts of intense anxiety when she awoke to the enormity of what she'd done and the situation she'd placed herself in. This happened early in the morning while Edgar was still asleep. She tried to push it away, she hated feeling the idyll disturbed, and she said nothing about it. This will pass, she told herself, they will forget, soon we will be able to slip quietly into the world and go unnoticed. This was all she was capable of, when she tried to think about the future. But most of the time she gave no thought to the larger reality outside. She tried, she said, not to dwell on Charlie, but without success, I suspect.

Housekeeping in the loft was primitive when she arrived. There was much to do and she was glad of it. It was work simply to stay clean, and the two men were less conscientious about it than she was. They only had one sink, one tap, and one lavatory. The sink was often full of paintbrushes. It didn't matter. She didn't care if they were dirty, what mattered was that they were together. Her identification with Edgar deepened daily. She told me she deliberately absorbed his tastes, his ideas, his feelings. His indifference to domestic comfort made her feel ashamed of all the years when the provision of domestic comfort for her husband and son had been her sole occupation. She began to write a little when no one was watching her.

She cooked them simple meals on a two-ring stove and made shopping lists and gave them to Nick, who shared the expenses with her. The nights when the three of them sat around the table drinking and talking, those were the best times of all. She was absorbing an entirely new way of thinking and feeling, losing what she thought of as her old, stale identity. Max and the hospital grew more distant with every day that passed.

This, she said, was her period of most rapid growth, for each day she understood more of what it was to think and feel and see as an artist, and the fact that they were fugitives, and that she and Edgar could not go out in daylight for fear of recognition and arrest, this only intensified her intoxication with this new way of being and gave it the flavor of danger that seemed to her intrinsic to the artist's existence.

. . .

She was astonished to discover that Nick and Edgar had visitors. How could a fugitive from the law have visitors? And yet, on her second or third day in the loft, as the three of them sat in the kitchen at noon eating sardines on toast, they heard a hammering at the door. Stella rose to her feet in dismay, but Edgar only glanced at Nick, who said, "That's Tony," and went to let him in.

"Who's Tony?" she whispered.

"Friend of ours," said Edgar in an offhand manner, returning to his sardines. Then he looked across the table at her, grinning.

"Don't worry," he said, "you'll like him."

She did like Tony. Like all the men who visited the loft, he was an artist, had unconventional manners, was poor (judging by the state of his clothes), smoked and drank excessively, seemed to take nothing seriously, and was apparently unimpressed that Edgar had escaped from a mental hospital, though fascinated that he'd been followed by the wife of the deputy medical superintendent.

Tony sat with them in the kitchen and was given a plate of sardines on toast, which he ate with his fingers, which he then wiped on his trousers, and the three men gossiped about people whom she'd never met but whose names were becoming familiar through repetition. Singly and in pairs these various characters appeared in the loft over the next few days. All were polite to Stella, whose flight to the city had clearly caught their imagination, and she, after her first spasm of uncertainty as to the wisdom of half of London, so it felt, knowing where Edgar was hiding, soon warmed to these odd, friendly men, so far removed from her experience, and their casual, sloppy ways. But one evening when it was just the three of them drinking in the kitchen she did voice her unease. Nick seemed surprised. It had clearly never occurred to him that Edgar might be betrayed.

"Why would someone want to do a thing like that?" he asked with genuine perplexity.

Edgar shrugged.

Stella thought, If he's not worried, why should I be?

They began to go out after dark. Edgar was growing restless after the days spent inside, so one night the two of them walked down to the river and gazed out across the water at the towers of Cannon Street and the dome of St. Paul's. They didn't yet go into any of the pubs but they felt secure enough out in the dark streets. If anyone came near they slipped into a doorway or an alley and embraced, and this aroused them so strongly at times that they ran unnecessary risks. She says it was starting to frighten her, the way their bodies flared at any contact, however slight. They seemed powerless to control this hunger they had for each other. Edgar slept soundly at night, but she often lay awake for hours in the darkness, staring at the ceiling and listening to the trains rumbling across the viaduct.

She remembers one night hearing Big Ben strike four and turning on her side and watching him sleeping. Who was he? Who was this stranger, her lover? She lit a cigarette. She remembered her first impressions of him, the man in the yellow corduroys mending their conservatory at the end of the vegetable garden. She remembered dancing with him and feeling his erection pressed into her groin, and being excited by his excitement, wanting him because he wanted her. Then the rapid escalation of the affair—the growing terror of exposure—and the escape. Now this. But who was he? From the fragmented episodes of the last weeks she tried to construct a man.

He was stronger now. No longer constrained, he spoke and acted with an authority she had never known in him on the estate. She saw how he was with Nick. Most of the time they appeared to be old art colleagues and close friends, but when anything serious came up Nick would wait to see what Edgar's attitude was before expressing his own opinion. The other men showed him deference too. When they talked Stella didn't join in, she just listened. She would take down Nick's battered books of reproductions and sit at the table turning the pages, gazing at the plates and watching for stirrings of response in herself.

She was drifting off. She thought about his word "likeness," and the idea of a being who was detached from the interests and feelings of others, capable only of returning the observer's gaze, impossible to know with any certainty. Could she see him like this? Would this be the truth? She leaned over the side of the mattress to crush out her cigarette. She adored sleeping with him under those rough blankets. She adored waking in the morning and finding him still there beside her.

During the day, when he didn't need her to model, she sometimes wandered out into the yard for fresh air. The fruit and vegetable market on the other side was enclosed under a high glass roof supported by slender metal pillars with elaborate filigree struts and bracework at the top. Various bays were fenced off, high piles of wooden crates and cardboard boxes stacked inside. One morning she watched two men loading sacks of potatoes onto the back of a dusty lorry. When she became aware that they had seen her she moved away, for it was rapidly becoming an instinctive thing to avoid drawing attention to herself. Shortly afterward, as she walked out onto Horsey Street and turned down toward the river, she came upon a big, shabby, neglected old church. She was surprised to find it there, at the end of that obscure warren of narrow streets and alleys. She was more surprised still when she discovered it was Southwark Cathedral.

She went in, and was immediately struck with the feeling that this was a good place, that for the hundreds of years it had stood on this site it had been untouched by violence or evil. She sat at the back and watched a tramp talking wildly to a young churchman in a long black cassock. She saw a middle-aged man, in pin-striped trousers and a black coat, deep in prayer in a side chapel. She counted twenty saints in their niches behind the altar, and paused by the tomb of the first English poet, his effigy in repose, his hands clasped in prayer on his chest, and his head resting on three books, one of which was called *Confessio Amantis*. She went back to Horsey Street refreshed by the quiet hour she'd spent there. She didn't mention her visit to Edgar or Nick. She suspected they would have little interest in the cathedral on their doorstep.

They began using the pubs at night. Nick or Stella would go up to the counter to buy the drinks while Edgar stayed at their table in the gloomiest corner of the room. Not that there seemed much risk. These were rough pubs with bare floorboards and wood paneling scuffed and splintered with age. Ill-lit and shabby, they harbored men and women anxious to drown the tedium of their dull hard days in cheap beer and spirits. Nobody paid any attention to Stella and the two shabby artists as they hunched over their drinks and their cigarettes, talking to one another in low voices at the back of the room. It thrilled her when they went down to the Southwark or the Globe, for it meant a sort of normality was entering their fugitive life, they were able to behave to an extent like ordinary people. She began to glimpse a future.

Being out in the real world brought its problems, however. One Saturday night they sat at the very back of a large, crowded pub, just the two of them. It was smoky and noisy and Stella felt at ease and a part of it. They sat side by side on a bench with a small round table in front of them, and she held his hand under the table. They were outsiders but they'd fetched up in this warm loud pub where to Stella everyone seemed somehow complicit with them. She thought then with a shudder of all the drawing rooms she'd been in presided over by the wives and mothers of psychiatrists, and remembered the horrors of strangeness and nonbelonging she'd felt in such rooms. Edgar picked up their glasses and pushed through to the bar, and she sat watching him with the glow of gin on her, filled with a sense of quiet elation.

There was no part of it she couldn't romanticize.

Suddenly a man appeared in front of the table and leered at her. She dropped her eyes and began looking through her handbag for cigarettes, lighter, anything.

"All by yourself, darling?" he said.

She looked up. "No, I'm not, actually," she said, "my husband's with me."

"Husband, is it, actually?"

He was a big man, a handsome man, but he'd been drinking and he was letting it show. He put his hands on the table and leaned toward her. She wanted him to go away. She didn't like that he mocked her speech, and she was angry with herself for giving him the chance.

"Yes it is, actually," she said, stressing the "actually," and this was a mistake, it amused him, and he pulled out a chair and sat down. Oh, she hadn't intended him to do this! It was then that Edgar came back from the bar with their drinks.

"Who's this?" he said.

The man had set his elbows squarely on the table and fixed his eyes on Stella. He now turned toward Edgar and looked up at him over his shoulder.

"This the husband, is it, darling?"

She shook her head wildly at Edgar. Nothing to do with me, she tried to tell him. He set the drinks carefully on the table, not looking at the man. Then he had the man's collar in his fist and his big black-bearded face was in the man's face. There was a sudden silence around them. Something passed between the two men, and she saw with startling clarity what was about to happen: a fight, smashed glass, blood, shouting, the police. Edgar let go of the man's collar and the man backed off. Edgar sat down. People returned to their drinks and conversations. But there was still a quality of hush around them, and she knew they were being listened to. He began rolling a cigarette and didn't look at her.

"What did you say to him?" he murmured.

"Nothing!"

He licked the paper. He shook his head. "Must have said something."

In a fierce whisper she told him what had happened. For a while he was quiet. Did he think she had led the man on? He was so cool, so distant, she had never seen him like this! She told him again that the man had sat down without any sort of invitation or encouragement.

"You won't play tricks on me, will you, Stella?" he said at last in an even, friendly voice.

"Of course I bloody won't!"

"That's all right, then."

But if it was all right, it left a bad taste in her mouth, this calm response of his that felt so full of threat. The old pride welled up inside her and she thought, To hell with you. She stared straight ahead, angrily smoking her cigarette in short rapid puffs. When she felt his fingers on her thigh and his lips at her neck she tried to ignore him, and pushed his hand away, but it did no good, any contact could overwhelm her.

"Give us a kiss, darling," he whispered.

"Piss off," she said and bit his lip.

Hurrying home a few minutes later, out in the damp night air, all now forgotten in the urgency to get back to the loft, they saw the policemen she had so recently imagined. There were two of them. They were at the far end of the street and walking slowly in their direction with their hands behind their backs. She drew close to him, both hands gripping his arm; he didn't break stride. She realized they would pass the policemen under a streetlight.

"They're going to see us," she murmured.

Still Edgar walked on. Stella could think of nothing, she was conscious only of a wave of black dread rising in her throat, she could taste it. The blur of the gin rapidly cleared and the tap of her heels on the wet pavement seemed to beat out a tattoo that said, Guilty, guilty, guilty.

Then he steered her off the pavement and past a row of capstans and down a flight of steps to the river, and there with the black water lapping at the stones he kissed her. She threw her arms around his neck and drank up his kiss as though her passion, if it were strong enough, could drive away the two policemen and leave them untouched. She was aware now only of Edgar's breathing and the approaching footsteps. They stopped at the top of the steps. Her fingers moved up the back of his head and she gathered his hair into her fist, her mouth still on his.

"Move on," said one of the policemen; then, after a moment, more loudly: "Move on, you two."

They did as they were told. They went off down an alley, huddled close like lovers disturbed and anxious to preserve their heat, and their pace quickened so that by the time they emerged from the other end of the alley out onto the street they were running.

They hurried in through the yard and came shouting up the stairs. She said she would never forget that night. Edgar felt it too, that a change had occurred, a shift into a new sort of security, despite the fright earlier in the night. The sense of panic, the sense of being only one step ahead, of the hot breath on the back of the neck: it had disappeared, replaced by a tentative confidence, the awareness that it was getting easier, hour by hour, day by day, to stay ahead of them and so allow the trail to grow cold and the hounds begin to tire. She felt for the first time that their blind leap into the unknown would be rewarded, that it would earn them the safe place where they could love each other without fear. They made love in that spirit, fearlessly and freely, as the trains rumbled over the viaduct through the night. She laughed aloud, she cried out, she gave her own sounds of life to the warehouse, careless whether Nick heard her or not.

This at any rate is how she described it to me.

7

Often, she said, she went to the cathedral. She sat in the shadows on a stone bench at the back, or wandered down the side aisle, past the tombs and chapels, her footsteps echoing on the stone floor. She always wore sunglasses and a head scarf tied tightly under her chin. She was vague about these days, about what precisely she was going through, but this is how I see her, as the sad woman in the cathedral. The problem was that the further she moved away from the hospital the harder I found it to reconstruct her experience, to mold it into something with a shape and a meaning I could recognize.

Edgar had started working in clay and it wasn't going well. At first she tried to tell him he must be patient, he hadn't done any sculpting for so long, how could he expect to command the old facility straightaway? But he didn't want to hear this. He wasn't interested in excuses, or in facility for that matter. He was angry and frustrated, and it seemed that no sooner had he begun to make any impression on the clay than he grew quietly furious with it and destroyed what he'd done. He worked on his feet, the clay slapped onto a wire frame in the rough shape of a head and mounted on a battered wooden stand. Nick had found him what he needed, the clay and the tools, and Stella had paid for it. She was feeling increasingly worried about money. Still nothing was coming in, apart from what Nick contributed in the way of groceries and drink and small sums of cash, and what did she know about getting money?

But these were the sort of thoughts she tried to block. They were not useful, and she was beginning to divide the world into what was useful and what was not, and talking to Edgar about money was not. She disregarded her own needs because she was reluctant to spend money on herself. She was without certain basics of body and skin care, she also lacked adequate supplies of clean underwear. She needed a warm coat but that was definitely out of the question, and all her other clothes smelled of stale air and cigarette smoke. The weather had turned damp and overcast and if she opened the shutters flurries of rain came in.

Edgar's utter absorption in his work had the effect of turning her in upon herself, especially if Nick wasn't there, and often now he wasn't. But one afternoon, while Edgar slept, Nick told her he was familiar with Edgar's mood; all artists were like this when the work went badly.

"You're not," she said.

"No, I'm not."

He was sitting on the edge of an old couch at the far end of the loft, frowning, his elbows on his knees, his hands clasped together. A cigarette hung from his lips. "But I'm not the real thing. Not like him."

She wandered about the room looking at his canvases. Nick's painting was turgid. She stopped by the window. In the yard below a potato lorry was backing through the gate of the vegetable market.

"What's he like when it goes well?" she said.

"The same."

She found this funny. Laughing a little she turned toward him, and he looked up, surprised. "Is that funny?"

"The way you say it."

He thought about this while she lit a cigarette, still standing by the window watching him.

"Don't you have a woman, Nick?"

He shook his head.

"I thought that's where you went off to, visiting your mistress."

He went on shaking his head, staring at the floor, twisting his long fingers. He shot her a glance, and though she didn't clearly understand it she didn't take the joke any further. What an odd, blocked fellow he was, she thought.

But more and more Nick stayed away from the loft, and with Edgar distant and distracted for hours on end, she was at times almost overwhelmed by anxiety, and it was only with difficulty that she roused the flame of her love and forced it to burn with enough fierceness that it crowded out the other feelings. She didn't want to tell him about any of this, none of it was useful. So while he worked, or slept, she fought terrible silent battles with herself and though they exhausted her she lay awake at night hour after hour as the trains rumbled over the viaduct and Big Ben chimed the hours. What began to disturb her was the thought that these were precisely the conditions that *killed* love, after first blighting its growth: squalor, fear, uncertainty, over-familiarity. How could she have failed to see this? What a fool she was, to have behaved so impulsively, and so naïvely! She thought of her old life and was aware that the hospital had receded into some misty mental realm where the sun always shone and order prevailed, where everybody knew their place and nobody suffered from want: a castle keep on a rocky ridge, and within its walls security and plenty. And while she knew this to be an illusion there was still enough truth in it that it gave her a sort of comfort to think about a place of refuge, a safe place in her mind if nowhere else. Later still she would find it ironic that this great good place (as it seemed to her then) was the place they had both chosen to flee, and that they were now seeking its very qualities of safety, warmth, and plenty in a street of derelict warehouses.

He began at last to make some progress. He now required her to sit for him for four or five hours every day. She saw her head and neck begin to emerge from the clay, strangely flattened and elongated but recognizable all the same. But his mood remained tense and preoccupied, and a day or two later Nick moved out. Stella was now more alone than ever, and found herself turning again and again in her mind not to the hospital, not to Max, but to Charlie. She couldn't help counting the days since she'd last seen him. She realized that while he must be missing her, at the same time he would be learning to hate her. He would see the depth of his father's pain, and know that she was responsible, and the longer she was away from him the deeper that hatred would root.

Eventually she allowed these feelings to infect her dealings with Edgar, and it backfired badly. The artist's psyche, when it achieves equilibrium, achieves it at such a pitch that any dis- traction, any disturbance by brute reality will destroy it in an instant; to make art it is necessary to turn away from life. Edgar's sensitivity in this regard was intense, to the extent that I thought of him as the pure type of the artistic personality. For him the making of art and the maintenance of sanity had a pre- cise and delicate relationship. Disturbance in one would create dysfunction and breakdown in the other.

One morning she awoke and found herself alone in the loft. Edgar had never gone out in daylight before. At first she was calm. She made some tea, then washed her underwear in the sink and hung it up to dry on the pulley. She went into the studio and opened the shutters. It was a clear, windy day, with a few high white clouds kicking across the sky. She wandered about looking at the drawings pinned to the wall. The clay on its stand was covered with damp cloths.

She went upstairs and read an old newspaper. After an hour she was sick with worry. He hadn't told her where he was going or how long he'd be gone, and it was too easy to imagine another chance meeting with the police, though this time without the cover of darkness and with no alley to slip down. How would she know? This suddenly struck her with force: how would she know if he'd been caught? Her helplessness started to terrify her. Without the two men she was lost. She depended on them utterly. This was a flaw in their arrangements, they must plan for contingencies like this, he must not abandon her again.

By noon she was desperate. She thought it now beyond question that he was in the hands of the police. She felt angry with him but she dimly recognized that this was the effect of anxiety, she'd felt the same when Charlie vanished into the marsh for hours. It was a mistake to think about Charlie when she lacked the strength of mind to resist the guilt he aroused in her, now that it seemed she'd lost Edgar as well. Eventually she could stay there no longer. She rushed down the staircase.

Where she intended to go she doesn't remember. But she does remember her urgency, her sudden burning conviction that by doing nothing she was losing everything. Perhaps, I suggested, she intended to return to the hospital, but she shook her head. She clattered down the stairs in her panic and stumbled along the passage and out into the sunshine.

She ran right into his arms.

"What is it, for God's sake!"

She realized what a state she was in: coatless, hatless, her hair a fright, her face puffy and unwashed. Her panic subsided, she let him help her back up the stairs.

He was badly rattled by her behavior.

She tried to explain that she'd felt sure he'd been picked up by the police. He moved away from her and paced about the studio, frowning and chewing at his thumbnail and casting wild glances at her. She had never seen him like this before, he had always been strong enough to absorb her anxiety and quiet her down. She didn't understand what was going on.

"Is that what you want?" he said.

She stared at him. He stood there in the middle of the loft watching her coldly.

"No! How could you think that?"

"You're missing your comforts."

He was standing at his table now, idly turning over sketches, not looking at her, still chewing his thumbnail.

"I thought they'd got you. I thought I was on my own."

"You wouldn't be on your own for long."

She said she didn't properly take in the meaning of this, all she heard was his pain, so she went to him and tried to take him in her arms. He pushed past her and sat on the chair by the wrapped clay and rolled a cigarette. She knelt by his chair. "I was frightened," she whispered. He wouldn't look at her. He lit his cigarette and shrugged his shoulders. She stood up and went over to the window and sat on the sill and looked out into the street. She was sick at heart. All this art, all this squalor, what was it for?

"Frightened," he sneered, but he sounded frightened himself, and it suddenly seemed so childish and petty and selfish of him to be angry with her for being frightened on his behalf!

"Oh, you don't love me," she said, "you haven't the imagination."

She didn't look at him as she said this. The next she knew there was a crash and he was on his feet, the chair on its side on the floor, and then he was standing in front of her with his fists clenched, huge and furious.

"Are you going to start hitting me?" she said calmly. She looked up at him without fear. It didn't matter now. Nothing mattered. She didn't care if he knocked her around. He was just another angry man, the world was full of them.

"You were going back to Max."

"Don't be absurd."

He turned to the wall and hit it once very hard with the side of his fist. The room was alive with violence. It was dreadful to feel his rage. Why had she never seen it before?

"So they were right about you."

"What?"

"You are a psychopath."

She didn't care if it made him angrier. She was past caring.

He turned back toward her and his pent fury filled the room and made everything tremble as though it were about to shatter.

Then his mood shifted. He let out a deep breath. He leaned against the wall, pushing with his hands, his eyes closed. His anger had subsided. "Oh, psychopath," he said. "This is Max, is it, or is it Cleave?"

Not me. Edgar is many things but he's not a psychopath. But she didn't want this, she didn't want him grouping her with the psychiatrists. She went to him and tried to take his hands. Without opening his eyes he resisted her and now she didn't blame him, he was right.

"I'm sorry," she whispered, "I was desperate. You didn't come back and I thought they'd got you. I didn't know where you were."

He opened his eyes. He absently touched her face. His mood shifted again. He became brisk. "Look at this," he said. He pulled an envelope out of his inside pocket and handed it to her. "Go on, open it." She slit it open with her fingernail. There was a wad of ten-pound notes inside.

"You were getting money," she said.

"Good old Nick."

She took the money out of the envelope. It should have made her happy, this wad of notes, it translated into food and drink, but the effect was the opposite, it depressed her. It was too brutal, the fact of his money and what it would buy them. Life was a squalid barter, cash for time. Cash bought them time, what did time buy them, the chance to watch love turn to ash? It was an awful sensation, to feel the meaning drain out of everything. She dropped the money onto the floor.

"What's going to happen to us?"

He reached down for the money and with his eyes still on her face he touched it to his lips. He put it back in his pocket.

"No good," she whispered.

"Money, Stella."

"Oh, money."

She stood at the window with her back to him.

"Yes, money." She knew what he would say next. He would tell her it hadn't been easy to get.

"You think it was easy?"

"I want to go to sleep."

She pushed herself off the window frame and without looking at him wearily climbed the staircase to the mattress. She lay down and closed her eyes. Immediately she felt it all begin to slip away. She was exhausted. She wanted to sleep for a year and when she awoke it would all be as it was before, she would have her child back. Then he was shaking her awake.

"I'm sorry," he said. She could smell wine on his breath.

She rolled onto her back, then sat up on her elbow and reached for the cigarettes.

"Oh what does it matter?"

There was a silence. He didn't understand her. Why not? He was so clever, he understood so much, why was he being so obtuse now? He sat on the end of the mattress, staring straight ahead. She lay there, propped on one elbow with her back to him, smoking.

"I got it for us," he said eventually.

This at any other time would have filled her with joy. Now she was indifferent. She said nothing. She shrugged. He was watching her closely; he saw her shrug, and it enraged him. He seized her wrists so that she half rose off the bed.

Immediately they became excited. They began kissing, and then they were pulling open their clothes. This overwhelming appetite they had, this ravenous lust, it alarmed her, she hated being constantly out of control. There was desperation in it now, and aggression, she worked off her anxiety and frustration in the sex, and this time, as they clung blindly to each other, she bit his shoulder hard. The effect was dramatic. He reared up and slapped her face, but they didn't stop, and it wasn't until a minute or two later, when they came apart, that she rolled away from him and buried her face in the pillow. She felt utterly numb. It was collapsing as she knew it would and she didn't care. She heard him muttering some nonsense and she didn't listen. She lay on the mattress with her face stinging and her mind blank. She expected him to beat her up and she didn't care. But after a few moments he went back down to the studio.

She sat up and found her powder compact. Already her face was red. There would be a bruise. She snapped shut the compact. You fool, she told herself, over and over again.

When she returned from the cathedral he didn't apologize. It was late afternoon and he had gone back to work on the clay. He hadn't turned the lights on, and with the shutters half closed the loft was gloomy. The day had seen enough clarity, enough grating exposure; it was time for gloom and gin and eventually sleep. A night of gloom and gin. They were both depressed; they didn't speak; they felt no inclination to go out. Stella lay on the bed, sprawled on top of the blankets in stockings and slip, a woman adrift amid a flotsam of old cosmetics and yesterday's newspaper. When it grew dark he didn't turn the lights on, he pushed open the shutters instead, and the streetlight diffused a soft gray glow into the studio. Stella wanted to get drunk and try and see things with some sense of hope. She went down to the studio with her gin and drifted over to the window. Edgar was at the clay, hunched over it, and didn't turn around.

"I wish Nick was here," she said, and saw him stiffen.

When she awoke at dawn she was still on top of the blankets and she'd spilled her gin. Edgar was asleep beside her in his clothes. She sat up, a foul dry bitter taste in her mouth and her head already thumping from gin on an empty stomach, and got him into bed. They both immediately fell asleep.

It occurred to her the next day as she listlessly set about cleaning the place that nobody rises above their surroundings, not for very long. Stay in shabby, constricted places and then look in the mirror, what you see is shabby and constricted, watch your own behavior and see it turn cheap and shabby too. She had been thought a beautiful woman: that had all been stripped away, there was no place for beauty here and the more she tried to restore herself with cosmetics the more she looked like a tart.

Edgar seemed not to notice it. It didn't bother him. What bothered him was her. Ever since he'd met her running into the yard he'd become suspicious of her. He thought she wanted to go back to Max. She tried to explain to him it was Charlie she missed, not Max, surely he understood that, but he appeared not to. He appeared to have lost the quickness of intelligence she had grown used to. She said he seemed coarse. Even his voice grew coarse when he was like that.

I think he was frightened. I think any expression of distress from Stella he took as a signal of imminent desertion. Like many artists, Edgar had the soft fearful core of a child.

They went out to the pub the next night and he frightened her, he was so strange, behaving as though every man they saw was trying to take her away from him. He sat there muttering angrily to himself, then caught himself doing it and broke off, shaking his head, embarrassed and bewildered by this other, foreign voice he heard issuing from inside himself, the distorted, ugly voice of jealousy and terror and need. It broke her heart to see him so miserable and helpless, for he didn't want to be like this, he hated what he seemed to be turning into. She held his hands and told him fiercely to hang on, to keep fighting, they'd be all right, she wouldn't leave him. Eventually and with great effort he got control of himself, and after that he became something like his old self once more. But now she couldn't trust it, because she didn't know how long it would last. She saw a divided man; she saw that the man she'd known on the hospital estate had not disappeared but had been invaded, rather, occupied, so it felt, by some other spirit that wasn't his. She told him it was because of the pressure they were under, and that a little time was all they needed. He didn't really take it in, he was frowning and rubbing his head as though he could dispel his illness as one shakes off a bad dream.

How much longer? She lay awake at night and asked herself

how long they could last like this. The bruising on her face was still noticeable, and on these streets there were no illusions about how such things happened. She saw the sympathetic glances she got from other women, and when they were out at night she saw how their eyes flickered to Edgar to see what sort of a brute her brute was. It made her so very uneasy. Any one of those glances might draw the gleam of sudden recognition. So the days passed, and all her efforts went into keeping Edgar steady, though when she went to bed, and he went back to his clay, her mind would turn to Charlie, and she wept silently into her pillow. She had to treat Edgar as a child now, a touchy, clinging child, and she wondered why she was looking after this child and not her own.

But it doesn't surprise me that she didn't leave him. At root, I suppose, in spite of everything she loved him, or told herself she did, and women are stubborn in this regard. She had made her choice, she had gone to him willingly, and it was unthinkable to run home because he was ill and his illness robbed him of responsibility. What did surprise me was that she could ignore the proliferating signals that an act of violence was imminent. It astonished me that her capacity for denial was so strong as to block the knowledge of what he was capable of. Even when she saw what he was doing to his work, even then she failed to recognize the danger she was in.

She was awakened at dawn by men shouting in the market. Edgar was asleep beside her. She got up and slipped on her coat and went down to the studio. She pushed open the shutters and admitted into the room a pale autumn light. She smoked a cigarette and listened to the market coming to life. The clay was covered in damp cloths as usual and on impulse she began to remove them. What she found was ugly and shocking. It was as she'd last seen it, a strangely attenuated head and shoulders, recognizably hers, but violently scarred and gouged now, she could see where he had gone at it with both his tools and his fingers.

She felt sick and quickly covered it up again. But instead of fleeing the place, instead of running for her life, she went back to bed and took him in her arms and held him.

And then he was all right, and there was, again, passion, and then tenderness. The sex, she said, was rather painful now. Her menstrual rhythm was disturbed, and she even thought at one time she might be pregnant. I asked her if she wanted medical attention but she said no, she was fine. She'd been the one looking after the contraception and she hadn't been truly worried. No, much more worrying was *him*. When his guard was down, when he trusted her, when he was himself, she regretted nothing. It was all worth it. At the smallest sign that he was receptive she surrendered. She only wanted to love him; her own will was crippled, the old pride had gone.

If only they had enough *time*, she thought, then they would be all right. If he didn't do something stupid. But it was so hard to reassure him. It was *his* photograph that had been all over the papers, not hers, this was his angry response, it was him they were looking for, him they'd put back inside, she'd be all right, she had Max to go back to. She no longer argued with him when he told her she had Max to go back to, there was no point in making him angrier.

And what of Max? Did she ever miss him?

Not once, she said; she had thought about him, of course, but she insisted she had felt not a single pang of regret, which of course made it so bitterly ironic that Edgar should feel jealous and think she yearned to return to him. No, she had no feelings for Max. She said that had he been a real husband none of this would have happened, there would have been no emptiness in her, no hunger, she would not have needed what Edgar had offered her and which she had been unable to refuse, even though it meant losing everything in the process: child, home, a place in the world. Max seemed to her now a sort of dead man, a bloodless creature who behaved toward human beings like an insect collector, skewering them in glass cases with labels underneath, this one a personality disorder, this one a hysteric. Only after leaving him, she said, did she become aware of the extent of the lack he had created in her. She hated him for that, for pushing her to the extreme of desperation. What would happen to her now she didn't know, but it seemed to her that all she could do was play it out to the end.

One day while she was sitting for him she asked about Ruth Stark. She asked him if he'd done her head in clay.

"No good," he said, without breaking the rhythm of his work.

"Why?"

"I couldn't see her at all in the end."

"Why not?"

He was absorbed with the clay and didn't answer her for several moments. When he did reply his tone was vague.

"All the men. I couldn't get through them."

"Get through them to what?"

"To what she looked like."

"Oh."

She was silent for a while.

"Her likeness," she said.

"I tried someone else but her head was all wrong too. I didn't want to know who she was, I just wanted to see what she looked like."

"How did Ruth take that?"

"What?"

"The other woman."

A small snort here. "She didn't like that at all."

"And?"

Another silence.

"I told her she could clear out if she didn't like it."

"Did you have sex with the woman?"

Now he stopped working and gazed at her for a moment, a smeared wooden spatula hanging from his fingers. He grinned at her.

"No."

"Did you want to?"

"No! I just wanted to do her bloody head in clay!"

And then she thought she detected good omens abroad. She had been reading the papers every day, and Edgar had not been mentioned for weeks. Nor had she been mentioned once, and certainly there had been no photograph. She assumed, correctly, that this was because the hospital didn't want it known that the deputy medical superintendent's wife was the lover of the escaped patient and had gone to join him. This would have been sensational indeed, and more sensation, more publicity, was precisely what Jack and the rest of us would be anxious to avoid. So yes, we hushed it up, and from her point of view this worked in their favor. It was progress.

Then Nick showed up again.

8

Dear Nick. She had grown fond of Nick, tall, lanky, earnest Nick. It was Nick who usually gave Edgar the money he brought back to the loft. He had a small income from somewhere, and he was generous with it. Also, seeing how things were with Edgar and Stella, he had borrowed a small flat in Soho so as to give them more room. Stella was relieved to see him again. I believe Edgar was too, in his way; he was aware that he was starting to lose control, and I believe it frightened him. Without me his work was his only lifeline, the only thing that gave any sort of structure or purpose to his existence. He discounted Stella now, for he was increasingly plagued by suspicion, and though he fought these thoughts they cast a shadow over his mind, a persistent pall of misery and doubt that only rarely allowed him to see her fully and clearly anymore, and that was when he was working.

He had continued with her head, and the disfigurement produced by his gouging and stabbing became a stage in the evolution of the piece. He was eager to show Nick what he'd been doing, and Stella saw how her head seemed now to be both itself and an account of his fraught and increasingly tortured relationship with her; it was, she thought, pathology in clay. Nick understood immediately that Edgar was doing something important. His reaction made Stella wonder if it was possible that all they'd been going through was simply the turmoil that attaches to any serious artistic project. No creation without suffering, the greater the suffering the better the art, was this it? They were certainly being put through it for this head, she thought, and then asked herself would she prefer to return to the drawing rooms presided over by the wives and mothers of psychiatrists. She would not. She was grateful to Nick for leading her to this insight; she realized she and Edgar had been too much alone together, and perhaps it was nothing more than that. Nick was fresh air. The tension eased dramatically.

Oh, and he was good for Edgar too; she saw how Edgar tried to conceal his pleasure when Nick expressed genuine admiration for the work. Nick's reaction mattered as hers did not: Nick was an artist, he knew what Edgar was up to. Later the pair of them went out and came back with a case of red wine and a box of groceries. That night was one of the happiest she'd known in the loft. The two men were in good spirits, there was plenty to eat and drink, they shouted and laughed and talked into the night, and Stella kept a quiet eye on Edgar throughout and secretly exulted in his mood. It was the old Edgar she saw that night, the funny Edgar, affectionate, spirited, smart, laconic, and dangerous. He argued with Nick about painters. A pad of paper appeared and Nick sketched out the paintings he was planning. Edgar made a series of rapid suggestions and Nick listened and nodded, chewing his lip in that way of his when he concentrated, getting it all down as fast as he could. Later, when Nick, drunk, was stretched full length on the couch smoking a cigar, Stella told Edgar she had no regrets. They were drunk too. He stood up unsteadily and came around to where she was sprawled in her chair with a foot on the side of the table and her skirt riding up her bare thighs. He held her shoulders and leaned in toward her and solemnly apologized for being such a shit.

"You're not a shit," she said.

"Oh yes I am," he said.

"He is," said Nick from the couch.

Nick passed out where he was and they slept late the next morning, which was a Sunday. Edgar was still unconscious when Stella got up and found the painter in the kitchen poring over his sketches and trying to decipher the notes he'd scrawled when Edgar was firing ideas at him. Stella said she needed some fresh air, she had a bad hangover, and Nick said he'd come with her. They left the place quietly so as not to wake Edgar.

They wandered down to the river. Nick looked awful. He was in his old tweed jacket and paint-spattered trousers and shoes, and he was unshaven, red-eyed, and baggy-faced. It was a gray, chilly morning with spots of rain in the wind, and after a few minutes watching the river they were both too cold to stay out. Nick suggested they stop in at the pub.

It was when they got back an hour later that the nightmare began. Edgar stood in the door of his studio glaring at them. He hadn't opened the shutters so the place was still dark and his face was indistinct. The couple of drinks in the pub had mobilized the alcohol still in Stella's blood from the night before and she was already squiffy.

"Darling," she cried, "we've brought you some breakfast!"

Nick held up two quart bottles of brown ale. "Hair of the dog," he said. "What's the matter?"

Edgar hadn't moved, he hadn't said a word; he just stood there glittering at them, his bottom lip pulled down and his teeth pressed tightly together. Stella moved toward him, her laughter dying and concern now clouding her features. The other one, the sick one, was there, that was all there was; there was no Edgar at all.

"What's wrong? Has something happened?"

"Don't come near me."

She turned to Nick, who was frowning at Edgar, as troubled by his behavior as she was. They were both quite sober now.

"Edgar—"

"Get out, Nick. Don't come back here."

"I don't—"

"Get the fuck out, Nick!"

"Look—"

Edgar moved toward him, clearly intending to hurt him. Nick backed away.

"Get the fuck out!"

Nick did what he was told. In silent amazement Stella watched him go.

"Bastard," muttered Edgar as Nick's steps were heard clattering down the stairs.

"Stop this, you're frightening me—"

"You little slut. With *Nick*." He had started talking with a public-school accent like Nick's.

"I don't understand." But she did.

" 'I don't understand.' " He mimicked her. "Yes you do understand, don't lie to me anymore."

A great weariness swept over her. She had seen the other one before but it had never been as bad as this. And he'd never turned on Nick before. How long would she have to wait this one out? She sat down and lit a cigarette. She felt sick and depressed.

"You bore me to death with this nonsense," she said quietly.

She picked up an orange from the bowl on the table and turned it idly in her fingers. The next thing, he was across the room and dragging her onto the floor. She was aware of the orange rolling away toward the window and she wanted to tell him not to tread on it as they were expensive. Just as he had before, he half lifted her up and held her there by the wrists, shouting that he knew she was fucking Nick, did she think he was a fool? She said nothing, there was no point, and he slapped her, harder than the other time, and she fell back onto the floor and turned over and buried her face in her arms.

She lay there, her breathing muffled, her body heaving. She couldn't hear him. She didn't know what he was doing. But he was still in the studio. Time seemed to slow down and she couldn't tell how long it was since he'd hit her, whether it was one minute or ten. She dared not sit up. She feared enraging him further. Then she heard a sort of scraping sound. She couldn't identify what it was. She lifted her head slightly and opened her eyes. She could see him on the other side of the room, standing at the table with his back to her.

"What are you doing?"

He didn't turn, he didn't answer. She again felt bored with it all. She sat up sighing and gingerly touched her face, which was throbbing painfully. She reached for her powder compact to inspect the damage. Still Edgar's back was to her, and still he was making that curious scraping sound.

"I said, What are you doing?"

Then she recognized the sound. He was scraping a blade against a stone. She flipped open the compact. She was deeply alarmed. She stared at herself in the little round mirror. One side of her face was already changing color. There were little pulsing jabs of pain.

"What are you sharpening?"

No answer to this. She wondered if she should run for the door. How little she knew him after all. In the garden she'd known who he was. Then she'd have said that whatever happened in the future, whatever he did, it would be consistent with the man she knew. But he wasn't the man she knew. He was somebody else. Or had she just invented that other man, created him out of her need?

"What are you sharpening?"

"A knife."

A knife to cut her head off with.

"What are you sharpening a knife for?"

She was strangely calm as she scrutinized her face. She

remembers thinking she should be grateful he hadn't broken the skin. Her eyes were smudged and she dabbed at them gingerly with a handkerchief. Her thoughts were of flight, for now he was going to murder her. Oddly, the idea held no terror for her, she was detached from everything around her. The scale of things had changed. The compact she held in front of her face seemed far away, as though it had been compressed to the size of a coin. Her reflection was tiny. She couldn't make out her features properly, her face was so small.

"To cut up the orange with."

He was tiny and far away too. She saw him as if through the wrong end of a telescope. He had stopped his sharpening. He still had his back to her but he was watching her over his shoulder. A tiny man a long way away on the other side of a vast room.

"To cut the orange?"

Her voice seemed to issue from an unknown source, toneless and metallic. He crossed the room with his hand extended, offering a slice of the orange. She put it in her mouth. He didn't want to murder her, he wanted to give her a piece of fruit. He watched her intently as she ate it.

"What's wrong?"

It was so strange, the way he was watching her. She couldn't imagine what he was thinking. He shook his head and turned away. She saw him cut another slice of the orange and tentatively bring it to his lips, as though he'd never tasted it before. And then she understood. She remembered something I had told her about the delusions he'd harbored about Ruth Stark. She remembered me telling her that he thought she was poisoning his food.

This affected her in a way that nothing else had. His violence she had rationalized. His jealousy she could explain. But for him to think she was poisoning him with an *orange*!—now she was alarmed. Now she knew that *for his sake* she must get away from him, and everything we'd told her, everything she had so far successfully suppressed, it all came flooding into consciousness, and for the first time she was mortally afraid of him. Or rather, not of him, but of the madness that was in him, this was a point she stressed. She knew she mustn't show her terror, for she believed now that at any moment he could become violent and do to her what he'd done to Ruth Stark. Perhaps with her he wouldn't need to get drunk first, perhaps he was already out of control. She felt that if he caught the smell of her fear it would set him off.

She wanted to flee but she didn't dare leave the room. She sensed that he would know what she was thinking, and once he knew it would be the end.

"I'm going up," she said.

She picked up her bag and slowly climbed the staircase and sat on the mattress. She wiped the stickiness of the orange off her fingers and resumed inspecting her face in her compact mirror. Then she reached for her book, settled back on the bed, and without once glancing down into the studio she began to read. She could feel him watching her. Will it be now? The calm she was projecting was utterly sham. Her heart was beating fast, her skin was moist with fear, and panic threatened at every moment to overwhelm her.

All afternoon he stayed in the studio. He worked on her head. I think I can guess what a superhuman effort of will he made to stay in control. I think by working on her head he was trying to see her clearly, to see the truth of her, and so master and defeat the madness that was in him. Upstairs Stella guessed nothing of this, she simply prayed for him to go out. She dared make only mental preparations for her own departure. She lay among the bedclothes, her back propped against the bricks, smoking cigarettes. Having for so long denied what she knew about the murder of Ruth Stark, she could now think of nothing else. That he should think she was *poisoning* him—oh, he was mad, he was mad, and despite her terror she still found it in her to pity him, for she understood his madness as disease. She had lived among forensic psychiatrists far too long to forget that.

. . .

He shuffled out without a word shortly after dark, she heard him go, that strong man. She wasted no time. She had planned precisely what to do. She packed her suitcase and got dressed in less than ten minutes. In her raincoat, head scarf, and sunglasses she ran down the stairs and along the passage at the bottom. There she waited a moment and then peered out into the yard. It was empty. She walked quickly out to the street. She paused by the wall to check that he wasn't on his way back. He wasn't. There was a cold wind off the river. She hurried away.

Half an hour later she cautiously entered the saloon bar of a shabby little pub near Waterloo. It was a clean, warm, empty, dangerous room; there were rooms like this all over London, she thought, rooms that appeared to promise safety but were in fact alive with the possibility that he would walk in. Just one man in a gray raincoat, up at the bar with his evening paper and a glass of beer in front of him. A carpet on the floor and a gas fire burning. Beside the fire, in the corner, a small round table with metal legs. Just the man at the bar, the warm fire, the warm low lighting, cigarettes and alcohol, and outside, cold and twilight, an empty studio, a madman. She would sit at that little table for a while and have a drink. The woman behind the bar sold her a packet of cigarettes and a large gin and tonic, and she carried them over to the fire and installed herself, bruised cheek to the wall. She poured tonic into her gin and lit a cigarette. She was aware after a minute or two that the man at the bar was watching her, but when she looked up he turned back to his paper.

It was warm and quiet and the lighting was subdued. There was tonic left in the bottle so she bought another gin. While she was up at the bar the man in the raincoat asked her if she'd like to join him for a drink. No, she said, she was waiting for her husband. He probably thought it odd, she told me, that she was wearing sunglasses. He probably wondered about the bruise on her face. She wasn't concerned with what he thought. She took her gin back to her table by the fire. She was waiting. She had chosen this pub because there was a phone box outside. She had called Nick's flat and been told he was out. She would try again in half an hour.

An hour later she was still there. The sadness kept welling up inside her, wave after wave of it, and she told herself fiercely, in a tone she recognized as Max's, not to be silly, not to give way to self-pity—to *pull herself together.* Ironic that one of Max's precepts for the management of unruly female emotion should come to her aid in this particular extremity. Pull yourself together, dear, you're in a public place, do you want to make an exhibition of yourself? This distracted her, the idea of making an exhibition of herself. Putting a frame around the little table and its weepy occupant, a somber black frame and under it the title of the piece, *Melancholy.* She smiled, her face hurt, soundlessly the tears streamed down. From the public bar came the sound of men's laughter. Enough of this, Stella, she said to herself, but it didn't help, it only seemed to make it worse, and at that point the man at the bar turned and brazenly scrutinized her, so the public exhibition rose to her feet and went out to try and reach Nick for the third time.

The flat was tiny but it was better than the loft. What a pleasure it was to have a proper bathroom! Nick had been worried sick about her. He had gone back to the loft and found it empty. He hadn't known what to think but he'd feared the worst. His relief was enormous when he heard her voice on the phone. He came to the pub, they had a drink together, then he took her back to the flat. She told him that more than anything she wanted a bath.

She undressed in the bathroom. She sank into the hot water and lay there with her eyes closed. She felt she hadn't been properly clean for a long time. Some of the unhappiness and squalor and anxiety and guilt of the last days lifted. After a while she examined her body, her white skin, her breasts, her limbs, her pale, delicate hands and feet. Max had lost interest in her body after three or four years of marriage, for he lacked the imagination to sustain sexual attraction. She had then been more or less celibate until Edgar. But she couldn't think about him now. She blocked him out.

She emerged from her bath and powdered herself in front of the long mirror in the door.

Dear Nick. He was not well equipped to offer hospitality and succor to a distressed woman but he was trying. He insisted she have the bed, he would sleep in the armchair. So she climbed gratefully into bed in her dressing gown as he fussed around her, getting her a drink.

"Would you like something to eat?"

"I'm not hungry, Nick."

She was demure and gracious, as befits a lady in straitened circumstances. She liked this weak, messy, good-hearted man. His paint-spattered trousers had always made her smile; she and Edgar had a private joke about them, they'd suggested he exhibit them as art. Poor Nick, he'd laughed, but the next time they saw him he was wearing clean trousers, though they didn't stay clean for long. Now he sat forward on the edge of the armchair, rubbing his long hands together and shyly telling her how he'd felt when he'd heard her voice on the telephone that evening, the enormous relief.

"I knew him when he started getting ideas about Ruth," he said.

"Oh, Ruth," said Stella. She didn't want to hear about Ruth now.

"Nick," she said as an idea occurred to her.

"What?"

"Has Edgar ever been here?"

Nick looked sick and said yes.

She couldn't sleep, and nor could Nick, sprawled in the armchair under a blanket, tossing about, trying to get comfortable; she wondered at one point whether she should invite him into the bed with her. Later she slipped over to the window and pulled back the curtain an inch or two. The rain was coming down steadily, slanting down through the glow of the street-lights. The narrow street, slicked and gleaming, was deserted. What had she expected, to see him standing under the street-light in the rain, gazing up at the window?

A little later she heard Nick groping for his cigarettes, trying to make no noise, and then came the flare of his match.

"I'm not asleep," she said into the darkness.

"I can't sleep either."

"Nick."

"What?"

"He'll come here, won't he?"

"I don't know."

"I'm frightened."

He sat on the edge of the bed and held her hand.

"It's not him," she said. "It's because he's sick. You know what he's like when he's not sick."

Nick didn't say anything. He was holding her hand tightly. She realized he was aroused. It had never occurred to her that Nick desired her. Had Edgar had seen it, was this how it had all started? Was it all Nick's fault?

"The door's locked," he said.

She squeezed his hand. He leaned toward her and she let him kiss her. He slipped his hand under the blanket and tenta-tively touched her breast.

"No, Nick."

"Sorry."

He went back to his armchair.

"Try and sleep," she said.

He came at dawn. They were awakened by the sound of the door handle being turned. They never did find out exactly how he got into the building, for the front door was locked. They sat up and stared with horror at the door.

"Nick, open the door."

His muffled voice terrified her. It wasn't him, it was still the other one with the strange artificial accent. Nick stared wildly at her, shaking his head. In the gloom she read the terror in his face.

"Open the door, Nick. Come on, man, it's me. I'm not going to hurt you."

Silence. They were utterly still. He won't want to create a disturbance, she thought. He won't dare try and break the door down, it would be the end of him. Unless he doesn't care anymore.

"She's in there, isn't she?"

Nick didn't know what to do. He was paralyzed. Stella stared at him, shaking her head. He mustn't get into a conversation with him, not even through a locked door. Nick was shrugging his shoulders like a schoolboy. With her finger at her lips Stella silently crossed the room. She sat on the arm of the chair and put her hand on Nick's mouth. With her other hand she gripped his wrist. He gazed up at her and she made a silent shushing shape with her mouth.

"It's not your fault, Nick," came the voice. "I know what she's like."

Nick's eyes grew wide. She couldn't tell what he would do. She took her hand away from his mouth and leaned forward and kissed him.

"She's no good."

Nick tried to turn his head toward the door but her fingers were in his hair, gripping him, as she kept her mouth pressed to his.

"*Nick!*"

He thumped the door very hard once. Nick almost jumped out of the armchair, but Stella held him, still kissing him, darting her tongue into his mouth. Her dressing gown had opened across her legs as she balanced herself on the arm of the chair, and Nick's hand crept under and began tentatively to touch her thigh.

There was silence now from outside the door. Had he slipped away, alarmed that all the noise he was making would rouse the house; or was he waiting in the corridor? Nick's hand moved up her thigh to her groin. She was becoming aroused too, by the situation as much as by his touch, but she pushed his hand away. She went to the door and pressed her ear against it. She could hear nothing. Nick had slumped deep into the armchair and turned gray. She went to the window and twitched back the curtain a fraction. She saw him emerge from somewhere along the side of the building, and she watched him walk away. Even his walk was different now, gangling, ill-coordinated. It cost her not to call out to him, to let him just walk away. It had stopped raining. She turned into the room and faced the slumped and shattered Nick.

"He's gone," she said.

"I want a drink."

"Poor old fellow."

They moved out within the hour. They slipped away through a side door, each with a suitcase. Nobody was about yet and the street was almost deserted. A little later they passed two loud men in evening clothes looking for a cab. Stella had only one pair of shoes now, her high heels, and she stumbled trying to keep up with Nick, who was still badly frightened. He took her suitcase and she clung to his arm. They caught a bus going west, away from Southwark, and sat among silent, sleepy men and women too preoccupied with their newspapers and ill humor to pay any attention to the bruised woman in the raincoat and the tall shabby nervous man beside her.

The day was overcast. Small flurries of rain swept against the windows of the bus. After a few minutes they got off. Nick said he knew where they were. He took her down a side street to a run-down square of large Georgian houses surrounding a patch of brown grass with a tree in the middle and a fence around it. The hotel was no different from any of the other houses. A tired woman took them up two flights of cheaply carpeted stairs and showed them a room that overlooked a high brick wall with glass shards cemented along the top and an alley with dustbins, washing lines, and cats.

.   .   .

She said that the two days she spent with Nick were the grimmest yet. Only a few details stand out in her memory. He was not clean in his person, she said, and his eating and drinking were messy. He was considerate and devoted but he watched her constantly, not with tenderness but with hunger. She wondered if he was capable of rape. She lay for hours on the sagging double bed, and the overhead light cast a weak yellowy glow that made everything in the room uglier than it was already, including themselves. She lay there worrying about Edgar. She feared he was too disturbed now to avoid drawing attention to himself. She thought he might do something stupid.

And their future together?

Oh, she said blithely, she was always sure of that. She knew the thread was unbroken; even in his worst fits of aggressive jealousy she felt him straining for her, she felt the passion, only it was confused and misdirected, it was as though it had been shunted off down some passage from which it emerged monstrous and unrecognizable. This was his illness. And she said that it was during the two days she spent with Nick that she attempted what she called her heart's prompting: she tried for the first time, not intellectually but emotionally, to separate the man from his illness, and yes, she could do it. Oh, it was easy, she was more than equal to the task: she imagined him clutching his head as the storm raged in his poor benighted mind, but the storm wasn't him! The storm would pass, he would recover, he would be himself again. But *for his sake* she must avoid him while he was mad; later she would go back to him. How all of this would come about she had no idea, but she chose to trust that it would.

Nick was too afraid to go back to the loft, he was afraid to go out at all, and the pair of them were too much together. She was soon deeply irritated with him, but by now she had almost no money left and no clear idea how to get more. At the end of the corridor there was a bathroom, which they shared with the other residents of their floor. She spent as much time in it as she could, if only to escape Nick and his smells and his anxiety and his lust. The house smelled of boiled cabbage and seemed occupied exclusively by shabby gray people who avoided her eyes when she passed them in the corridor or on the stairs.

At last she'd had enough. She took it all out on Nick. She admitted that on the morning of the third day, after another restless, unhappy night, in a weak moment she acquiesced in his constant doglike lusting and took him into bed. She was passive. She was also rather sore. Her only satisfaction lay in being reminded of how it was to make love to Edgar. So in her debasement and despair, as Nick laboriously went about his pleasure, she summoned the image of her lover.

Afterward Nick was pathetically satisfied with himself and that was the trigger. She turned on him, she belittled him, she mocked his weakness, his failure to be a hard surface she could grind herself against. He tried to protest his sympathy and concern but what did she need his concern for, or his sympathy? He could keep it. She went to the bathroom and came back and got dressed in front of him, provocatively, and went out without telling him where she was going, because she didn't know. She left him like a kicked dog to lick his wounds.

She wandered the streets, a sad slow woman, her coat hanging open and a cigarette dangling from her fingers. She didn't care what she looked like or whether anyone noticed her. A sad woman drifting down sad streets, insubstantial, not quite real, not quite there, a ghost. She came to a decision.

It seemed suddenly absurd to her, she said, to be running and hiding not from the hospital authorities but from *Edgar*! She caught a bus as far as Blackfriars and walked to Horsey Street in the rain. In the street the boys were kicking a ball against the wall. They stopped their game and stared at her as she turned up the alley to the yard, and their silent scrutiny did nothing to relieve the dread she felt, a dread so palpable it made her nauseated. More than once her step faltered and she thought she couldn't go on.

She reached the passage into the building. The children had not resumed their game, they had followed her into the yard and now stood silently staring at her. She soon understood why. At the top of the stairs the door to the loft was open and there were men inside. She immediately started back down but she'd been seen. She heard a voice calling; she did not stop. A man came after her and caught up with her halfway down. Just a moment, please, he said, as he put his hand on her shoulder. She turned. He recognized her. Christ, he said, it's Mrs. Raphael. You're Stella Raphael. She stared at him. She had never seen him before in her life. He started shouting to the other men. Within moments two more of them had appeared on the stairs, and they were both as surprised as the first one. They led her back up to the loft. Edgar wasn't there, nor did they appear to know where he was. They wanted to ask her a few questions, they said. If she didn't mind.

9

With this dramatic development Stella swings back into my field of vision, she comes into focus once more, and the account is again grounded in my own observations. She says she was grateful they weren't rough with her. Actually they were more surprised than anything else, I think because it hadn't occurred to any of them that she would so clumsily blunder into their clutches. They didn't attempt to question her there and then, once they'd established that she didn't know where Edgar was.

The events of the next hours have an unreal, nightmare quality for her now. She remembers a room in a police station and a woman in uniform giving her a cup of tea. An hour or so later Max arrived. He, like the police, had clearly decided that the best approach was the gentle one: Stella the victim, seduced and abandoned, a pitiful woman led astray by a cunning man who had manipulated and entrapped her then cast her aside. When he came into the room she tried to be calm and cool but she hadn't the resources, and even before he could open his mouth she found herself in his arms and clutching him tightly. She had been so weak and alone and desperate these last days. He stroked her head and she didn't care that he stroked her like a doctor, like a psychiatrist, because that was what she needed then. It wasn't until later that the doctor receded and the husband advanced, and a new nightmare began.

She allowed herself to go limp. She became passive and pliant, like a child or a sick person. They talked to her gently, and she answered their questions. She saw them frowning, murmuring to one another in low tones, and she didn't even try to understand what was going on, she made no attempt to take any active part in it at all. All she wanted now was to be looked after.

That night she slept in a cell in the police station. They were apologetic but she didn't care. Sleep was sleep and they'd promised her a pill. The room was bare and the sheets were clean. She swallowed her pill and closed her eyes, her mind empty of thought, clear of all feeling, and slept a long, deep sleep and the only dream she could remember in the morning involved the conservatory in the vegetable garden, but she couldn't remember anything more than that.

The sense of numbness gradually wore off. The next day she had to submit to a lengthy interview with a senior policeman, who was polite, she said, in a brisk sort of way. Her eyes wandered about his office. The walls were a shiny green to shoulder height, cream above. There were two large, dusty arched windows, several gray metal filing cabinets, a wall map with pins in it, and a large clock over the door. He asked her where she had lived with Edgar Stark, what they had done, the people they'd seen. She told him all she could remember, she didn't see how it could hurt him now, but she couldn't remember anybody's name. He nodded, he made notes, he moved her in a straight line through the days and nights since she'd first come to the warehouse on Horsey Street. She told him her story and paid no particular attention to his reactions. She did not talk about the fits of jealousy, and she tried to leave Nick out of it as much as possible. Some parts of her account seemed to interest him more than others, she didn't know why and she wasn't interested in finding out. It was over, that was all, and as she experienced relief and blankness so did she glimpse as though through fog the encroaching fingers of loss, and understood dimly what would come next. She began to brace herself for the darkness.

Max drove her home the next day. The white Jaguar was parked in the yard at the back of the police station. As he opened the passenger door for her she glanced up at the back of the building and saw the barred window of the cell in which she'd spent the last two nights. In silence he pulled out of the yard and into light London traffic. It was the first time they'd been alone since she'd been picked up.

"You look tired," she said.

He didn't reply. He was smoking, staring straight ahead.

"I talked to Jack on the phone last night. We think the police won't press charges," he said eventually.

"Against who?"

He glanced at her. She was huddled up in the front seat, wearing his overcoat. When she felt his glance she turned toward him. His eyes slid back to the road.

"Don't you know what you did was criminal?"

She didn't like his tone of voice and she wasn't interested in what he was saying. She didn't reply. They both stared straight ahead at the road.

"Nobody wants a scandal," said Max.

She said nothing.

"I didn't expect you to be grateful."

A lorry pulled out in front of them and Max had to brake sharply to avoid running into the back of it. It took him a few moments to overtake the lumbering thing, and by the time they were once more moving at normal speed he seemed to have forgotten the demand for gratitude he'd embarked on. She glimpsed then just how delicate and complicated their negotiations would be, now that it was all over. If it was all over. Was it all over? He was apparently being chivalrous. He was saving her from prosecution. He was standing by her. For all of this a price would have to be exacted. Gratitude was just the beginning.

She and I talked one morning in late October, a cool morning with the mist still clinging to the trees. We walked through the vegetable garden, where it had all begun. The men were burning dead leaves and there was a smell of bonfire in the air. She told me she was sad that she wouldn't see another spring, or another summer, here in the garden. The change in her was noticeable. She was paler, slower, heavier; there was a gravity about her now. The apple trees were heavily laden, and the ground beneath was scattered with fallen fruit, soft, spongy apples, pale green and yellow, dimpled with black spots of rot. As we picked our way among the the fallen apples she took my arm. I was her first and only visitor, she said; all the rest nodded at her and said good morning but they couldn't look at her, she was an affront to their sense of decency. There had been no word from the Straffens, and she'd assumed, she said, that her old friend Peter Cleave was with them.

"So how are you, my dear?" I said.

"Oh, Peter," she said, "I've been better. Really, how lovely of you to come and see me. I did think you were up there in the stands, booing with the rest of them."

"I?" I said. "I boo you? I don't take my friendships as lightly as that!"

"I should have known."

"Anyway," I said, "I'm a doctor, I don't blame someone for becoming ill. So how could I blame you for falling in love?"

"Nobody else seems to find it very difficult."

"Ah, but that's because they were hurt by what you did. It's only when we feel pain, or the prospect of it, that we start to make distinctions between right and wrong."

"Is that what it is?"

"I think so. Don't you?"

We reached the bench by the conservatory and sat down. She tilted her head back and closed her eyes.

"Oh, I don't know, I'm too tired to think."

We sat there in silence for some minutes. Later she said it was heaven to feel that sense of simple companionship, she hadn't realized how much she'd missed it.

"How are things with Charlie?" I asked quietly.

She opened her eyes.

"Dear Peter," she murmured. She was grateful for my tact, grateful that I didn't ask how it was with Max; I had identified, she said, the relationship that really mattered.

"I'm winning him back. He wants to love me."

"I shall miss you," I said.

"You've heard then?"

"About Cledwyn? Yes."

"Do you know the place?"

"I saw a patient there once. It's all sheep and tractors. I'm afraid you won't like it."

She smiled.

"Sheep and tractors. I shall be the country wife. And no one will know about my sordid past."

Before I rose to leave I told her what I'd come to say, that in all seriousness I was greatly relieved she had come to no harm.

"You don't know what harm I've come to," she said.

"You're in one piece as far as I can see."

She touched her breast. "Not in here."

"You'll heal," I said.

"Please come and see me again," she said. "You're my only friend, you know."

I said I would, and then, as I was leaving, she quietly asked me if I knew where Edgar was.

I told her I didn't know.

She said later that she was much happier after my visit. A certain darkness lifted from her mind. She said she thought that before they moved to Wales she might lean rather heavily on me for support, so as to nourish her spirit for what lay ahead.

I came to see her frequently in the days that followed. She was frank with me about her relations with Max. He was taking a ghastly grim satisfaction, she said, in seeing her suffer the consequences of her defection. You did this, this is your fault, he seemed always to be implying. Damn you, she thought, I shall endure this but I won't put up with this false calm of yours, this façade of neutrality and the poisonous moral superiority it masks. Max would be sure to be seen to do the right thing, she said, but he would never let her forget that she had hurt him, or rather that she had humiliated him publicly; the needle would be inserted whenever he chose. He assumed, she said, that a woman as much in the wrong as she was wouldn't have the audacity to protest his toxic pinpricks. We'll see about that, she thought, and lifted her chin, prepared for the worst.

How had the homecoming been?

They felt so *stale* to her, she said, with a shiver, those familiar rooms, more like cells than the police cells she'd just left! With his usual dry asperity Max said the one word, "home," and went over to the drinks cabinet. She said nothing, just felt the fingers of the coming darkness plucking at her.

The house was strangely silent that night. Summer was long over and the weather was damp and misty. The house seemed too large for them, and they drifted about it like strangers in an empty hotel. Max was unable properly to begin his punitive campaign, perhaps, she thought, because the magnitude of her guilt awed him. That she should still eat, and drink, and move from room to room, burdened as she was with sin, this struck him dumb with amazement and even a sort of admiration. He could not quite believe that she wasn't crawling about on her hands and knees, weeping and tearing her hair out and begging his forgiveness. He was aghast with a sort of furtive pleasure that she didn't behave with shame, which made her in his eyes more shameful still, and so compounded his sick delight in the whole sordid performance. It was a cool evening but she took her drink onto the back lawn and stood staring out into the darkness. She heard him behind her in the house, moving about, getting ready.

She made up the bed in the spare room, and she could tell he thought she was sparing him the embarrassment of having to refuse to sleep with her. Nothing of the sort, it was her decision, had she wished to sleep in her own bed she would have done so. She wasn't afraid of him, and she wasn't going to do his work for him. If she was to be punished he would have to do it himself. How would he do it? She didn't trouble herself with his problems. She felt the ground tremble beneath her feet and the abyss begin to open.

For the next few days everything seemed imbued with a solemn, heavy formality. She remembers one wet afternoon lying a long time in a hot bath with a gin and tonic then drifting about the house, going from room to room, doing nothing, not bored, just passive, numb. She went into Charlie's room and lay on the bed, and she must have fallen asleep, for that's where Max found her when he came home from work. He was, as usual, irritable, but there was something else, his mood was compounded with an anxiety that came from a source other than her.

"What's the matter?" she said. "What's happened? Is it Charlie?"

He was leaning against the door frame. He pulled out his cigarettes. He wasn't looking at her.

"Are you sure you're interested?"

"Of course I'm interested. Tell me."

She was sitting on the side of the bed. Max lit his cigarette, tilted his head back and blew smoke at the ceiling.

"You've finished me," he said.

"What do you mean?"

"He's fired me."

She didn't know what to say.

"Oh, he can't do that."

He rubbed his face and sighed.

"Don't you want to know why I've become an embarrassment to the hospital? Why the fact that my wife ran away with an absconding patient makes me a liability?"

He was suddenly angry.

"What will you do?" she said.

He didn't speak for a few moments. He was simmering silently once more.

"Jack believes the hospital's mission will be compromised if I remain on the staff."

She yawned.

"There's a ham," she said.

He looked away and shook his head then went downstairs. She heard him go into his study. He didn't come out for the rest of the evening, and he was still in there when she went to bed. She was terribly tired.

The next morning she telephoned Charlie. He had been staying with Brenda and she hadn't seen him yet, but she'd called him every day. He was hurt, of course he was hurt; she'd gone away without preparing him for her departure and he'd naturally felt abandoned. He must have thought it was his fault, she said; until, that is, his guilty bewilderment was given definition by Max and Brenda, so that by now he'd be blaming her for his unhappiness. But she knew he wanted to come home. He wanted to love his mother, and to know that she loved him. Brenda, however, was being obstructive.

"He's not here," she said, and Stella knew she was lying.

"Let me talk to him, Brenda," she said.

"He was very upset last night. I think you should let him come to terms with this whole thing gradually."

"Just put him on, please."

"Have you really thought what's best for him?"

"Please don't interfere. Let me talk to him."

Silence then, and a few moments later Charlie was on the line.

"Mummy?"

"Hello, darling. What have you been doing?"
"Oh, going to see things. I want to come home now."

She drove through with Max in the afternoon to meet the train. Max was silent. Stella was sure he would want a divorce, but he had said nothing yet and she certainly had no intention of raising the topic. She didn't want any fresh upheaval, she wanted a haven, and time to heal, for she realized that she was still in shock and the pain of losing Edgar had not properly begun to make itself felt yet.

Charlie was nervous when he got off the train. But then, as they came together, all four of them, for Brenda was with him, on the platform, and Stella crouched and took his hands, he fell into her arms and kissed her on the lips. She glanced up and caught the look that Brenda shot Max, the lift of a thin plucked eyebrow.

The car was parked just outside the station. Charlie and his mother went first, hand in hand, with Max and Brenda following. Stella said she felt as though a great weight had been lifted from her. It seemed to her that if Charlie and she were all right then some semblance of a normal life could be sustained. Max would continue to stew quietly in his own watery juices, and Brenda would doubtless tell her smart Knightsbridge friends that her son was married to a slut, but none of that could touch her, none of it mattered.

She took him up to his room while Max gave his mother a drink in the drawing room.

"I'm so happy you've come home," she told him while he got ready for bed and she hung up his clothes.

"Are you going to London again?"

"No, I'll never go away again. I'm very very sorry. Do you forgive me?"

She sat on the bed as he buttoned his pajamas. He turned to her and again kissed her. She hugged him tight; she clasped his plump little body close to hers and wondered how she could ever have left him. She told him how much she'd missed him, and the tears flowed. Charlie was a gentleman; he comforted her; as she sobbed out her remorse he stroked her hair and solemnly told her that everything was all right now, and please not to cry.

That night she was flooded with memories of Edgar. Why that night? The crust of numbness on her heart, why did it crack open that night? She thought it was because Charlie was back, and loving Charlie roused her to the other, greater love, and so the loss and longing came. She had gone up to the spare room, her room, straight after dinner, and left Max to give his mother coffee and drive her to the station. The meal had been eaten in an atmosphere of ghastly politeness, nobody willing to give voice to the terrible currents roiling among them; there was only the clatter of cutlery on china as they ate ham and boiled potatoes, with Brenda murmuring civilized banalities all the more difficult to respond to because they assumed the family's continued residence here on the estate: Max had not yet told her he had lost his job. Too ashamed to, Stella supposed; she was glad of it, that he hadn't told his mother yet; Brenda would of course blame her, see her as the ruin of her son, and Stella simply wasn't strong enough to cope with that yet. So there they sat, the family, that cool autumn evening, and Brenda made the small talk that held at bay the silence that loomed in the corners of the room and threatened to tear them to pieces. She fled upstairs as soon as she decently could. Nobody thanked her for the meal.

After looking in on the sleeping Charlie she lay on her bed and a wave of pain swept through her and left her feeling desolate and tearful. Later she stood at the open window, a cardigan around her shoulders, for the night was cool, and hugged herself and remembered the nights they'd had in London, and how alive she'd been, alive with passion for that poor disturbed man and for the life they'd led those few glorious weeks until it fell apart. Where was he now? She held him clearly in her mind's eye, and though it gave her a jolt of pain to do this she wouldn't let him go. She knew then that this would not end quickly. She heard Max and Brenda leave the house, and she heard the car. Some time later she heard Max come back in and turn the lights off and come upstairs. He paused on the landing; thank God he didn't tap on her door.

They had their talk the next day. Max initiated it. She was alone in the kitchen when he came home from the hospital at noon. He said they had to talk in the study and it wasn't possible to say no. He didn't seem angry, nor was he heavy with resentment, just weary and troubled and sad, and she almost felt sorry for him. She wiped her hands on a dish towel and followed him down the hall and into the study.

"Sit down," he said. "I've been thinking about our future."

Obediently she sat down and waited for what he had to say.

"I've started to look for a job. There are a number of possibilities. Staff jobs, not superintendencies. I'm not regarded as a particularly good prospect for a position of responsibility just at the moment."

This was allowed to hang in the air for a few seconds.

"I'm afraid we shan't be living in London."

This too hung in the air. He regarded her with a cool, studied expression, as though she were a specimen. He wanted a response.

"What a pity," she murmured.

"Quite."

He frowned as he busied himself with cigarettes and matches. He didn't offer her one.

"Can't be helped, I'm afraid. You've brought this one on your own head."

"Could I have a cigarette, please?"

"I'm sorry; of course."

They smoked.

"Stella, I take it you do wish to continue living with me? If you have other plans I'll of course hear what they are. Naturally Charlie would stay with me. Have you made other plans?"

"I have no plans, Max."

"We are still married. We'll talk about what happened when you're ready. I don't see any point in trying to rush you. You seem to be in a state of shock still. In the meantime I suggest we try to put up as good a front as we can."

She said nothing.

"I think we can at least try and treat each other with common decency. God knows it's hard enough for me. You hurt me very badly, Stella."

"I made you look a fool, you mean."

"No, that's not what I mean."

He struggled to contain his irritation.

"That's not what I mean," he repeated. "We will talk it all through in good time. Not now. Now, I suggest, we simply make some preliminary agreements. I think it best if you continue to sleep in the spare room. And I think you should take responsibility for the house, the cooking and cleaning and so on. I'll find a job and see to the move. I suggest we take it a day at a time and try and rebuild some sort of a life."

There was a tree outside the study window. Most of its leaves had fallen already, though a few were still drifting down.

"Do you agree with what I've said?"

"Yes."

He took off his spectacles and rubbed his face.

"I suppose it's too much to ask that you make an effort to make this work?"

"I will look after the house."

"That isn't what I meant. Never mind."

He glanced at his watch and said he must go back. They both rose. They stood there a moment in the middle of the room face to face. He seemed on the point of saying something more but the telephone rang. He picked it up.

"Hello?"

Silence.

"Hello?"

After a moment or two he replaced the receiver.

"Who was that?"

"Nobody there."
She knew it was him.

Three days later Max told her he was applying for a staff job in a mental hospital in north Wales. He imagined, he said, that it was his for the asking. She knew what he was telling her: he was too good for it. He had not yet told his mother about any of this. She wondered how he'd break it to her. Would he tell her he'd been ruined by a slut?

Memories of Edgar would take her by surprise, catch her unawares and leave her gasping with pain as though kicked in the stomach. But the pain was tempered now by her conviction that he was trying to reach her, by the spurt of hope this aroused. Though when Max was at home she found it impossible to sustain even a numbed façade. She believes he knew what was going on, any psychiatrist could diagnose a broken heart at this close range. He didn't attempt sympathy, and she hated him simply because he wasn't Edgar. He wasn't Edgar, yet he was there, and because he was there he was hateful. It was unfair but there was nothing she could do about it. When she didn't hate him actively she was filled with a blank, dead, unfeeling indifference that she recognized as a form of passive aggression. Had she not been so exhausted she couldn't have tolerated living like this. But she needed shelter, and she needed Charlie, so she shuffled through her days and kept the house going and waited without interest for what north Wales would bring, and at the same time felt her heart leap every time the phone rang.

But it was never him. The weather grew darker and wetter and the prospect of winter gave her an odd sense of comfort. For one who craved sleep, the chilling air and the lengthening nights promised an easy drift into darkness. She thought she might wake up in the spring, if she had the inclination. Sleep promised oblivion, and that would at least release her from the constant hovering phantom of Edgar. Where *was* he? Often she lay on her bed, or wandered in the garden, these damp autumn days, and constructed scenes of his return, their reunion—would he reappear, or would he send for her as he had before? And wouldn't she go? Wouldn't she do it again, without hesitation? She didn't know. She didn't know.

Though what lay most immediately ahead was the storm she must face when Brenda was told the news. Max was reluctant to do it, this was clear, and kept putting it off; but it couldn't be put off forever. He drove up to Cledwyn a few days later and came back less dispirited than Stella had expected. He said there were interesting possibilities. Interesting in what way, she asked him. Oh, he said, the hospital. It's run by a man I used to know. He has some good ideas. He wants to make changes.

"Where will we live, Max?"

"I thought we might buy a farmhouse and fix it up," he said. "They have big stone farmhouses up there. Quite handsome in their way. It might be fun."

Since when had Max wanted fun? Ambition thwarted, was he attempting a new philosophy of life, one that involved fun? It appeared the work would not be as grim as he had anticipated, therefore he would have fun; or he would during the day, at least, while he was at the hospital. As to whether he would have fun when he came home in the evening, that was a different question.

"What did you say?" he said.

"I said, Why not?"

They were in the dining room finishing the wine after supper. Charlie had gone up to his room to read.

"When will you tell Brenda?" she said.

Max had produced a weary sigh when she said, Why not? He expected enthusiasm from her, or at least an attempt at it. He felt that if he was trying to sustain the appearance of domestic

normality, then surely she, as the one who had so violently disrupted that normality in the first place, could do the same. But
he knew it did no good to get angry with her. Hence the sigh.

"I think I'll call her tonight," he said. "Get it over with."

"She'll be terribly disappointed."

"I'll try and soften it. But she'll be horrified at the idea of us
being in north Wales."

"Not us. Just you and Charlie. She won't mind me being up
there."

He didn't trouble to contradict her. He took his glass and
went off down the hall to the study. He closed the door behind him.

She sat at the table, oddly lethargic, unwilling to move. How
Brenda would hate her now, she thought, the woman who was
dragging her son and grandson into exile with her. Dragging
them down, depriving her of them. Yes, she would hate her
more than ever.

It didn't go well, she could see this as soon as Max emerged
from the study. He sat down heavily and to Stella's mild surprise filled his glass again.

"We won't have a farmhouse to fix up," he said. He couldn't
meet her eyes.

"Oh?"

"If we go to Cledwyn we don't see another penny from her."

"What about your salary?"

"The salary won't begin to support the way we live. Staff
psychiatrist in a little bin in the back of beyond—"

He was ashen as he contemplated their imminent poverty.
Stella remembers feeling as indifferent to this as she was to
everything else at that time. Then something occurred to her.

"Max," she said. "If you divorced me. If you and Charlie went
to Cledwyn without me. Would she cut you off then?"

He didn't answer. This meant no.

"I see," she said. "She's given you the choice. Get rid of Stella
or there's no more money."

Still he said nothing.

"It's me or her, Max," she said. "Up to you."

Poor Max. She almost felt sorry for him. What a position his mother had put him in. Though he didn't have any real choice at all. Having made up his mind to do the gallant thing, he couldn't change course for money. It was a matter of principle.

"We can keep the car, I suppose?" she said.

He looked up at her then, bitterness and disgust twisting his weary features.

"Yes, Stella. We can keep the car."

She didn't care. "Well, that's something," she said.

She began to pack up their things. It was mindless work, and it was predicated on the idea of a family that moved from place to place and cohered throughout. But what bound them together, what sort of future made this thinkable? She could conceive of none, but felt she had no alternative. So she wrapped their china and glassware and put it in cardboard boxes, taped up the boxes and labeled them. Then their pictures, their clothes, their bedding, all packed up, all labeled. Mrs. Bain helped her, not because she wanted to, for she didn't, she made that clear, but because she thought she should. Room by room their possessions went into boxes and packing crates and cabin trunks and suitcases, and it somehow felt like a proper thing to be doing, this packing up of the old life to ship it elsewhere.

One morning as she was working with her tape and boxes I came to see her again. She made me a cup of tea and told me she couldn't stop working, she had too much to do, but I was welcome to talk to her while she packed books in the drawing room. So I watched her for a while before telling her what was on my mind.

"Stella, is Max giving you medication?"

She stood bent over a box of books and stared at me. She was genuinely surprised by the question.

"No, of course not," she said. "Why would he?"

"I think you're depressed."

"Well of course I'm depressed, wouldn't you be depressed?"

She straightened up and pushed a hand through her hair. Now it amused her, to have me sitting there frowning and telling her what she would have thought perfectly obvious.

I wasn't amused.

"It'll be hard for him to see the signals," I said.

"What signals?"

"Someone should be keeping an eye on you. Someone other than Max."

"What is it you're saying to me?"

She sat on the edge of an armchair and lit a cigarette.

"You're vulnerable at the moment. You're about to move to a part of the country not known for its warmth to strangers, where you know no one, and with a husband who's still very angry with you. It worries me, Stella."

"I shall cope," she said quietly.

"I hope so. I expect you to write to me."

"I will."

"Regularly."

"Yes, all right!" She was laughing now. "Can north Wales really be so bad? You make it sound like Siberia."

"For you it might as well be Siberia."

"Oh nonsense."

At the front door she asked me her pressing question.

"Have you heard anything of Edgar?"

I took a moment to decide how to respond to this. She assumed our common interest in his welfare; assumed too that I was as preoccupied with his whereabouts as she was. I curbed my impulse to tell her to put him out of her mind altogether. Instead I just shook my head.

"Poor man. Peter, where does his son live?"

"His *son?*"

"Leonard."

"He has no son."

"Yes he does."

"Stella, he has no son. Don't you think I would know?"

She gave a small brittle laugh.

"We shouldn't talk about him, should we?" she said.

. . .

She wandered through the empty rooms and remembered the events of the summer. In less than a week they would be in Wales, and she would never see this house again. Max had found them somewhere to live, not a place of their own but part of a large farmhouse divided in two. They would rent one half of it from the owner, who lived with his wife in the other half. Max said it was on the side of a hill and looked out over a valley. There was no real garden, he said, but there was plenty of open country around, fields, woods, a quarry. Charlie listened closely, wanting to believe they were going to a better place.

There were no farewell parties. Jack Straffen gave Max a glass of sherry in his office. I was there; they murmured platitudes to each other, the mansion of psychiatry having many rooms and so on, and Jack expressed his sympathy; though what sympathy could you offer a man who wanted your job and would probably have gotten it had his wife not sabotaged him so decisively? People had begun to question Max's judgment in marrying a woman capable of doing what Stella had done. Could he be *sound*? I tried to keep an open mind, and encouraged others to do the same. Though I thought then, and still think, that Jack was right to let him go. This is too sensitive an institution to have a man like Max Raphael occupying a senior post.

I did stand by her, I can hear him saying; I did stand by her, despite everything.

It was raining the morning they left. The removal men had come the day before and carried their furniture out to a huge black van, and then the packing crates, and then the neatly taped and labeled boxes that held the rest of their possessions. When they were finished Charlie and Stella watched them drive away, while Max went around the house locking up. They drove to the Main Gate for the last time and handed in the keys. Then they left for the north.

. . .

The journey took several hours. Charlie was more interested in the scenery than Stella was, so he sat in the front seat and Max did the driving. At least they still had the car, Stella remembers thinking; she was fond of that comfortable car. Somewhere north of Birmingham a terrible thought occurred to her: how will Edgar find me? When he comes looking for me, who can tell him where I've gone? Who can he ask? She stared out of the window and willed the tears not to come. She caught Max's glance flicking up at the rearview mirror, watching her, always watching her, waiting for moments of weakness like this when he would have it confirmed, again, that she was still elsewhere and unrepentant. Oh, Edgar, why have you done this to me, why have you left me here to twist and weep under the cold eye of this unloving man? She was angry with her lover then, she could afford to be: she knew he was trying to reach her.

It was already dark when they arrived. They would spend the night in the town and meet the removal men at the house the next morning. Max was tired; he was also angry, for it had not escaped him that Stella had been crying, and he knew she cried for Edgar Stark. He had distracted himself by having a long conversation with Charlie, and when after a while she paid attention again she discovered she was indifferent to what they were talking about but fascinated and horrified at how he was shaping the boy's thoughts, imprinting him with the patterns of his own logic, drawing him beyond the reach of her influence, though whether he was doing this from a conviction of her unfitness as a mother or from a more primitive impulse to punish her, she was not sure; she suspected the latter. For a while she was disturbed by this; Charlie was at just the age to take the impress of a grown-up mind, he was like soft wax.

They were in the hotel, eating together in the dining room, and Stella had leisure to examine the shabby provinciality of their surroundings. She was suddenly convinced that the house they were moving into the next day would be ugly.

"Max," she said, "is it ugly, this house? Will I hate it?"

Father and son stopped talking and looked at her. She had interrupted them. Good, she thought. She must interrupt them as often as possible. She must not allow Max to have the boy for himself. To steal his soul.

"I don't think it's ugly, no," said Max. "On the contrary, it's rather a handsome house."

"What is it made of?" said Charlie.

"It's a stone house," said Max. "They build with stone here."

"It sounds cold," Stella said to Charlie. "Don't you think so, darling? Doesn't it sound cold?"

Charlie was uncertain.

"Is it cold?"

"There's a wood-burning stove in the sitting room, and storage radiators, and all the rooms are carpeted except the kitchen."

"That's not what I meant," said Stella.

"What did you mean?"

"I meant cold for the spirit."

Max said nothing. He lifted his glass and watched her over the rim as he sipped his water. His eyes said, Be careful, stop now. Charlie looked from one to the other, not understanding.

"We'll make it warm, won't we, darling?" said Stella.

"What do you mean?"

"Mummy means we're going to be happy in the new house," said Max. "Don't you?"

10

You could see the house from the road when you were still a mile away. The valley was broad, contained by long, low hills crested with stands of trees. It was a clear, blustery day and she was filled with dread. Banks of cloud rolled across the open sky. The road was narrow, and splattered with dung, and there were thick, bristling hedges and stone walls on either side. When they were three or four miles outside the town Max pointed it out, a gray square block of a house high up the valley. It seemed built for defensive purposes, to protect its occupants, but against what? Max glanced at her in the rearview mirror.

"What do you think?" he said. "Think it's handsome?"

There was, she said, a jaunty tone in his voice now; he knew she was trapped.

"I don't know," she murmured. She couldn't decide if it would shelter her or not, this big gray house. Five minutes later they turned in through the gate and emerged cautiously from the car. The sign on the gate read, "Plas Mold."

The removal van had already arrived and was parked in the yard behind the house with the tailboard down and the men standing around smoking cigarettes. One of them came forward, a small lean fellow in a rough tweed jacket. It was windy up there, and there was a strong smell of manure in the air, so Stella got back into the car and watched as Max and Charlie shook hands with the man in the tweed jacket, who then produced a set of keys. They moved to the back door of the house, unlocked it, and disappeared inside. Somewhere out at the back of the house a dog was barking. The removal men climbed into the van and began passing boxes out. Max came back out to the car a few minutes later.

"Come in and see the place," he said. He seemed genuinely confident she would like it.

The man in the tweed jacket was Trevor Williams. He owned the house and lived in the other side of it with his wife, Mair. They had no children. He showed them around. He was a silent man, and he gave Stella the distinct impression that the less they had to do with each other the better he'd like it. The wind howled about the house and made it creak and bang like a ship. The kitchen was a long room on the ground floor. The sitting room, one floor up, matched its dimensions, and the top floor was divided into two bedrooms with a bathroom off the landing. Stella realized immediately that she and Max would have to share a bedroom: why hadn't he mentioned this? How could he expect her to sleep with him? She said nothing for the moment, however; Trevor Williams was watching her.

She didn't like the look of the master of Plas Mold. She told me she was to meet this type of character often in the weeks to come, suspicious, watchful men, dour and sly. They didn't like the Raphaels because they were English. They bore old grudges. The women were hard-worked and bitter. Stella met Mair a little later when she came out of her end of the house with a basket of damp laundry to hang on a line strung across a patch of grass at the side of the house. The laundry flapped and snapped in the wind as Mair moved along with her basket, a couple of clothespins in her teeth. She was as lean as her husband but lacked the spark of furtive vitality Stella had seen in his eyes, evidence of an appetite for whatever secret pleasures spiced his dry life. Mair's eyes spoke only of work and disappointment and bitterness and sterility; she had no children. She introduced herself and they stood there in the wind, the women, Mair clutching her basket of washing with both hands as at the back door the removal men grunted with the double bed. She asked Stella had they come from London and Stella said no, not London, but not far from London. Ah, she said, and Stella realized that the smell of their scandal had not yet reached those thin pinched nostrils.

"How old's your boy?" she said.

"Ten."

"Still a baby."

"Yes."

The frame of the bed went through the back door with a man at either end. Stella offered Mair a cigarette. Mair put down the laundry. She knew how to light a cigarette in the wind. Her eyes were pale blue and her skin had once been soft. She was probably only thirty-five or thirty-six, but her good looks had long since been leached out and she gave the impression now of agelessness and sexlessness, a piece of fruit so long neglected it had lost all juice and sweetness.

"He showed you where everything was, did he?" she said.

"Yes he did."

She nodded, picked up her laundry basket, and with the cigarette dangling from her lips and her eyes half closed against the smoke she trudged off around the back of the house, where the dog was still barking. The removal men emerged from the back door. Stella hadn't yet spoken to Max about the bedroom.

She didn't have a chance until Charlie had gone up after dinner and they were sitting at the table in the kitchen. She hadn't hung any curtains and the window at the end of the room looked out into the dark valley and a night sky full of stars. Above the steady roar of the wind she could hear the cattle in the field below. The headlights of a car moved slowly along the main road several miles away.

"How did you imagine our sleeping arrangements?" she said.

He put down his newspaper. They no longer made any attempt at conversation when Charlie wasn't in the room.

"I won't sleep with you," she said. "If you can't think of a solution we'll have to find somewhere else. It won't work like this."

"We're not moving again," he said. Oh, she could make him angry in a moment, no matter how determined he was to stay calm and reasonable. She heard the rising irritation in his voice, the barely controlled whine of indignation that she should be dictating terms to him, she who was entirely responsible for their upheaval. He was trapped in an idea of where his moral duty lay, but I'm afraid he hadn't the strength of character fully to believe in it.

"Why won't you help me?" he said tightly.

She was without mercy. She hated him because he wasn't Edgar.

"Someone has to sleep in Charlie's room," she said. "I don't care who it is."

He got up and walked to the window and stood staring out into the night, his hands in his pockets and his fingers twitching with the effort to keep his temper under control.

"I'll sleep on the couch tonight," she said. "It doesn't matter to me."

"No," he said, with his back to her, "I will."

"Why?"

Now he turned. "Because I don't think Charlie should see you sleeping on the couch. He shouldn't see either of us sleeping on the couch. Why can't you wait till I get the spare bed moved into his room?"

"No," she said. "Why didn't you think of this?"

He turned back to the window. He wouldn't tell her why he hadn't thought of it. Perhaps he'd hoped she'd start sleeping with him again. She saw then with a small dark surge of satisfaction that her power was far from extinguished, and that despite everything she was still stronger than he was.

Trevor Williams came over the next day and Max talked to him about moving in the spare bed, which had been put in the barn. As Stella came downstairs to the kitchen he cast a quick glance in her direction. He may not have known about her scandalous past, but he was certainly drawing conclusions about the state of her marriage.

They started Charlie in the local school the following Monday and he came home rather miserable. He didn't like the other children in his class. He said they were rough and unfriendly. Stella spent a long time with him. She listened to his troubled account of his loneliness in the playground and his trouble with unfamiliar classroom routines. It would all get better, she said; starting again in a new place was never easy but it was something he would have to do all his life. It was useful to learn how to do it now.

"But why do we have to start again?" he said.

"Because of Daddy's job."

Charlie thought about this and then explained that since he planned on becoming a zoologist, and intended to travel a good deal, it was probably best if he never got married. Stella said she thought this was wise. As for Max's job, it didn't seem to be as interesting as he'd hoped. Perhaps he had deceived himself, eager to believe that this wouldn't be dull work, but she saw that he was already bored, and felt rather as Charlie did about their new situation, though he wouldn't admit it. For he couldn't afford to think that he'd been shunted off into a psychiatric backwater, where his career would languish while other men with less talent moved into the jobs he should have been offered. No, this was much too painful to contemplate. Max was an ambitious man, and at times Stella wondered if he cared more that she had damaged his career than that she had been unfaithful to him.

Winter came hard and early in north Wales. Max drove Charlie to school in the morning and went on to the hospital, leaving Stella stranded. If she wanted the car she had to get up when they did, but she slept late now for she was awake most of the night. It rained for days on end and she woke each morning to banks of gray cloud moving ponderously across the valley, and the sound of rain on the roof, and of course the Beast That Never Stopped Barking, as she and Charlie called it, a black-and-white sheepdog that Trevor Williams kept chained to its kennel on the far side of the house. One day they went around to have a look at it and it leapt at them in a fury, and but for the chain would clearly have torn their throats out. Charlie was very upset, he thought it a great cruelty to keep an animal chained up all day. He tried to make friends with it but each time he approached the kennel the dog leapt at him with teeth bared, wildly barking, and eventually he grew afraid that one day the chain would snap, and he left it alone after that.

For Stella the days seemed to slip by without anything happening. It became an effort to keep the house clean and provide a meal in the evening. She was gaining weight and she didn't care. She gazed out of the kitchen window for long periods, watching the rain falling on the fields, and on awakening from her reverie she couldn't remember what she'd been thinking about. When the rain let up she would go for a walk up the lane behind the house as far as the top of the hill, where she had a view across the next valley with its scattered farmhouses and the quarry in the distance. The rain went rushing along the ditches and beyond the thick clipped hedges the sheep gathered as she went by and bleated at her. She rarely met anybody; sometimes a farmer; occasionally Trevor Williams passed her in his rusty, mud-caked Land Rover. He nodded at her but never stopped. Leaves fell and drifted in soggy masses by the drains. Water dripped from the bare branches of the trees. Once as she stood in the wind at the top of the hill, and gazed off to the west, the clouds parted and the sun briefly appeared, and its watery radiance seemed like a miracle, like a glimpse of God. She wore Wellington boots that blistered her heels and a long gray raincoat. It was weeks since she'd had her hair done but it didn't matter, she never saw anyone. She tried to imagine

Edgar still out there somewhere and drawing closer, coming for her.

On Saturdays the three of them went shopping. She didn't like the weekends. The house felt crowded and she was disturbed by their noise. There were more meals to prepare and she was becoming less and less interested in cooking. She herself ate erratically, whatever came to hand, which was why she was getting fat. She looked forward to Monday, when the house was empty and quiet again. Sometimes Mair came in and they had a cup of tea in the kitchen. Mair didn't disturb Stella, for neither of them felt any need to make conversation.

She first had sex with Trevor Williams in the middle of November. It was not her doing, it hadn't occurred to her to think of him in that way. It happened the morning Mair left to spend a few days with her mother. Stella was sitting at the kitchen table with a cup of tea, idly turning the pages of a magazine. There was a knock at the back door and when she looked out of the window over the sink there he was. She was still in her dressing gown. She opened the door and he asked if he could come in for a moment. She stepped aside and he came in and went straight to the window at the far end and stood staring out across the valley. It was one of those days when a profound stillness settled on the countryside, not a breath of wind, the trees motionless as though listening intently to movement deep in the earth, perhaps the sluggish blood of dead Welshmen, the murdered sons of Owen Glendower. She hated those still days, they filled her with dread, she felt menaced by unnameable things. She stood at the stove with her arms folded and watched him.

"Why is it so still?" she said. "I hate days like this."

He turned. "Do you, Stella?" he said.

He'd never called her Stella before, he'd never called her anything. She knew then why he was there. She wondered idly what she should do. He was standing in front of her now. She still had her arms folded.

"You're a lovely woman," he said.

His voice with its burr of an accent was hoarse and low. His eyes seemed to be feeding off her. She felt something stir inside her, the merest flicker of inquisitive desire, a response so slight it could have been snuffed out in a second. She waited. He told her what he wanted to do. The flicker flared and he saw it. He touched her hair, then his fingers cupped the back of her head and he came a step closer so their bodies touched and as his other hand went to her breast he angled his face at her and kissed her. She pulled away from him slightly. There was warmth inside her now, though at the same time she was aware only of a mild dispassionate curiosity about the man, this dour farmer who appeared at the back door in the middle of the morning and started talking about sex.

"Is this how the world does it?" she said.

"What?"

His groin was pressed lightly against hers. She laid her palms flat against his shoulders as though to push him away. His skin was rinsed bone white by the wind. His eyes were small and narrow, deep set and slate gray. His breath smelled of tobacco.

"As you do it, I mean," she said. "Walk in and say what you want."

He didn't speak, just held her eyes and began to stroke her in the cleft between her hip and her belly, and without really meaning to she set her legs slightly apart. He slipped his fingers inside her dressing gown and up between her legs and pressed gently. She thought she might as well let him have what he wanted, why not? He was so eager and it was so long since she'd felt even vaguely alive, sexually, and it would be so much trouble to try and stop him now, he would probably rape her.

"You'll come upstairs then, will you?" she said, and he gave her a weasely sort of smile as though he'd tricked her.

When they got up to her bedroom she knelt on the bed holding the headboard and pushed against his thrusts with her eyes closed and her mind empty, and she only spoke once, to tell him he couldn't have his orgasm inside her. She hadn't had her cap in for weeks, there'd been no point.

"Don't you do it with Mair?" she said afterward, lying there watching him pull his trousers back on.

"Not so often," he said. "And you don't do it with him at all."

She didn't say anything. He sat down on the bed and watched her like a man counting his profits. She could see what it looked like in his ledger, a woman under the same roof who'd let him do this to her.

"Lucky fellow, aren't you?" she said. "You didn't think it would be so easy."

"I could see you were lonely."

"I'm not lonely."

He left after that. He tried to make what he called arrangements but she wasn't interested, she wasn't going into his timetable as well as his ledger. Her curiosity was satisfied and she felt as indifferent to him as she had before. She thought it remarkable that a man could walk into a woman's kitchen in the morning, tell her what he wanted, and get it. Was that really how the world did it?

When Max came home he was irritable, as though he knew he'd been betrayed again; but it was their sleeping arrangements that annoyed him. The spare bed was in Charlie's room now, but it wasn't really satisfactory. There wasn't enough cupboard space, so he had to hang his suits in her room, and she made him take out at night what he would need in the morning as she didn't want him coming in early and waking her. Nor did he have a proper place to work, for if he spread his papers on the table in the sitting room he was disturbed whenever anybody went upstairs: the stairs from the kitchen went up against the back wall of the sitting room and from there to the floor above.

He was starting to express his sense of injustice, and now something shifted in the balance of their relationship. No longer bound by a code of gallantry toward the fallen woman, Max seemed concerned only about Charlie, and she realized that her security would one day come to an end. He would leave her, not tomorrow, perhaps, but one day, and take Charlie with him; and their semblance of family life, the form of it if not the substance, was her sole structure and protection now, while she waited. The prospect of losing it should have alarmed her acutely, but even then, even as she saw it start to slip away, she couldn't pretend to Max that she felt toward him anything but indifference.

Max behaved now like a man who no longer believed in doing his moral duty, and had decided to start to look to his own needs instead. She watched him anxiously, she saw how his eyes never settled on her now, but passed across her, as though she were invisible. He never spoke to her if he could avoid it. He wasn't angry with her anymore, just weary, impatient, irritable, distracted. He had given up.

She couldn't rouse herself to change any of this. She seemed to exist in a fog through which she saw the others as dim spectral figures, phantoms who possessed no real substance. Nor apparently did she possess substance in their eyes. When Trevor Williams came back some days later she was as pliant as before, for she came at least half to life with him, and the sex made her calm and sleepy and took away the anxiety for a while.

Mair knew that something was happening. She understood her husband well enough to realize that an unhappy woman under the same roof would not escape him for long. She didn't seem to care. She came over as usual, and they sat with their cups of tea and said very little, and it didn't really matter to Stella which one of them came to see her, it relieved at least for a little while the numbness muffling the world and turning everything colorless and indistinct. She still hauled on her Wellington boots and raincoat and went tramping up the hill behind the house when it wasn't raining, for she had become fond of the lonely lanes and their thick hedges, and the sheep, and the bare dripping trees, and the stone walls with pale green fungus growing on them, and the delicate little white mushrooms. It was all so wet! In the narrow ditches beside the lane the water went rushing down over the stones, and when she was near the top, and turned to look at the valley spread below her, she saw the stubbled fields raked with furrows in which rainwater puddled and gleamed like glass. She thought: he is out there somewhere. Crows flapped up from wet earth trodden to mud by the cattle, and when she passed through the woods at the top of the hill she came upon sudden steep-sided glades overhung with ancient trees, and felt the age of the land, and how it brooded on its secrets, and in an odd way she felt at home.

One morning while she sat with Mair in the kitchen the telephone rang and it was someone from the school who told her that Charlie wasn't well and could she come and take him home? Max had left the car that day so she said yes, she could. He said there was nothing to be alarmed about and she said she wasn't alarmed. Mair offered to come with her.

The car had lost its clean, sleek appearance, for the roads around Cledwyn ran with mud and dung which had so splattered and encrusted it that it looked like a farm vehicle. Also, she had scraped it against a wall a week earlier, and they couldn't afford to have the panel repainted. So it was a shabby, battered white Jaguar that pulled up in front of the school later that morning, and a shabby, battered mother who emerged from it and walked to the main entrance of the school.

This was a large, Victorian brick building with three floors of high windows, and a playground off to the side, and Stella felt a little intimidated, never having set foot in the place. At the reception desk she told the school secretary who she was, and was then asked if she'd wait in the staff room while Charlie's teacher, a Mr. Griffin, was located. Several children had appeared and were waiting to give the secretary a message; they eyed Stella curiously then fell to whispering among themselves, darting furtive glances at her and giggling. Did she look so odd? she wondered. Was it because her legs were bare that they found her odd, or because she had an English accent? It didn't matter, she didn't care. She went into the staff room as the secretary turned to the waiting children and silenced them with a look.

She was reading the notices on the notice board and smoking a cigarette when Hugh Griffin came in a few minutes later. He introduced himself and apologized for keeping her waiting. They had the room to themselves. He cleared a heap of textbooks off a couch and motioned her to sit. He was a tall young man with a shock of blond hair that stood up off his head in thick waves. He had a long, thin, pointed nose and a green tweed jacket with chalk dust on the lapels.

"I hope I didn't upset you," he began.

"Not at all. You said there was nothing to be alarmed about so I wasn't alarmed."

"Good."

She knew she flustered him. He was attracted to her, she said, and he was uneasy about it, for she was the mother of one of his pupils and quite unlike the farmers' wives and schoolteachers who otherwise made up the female element of his world. Amused, she watched him, this lanky young fellow with his long fingers and chalk dust all over his clothes.

"Mrs. Raphael," he said, "why is Charlie so unhappy?"

"Unhappy?" she said with some surprise. It hadn't occurred to her that he would say anything like this. He frowned and looked at his shoes and pushed his hand through his hair. Then he gazed straight at her.

"He's a clever boy," he said, "but he won't make the effort, and I think it's because he's so anxious. But he won't tell me what's wrong."

"I wasn't aware there was anything wrong."

"You don't see it then?"

"Maybe you should talk to his father."

"Can't you help me?"

"He's the bloody psychiatrist!"

This came out with more bitterness than she'd intended, and the laugh she laughed was brittle even to her ears. Hugh Griffin sat forward on the edge of his chair, long legs splayed wide and his fingers clasped together between his knees. He reminded her of Nick.

"Doesn't he talk to you, Mrs. Raphael? Why wouldn't he talk to his mother? Is this the problem?"

"What the hell does it have to do with you?" she said, rising to her feet. She fumbled in her bag for a cigarette.

"Sit down, please," said this offensive schoolteacher in his wheedly Welsh voice. "Please."

"I don't have time," she said. She had turned her head away from him and stared unseeing at the notice board, smoking with short rapid puffs at her cigarette. He sighed. He seemed unwilling to let her go. He was about to say something more when the door opened and two women came in clutching piles of exercise books to their bosoms and talking loudly. They cast no more than a cursory glance at Hugh Griffin and Stella as they settled themselves at the far end of the room. Hugh Griffin wearily stood up and said he would go and fetch Charlie.

As she left the school with Charlie and walked rapidly to the car she was still so angry with the man she could barely speak. She pulled out onto the road and almost collided with another car, and had to sit a moment and bring her breathing and her temper under control. Nobody spoke. Driving home she said to Charlie without turning her head that his teacher thought he wasn't working hard enough.

He said nothing.

"He told me it's because you're unhappy," she said.

Still nothing.

"I said I thought you were fine."

She glanced at Mair, who was sitting beside her in the front seat staring straight ahead.

"Are you unhappy?"

Charlie shrugged his shoulders and looked out of the window. They drove the rest of the way home in silence. He went into the house without a word and straight upstairs. Stella asked Mair if she wanted a cup of tea but she didn't. So Stella sat in the kitchen and stared out of the window. After a while she poured herself a drink. She knew what was happening, she was starting to see Charlie as an extension of his father, and so a part of the conspiracy against her. She didn't want to feel this way about the boy, she knew it was unfair, but she couldn't seem to help herself.

When Max got home that evening she didn't tell him what had happened. She'd decided she would let Charlie explain it in his own way, and then she'd hear it from Max. But when Max came downstairs after saying good night to Charlie he didn't talk to her at all, just settled down in the sitting room with a medical journal.

She couldn't sleep at all that night, and she had the feeling that Max was awake too and listening to her pacing. It was a windy night, the house heaved and shuddered, and though she had a jersey on over her nightdress, and thick wool socks, and her dressing gown on top, she was still cold. She stood shivering at the window and stared at the stars in the wintry sky, her thoughts racing as she smoked one cigarette after another. She remembered the children laughing at her at the secretary's desk, and that teacher telling her she was making her own child unhappy. She thought about Trevor Williams, asleep on the other side of her bedroom wall, and their dispassionate sex together. Since Mair's return he had twice coaxed her into a small stone outbuilding and had her bend over a stack of hay bales. He said she had a lovely white arse. His penis always seemed to be hard. Making her way back across the yard she hadn't dared look at the house in case Mair was watching from a window, though if she was it seemed to change nothing, for she still came over for her cup of tea.

She thought about Edgar and their weeks in London, and saw how her memories were starting to fade like old photographs. But she had her other signs. Certain cloud formations, snatches of birdsong, flowers: by means of phenomena once shared with him she sustained a sort of contact with him. Whenever she went shopping, alone or with the others, in Cledwyn or Chester, she scanned the streets for a glimpse of him. A dozen times she'd seen him, and a dozen times been disappointed. It didn't matter. The flare of feeling, the lift of the heart, this was enough, even if it was in response to the broad black back of some big Welsh farmer going into Woolworth's with his wife.

She climbed back into bed and still she couldn't sleep. She turned from side to side and she was sobbing now. Nobody came to her door. Nobody tapped on her door and whispered, What's the matter? Are you all right? She thought about her father and remembered how she would drift to sleep feeling his bulk and strength as he sat on the side of the bed and stroked her hair and listened to her murmuring the last of the day's thoughts. Again she thought about Edgar, she saw them dancing in the hospital, gods among mortals, and she felt no regret, no remorse, it didn't occur to her to want to change a thing.

She saw the sky grow lighter and then she fell asleep. She awoke late in the morning and after her bath she made a cup of tea and put three spoons of sugar in it and a splash of gin. She felt better after that. She filled a thermos flask and walked to the top of the hill and spent the afternoon up there.

When Charlie came home from school he brought her a letter from his teacher. She asked him if he'd been talking to Mr. Griffin about her, or if Mr. Griffin had said anything to him about her. He shook his head. He looked frightened, as though he didn't know who she was anymore. She asked him if that meant yes or no and he said no. The letter was polite. He apologized for upsetting her. He repeated that he was concerned about Charlie. Would she and Dr. Raphael like to make an appointment with him, to talk about it? She thought not. She crumpled up the letter and threw it away.

Weeks passed. Christmas came and went. She spent it alone in Plas Mold, she said, getting drunk. Max and Charlie went down to London for three days to stay with Brenda. Max was unsettled when they returned; Brenda had clearly wasted no time in urging him to leave her. But he did nothing, and life went on as usual. She heard no more from Hugh Griffin, though she thinks he may have written to Max at the hospital, this suspicion aroused by a conversation they had one night after Charlie had gone to bed.

"You have no cause to hate Charlie as well," he said, with no preamble at all.

They were in the kitchen. She was washing the dishes. He was at the table, turning the pages of the newspaper.

"Has his teacher been talking to you?" she said.

"No, why should he?"

She didn't believe him but she said nothing, just went back to washing the dishes.

"Has his teacher been talking to *you*?" said Max.

"Not recently."

"Then when?"

"Oh, it's too tedious. I saw him in the autumn, I don't know when, before Christmas. He tried to tell me Charlie was unhappy because of me."

"But don't you see how miserable he is?"

She shrugged.

"Stella, don't you see it?"

She ignored him.

"Christ!" he said. She turned. He was struggling to keep his temper. "Listen," he said, "I stay here, with you, for one reason only, and that's because I think that child needs a mother. But if you never show him any warmth there isn't much point. Well, is there?"

She gazed at him silently.

"Is there?"

"He's your son," she said. "He feels about me as you do, you taught him to."

"That's rubbish."

"It's the truth."

"My patience is wearing thin," he said. "For weeks you've been like this, no use to me, no use to him."

"Our arrangement was I look after the house," she said.

"Yes, you look after the house, but you're never properly *in* the house, not body and soul. Can't you get over it? Or don't get over it, do whatever you want, but why must you take it out on him?"

"You taught him to hate me."

It was then they both realized that Charlie was standing at the bottom of the stairs, pale and bewildered in his pajamas. Max glared at her then crossed the room and took the boy's hand.

"Come on," he said, "upstairs. Time you were in bed, young man."

He came down to the kitchen half an hour later.

"He doesn't understand," he said. "He doesn't know why you're like this. Talk to him, Stella, for God's sake. There isn't much time left."

She was far from convinced by any of this and wearily said so. Max went to the window and stared out, his fingers clenching and unclenching in that familiar way. She saw that he couldn't tolerate this failure; the idea that Charlie was suffering because of his parents' collapsing marriage embarrassed him acutely. She went upstairs without a word. Charlie's bedroom door was open. She stood in the doorway. He was lying in bed with his back to her. She knew he was awake and aware of her there, but he wouldn't turn and face her, and after a moment or two she went into her own bedroom and shut the door.

The following afternoon she was at the sink peeling potatoes when Charlie came shuffling in from school and dumped his satchel on a chair and sat down to change his shoes.

"What are we having?" he said.

"Beef stew."

"Mummy."

"What is it?"

"Can I ask you something?"

"If you want to."

She went on with the potatoes. The window over the sink

looked out across the road to the barn where Trevor Williams kept his tractor. There was a window high in the wall that had no glass in it. A crow landed on the sill with a flurry of flapping wings and hopped around two or three times pecking at the sill. Then Trevor Williams emerged from the building. It was twilight, and she was sure he couldn't see her clearly through the kitchen window, but he put his hand on his groin and rubbed it, and she couldn't help smiling.

"Mummy?"

"What *is* it?"

Trevor opened the gate into the field beyond the barn where he'd driven his cattle earlier. She could never understand why he moved them from one field to another, something to do with the grazing, she supposed. He latched the gate after him and set off across the field to where the cattle had gathered at the top end.

"I want to be friends."

She turned from the window, delighted with his plaintive request but pretending to be dubious.

"Are you sure?"

"Yes."

"Hm. Did Daddy tell you to say that?"

"No."

"Did Mr. Griffin?"

"No."

She sniffed and turned back to the sink and began cutting up potatoes on the draining board. He sat there with a sulky, angry look on his face that she recognized as Max's. Another long silence as she put the potatoes into a pot and filled the pot with water and salted the water, turning every few seconds to glance at him with mock suspicion. The boy was not sure how much of a game this was. She could hear the cattle out there in the thickening dusk.

"Turn the light on," she said, "it's getting dark in here."

She started to chop an onion. No sound from behind her, and no light either.

"Charlie," she said, turning, and saw his little face pucker.

"Oh, darling," she cried, darting to him and taking him in her arms, "of course I want to be friends! Aren't we friends already? I thought we were!"

The next day she stood by the house gazing out across the valley. Another windy day, but dry, with an armada of white clouds moving across the sun so that one hill was lit by a pale watery sunlight while the one beyond was plunged in shadow. It was a restless, active sky, and she watched it contentedly for some minutes. Electricity pylons, recently erected, marched across the valley and climbed in a line across the far hills. When she walked beneath them she heard them buzzing and crackling. The sun was higher in the sky, the first hint of spring, and white smoke poured from the chimneys of the brickworks to the east. For the first time in months she felt something stirring in her that might have been hope.

That night she suggested to Max that he look for a job in London. She saw the flash of pleasure in his face as he told her he intended to stay at Cledwyn for at least two more years.

"So you'd better get used to it," he said.

That night she got drunk. At times Max's cruelty cut her deeply, she said. There was a certain thrust of the blade he had perfected by now, one that slipped between the plates of her armor and went right to the heart. He left her feeling a fool that she had momentarily forgotten that this was a mortal struggle, a fight to the death. So after dinner she poured herself a large gin and put her coat on and went outside and leaned against the gate looking at the stars. After a while it was too cold to stay out so she went on drinking in the kitchen, gazing out of the window from a wooden chair tipped back on two legs, her feet up on the sill, the bottle on the floor beside her. The trouble with getting drunk was that it made her think about Edgar and thinking about Edgar made her maudlin. When Max came down to the kitchen she told him he was a shit and he said to her in his quiet, furious voice that his patience was almost exhausted, which provoked a further stream of abuse from her, which quickly sent him back upstairs to his medical journals. Soon enough the tears came but of course nobody came down to see if she was all right, it was just the slut in the kitchen who'd ruined their lives, getting drunk on neat gin and howling for her lost lunatic lover.

On her way upstairs, after a last expedition out of doors, which culminated in her hammering on the Williamses' door and shouting for Trevor, she paused in the sitting room. She had the bottle with her and she was tempted to hurl it through the window, just to see Max's face when he came out of his room, but it wasn't worth losing the gin for. Laughing boisterously she made her way upstairs and fell asleep in her clothes.

Max was furious in the morning, so furious she had to apologize. Fortunately she hadn't announced when she banged on the Williamses' door in the middle of the night what it was she wanted Trevor *for.*

This, she said, was the pattern of their days, in Plas Mold.

And what of Edgar, what of her lost lunatic lover? To my deep consternation I had heard nothing. He seemed to have disappeared off the face of the earth, and more than once it occurred to me that he was dead. I was intensely relieved, then, at last to get word of a reliable sighting: he had been spotted in the vicinity of Euston Station. This suggested the possibility that he was going north, and I immediately called Max. I told him we suspected that he'd found out where he and Stella were living. What he intended to do, if he was indeed heading for Cledwyn, we could only guess. I told him of the security arrangements the police were making, which put his mind somewhat at rest though not much. It was worrying news, and I didn't hide from him my own unease.

Then I asked him about Stella. I had talked to her recently on the phone, and I was concerned that she was not being properly looked after. Max was guarded, and when I pushed him, and at last heard the immense weight of suppressed anger in his

voice, I tried to suggest gently that he adopt a different perspective, a more detached, more *psychiatric* perspective. She
had suffered a hysterical illness, I told him. She was trying to
deal with a huge burden of guilt, and clearly she was having
trouble coping. She needed his help.

He said nothing, and I took his silence for assent.

I assumed he would tell her what the police had said about
Edgar, but I discovered later that he told her nothing. Did his
silence issue from some misguided impulse to protect her from
distressing news?

Or was it, rather, cold passive aggression: concealing from
her that a man was coming for her who quite possibly intended
to murder her?

A few days later another letter came from Hugh Griffin. She
almost threw it away unopened, expecting it to be a further plea
that she hug her child more often, or some such nonsense, but
she thought of that lanky young man sitting forward on the
edge of his chair, peering earnestly at her as he clasped and
unclasped his long bony fingers, and she opened it. She was in
the kitchen, still in her dressing gown, boiling the kettle to make
tea. She'd just washed a pair of stockings and hung them over
the back of the chair as she couldn't be bothered to go out to
the line. She sat down and read the letter: no plea for kindness
and understanding, however, nor a request for an appointment
to "talk things over," instead an invitation to join a class outing
to Cledwyn Heath, a tract of wild land a few miles west of
the town. It was part of a class project on local flora and fauna.
Her first reaction was negative, though as she drank her tea and
gazed out across the valley she thought she might be persuaded
to go, if they were nice to her.

She announced all this at supper that night, and Charlie was
excited; clearly he had been pessimistic about his chances of
producing a parent for the event. Max, seeing this, also took
heart; poor man, she had worn him down badly over the winter,

he had been depressed for weeks, though it was as much the job as her, she believed. She knew something of his caseload, she knew that the block he was responsible for housed a high proportion of female schizophrenics, women in middle age or older who had been institutionalized so long there was no real hope of change. There was little there to stimulate a man like Max. He would have liked to run the wards with the younger, more acutely disturbed patients, but John Daniels, the medical superintendent, the man Max had hoped would make the work interesting, had taken those cases for himself. John Daniels is an old friend of mine. Max came too late, he told me; it was as simple as that.

The situation remained unchanged through the first two weeks of February. The police had no further reports of Edgar, and Max kept to himself the knowledge that he was out there somewhere and quite possibly heading in their direction. The family sustained its delicate explosive equilibrium, lurching somehow from day to day without detonating the enormous destructive energies at its heart. It was hardest on Charlie, of course; he stayed in his bedroom when he couldn't be outside, and was silent and gloomy at mealtimes.

Then came news guaranteed to do nothing but exacerbate an already fraught situation: Brenda was coming to visit. Oh, it was with grim foreboding that Max heard this news, which came in a phone call to the hospital one Thursday morning; and it was with sardonic humor that Stella heard it from him that evening.

"And where will she stay?" she said.

"She's booked a room in the Bull."

"How appropriate."

She could all too easily imagine Brenda's strategy. She had no intention of allowing her son to waste his life and ruin his career moldering in this damp, forgotten pocket of north Wales, but she knew too that inertia was the enemy, inertia and Stella; these were the forces she must fight, if Max were to shine once more in the psychiatric firmament. All of which obliged her to act, to intervene, to prevent inertia and Stella from dragging him down into a slough of mediocrity from which he would eventually be unable to extricate himself. Stella would *coarsen* him, Brenda told me; that was her great fear. I myself was adamantly opposed to this projected visit, but Brenda's mind was like a piece of forged steel, once she'd made it up.

Max would bear the brunt of it, of course. It had been difficult enough in the early days to sustain wife and mother in any sort of harmony. Now, with Brenda so vividly vindicated, when it was clear to all that Stella was a tramp and a slut and an unfit mother, how was he to oppose his mother's argument that he must leave her, that he must stop making sacrifices she didn't deserve? Stella watched with secret pleasure as Max grappled with all this. She suggested they give a dinner party.

"Christ, no!" he cried.

"Why not?"

"You know bloody well. Don't twist the blade."

Don't twist the blade. Was that what she was doing? Charlie at least was happy about the visit; he liked his grandmother, she gave him money and made it clear she adored him. He was all right, in fact he was more animated than they'd seen him for weeks. But not Max. He dreaded this visit.

One wet Saturday Max and Charlie drove to Chester to meet her train. Apparently the first thing to arouse her displeasure was the state of the car. She hadn't seen it, of course, since they'd come north, and a winter on farm roads had not been kind to it. Nor apparently was she impressed with Max's state of mind, and she didn't have anything good to say about the town either. It was just as well she didn't come out to the house, Stella reflected, for even in Brenda's bleakest imaginings she didn't see a messy kitchen with dirty dishes piled in the sink, stockings draped over the back of a chair, and her daughter-in-law still in her dressing gown at half past eleven in the morning, lacing her tea with gin.

Her demands were of course immediate and excessive, and Max had never found it easy to say no to her. She wanted him to eat dinner with her every night, and had realized at once there was no decent restaurant in Cledwyn, which meant they had to drive the twelve miles into Chester. She was also eager to see the hospital, and meet the superintendent, and she failed to understand that Max's position now was very different from what it had been down here. Nevertheless she got her way, and it was arranged that Max would take her to see John Daniels.

And what of Stella? What of her tear-stained, gin-sodden tramp of a daughter-in-law? Did she want to meet her as well? No she did not, which suited Stella fine, as she had no desire at all to meet Brenda. I wouldn't have expected Max to be in favor of their meeting either, but here I was wrong. Max had realized (correctly, as it happened, for Brenda took me into her confidence over this) that his mother's motive in coming to Cledwyn was a divisive one: she hoped that by spending time with her son and grandson, and excluding Stella, she could establish an alternative family structure. She wanted to demonstrate that this alternative family was viable, that she could assume Stella's place and take care of them, Max and Charlie both. She hinted that she might be prepared to reinstate his allowance.

Max disliked the suggestion of blackmail, and thought he saw a better way of resolving the situation. He explained it to Stella one evening after supper. His point was, they should seize the opportunity to reverse his mother's impulse of exclusion and try, now, to bring them together, all four. It was his last brave, doomed effort to save his family. They would have Brenda to dinner and there would be a reconciliation.

How queer she found it to hear him say "we." Why did he still want her? Why didn't he accept Brenda's offer, take up the idea of the alternative family and push her out into the darkness? God knows she deserved it, the way she'd been behaving, and God knows he would have a better life under Brenda's wing than on his wife's cold breast. But she agreed to do her best.

Persuading Brenda, Max knew, would not be so easy. During the conversation that I had had with him in January, when I'd heard the suppressed fury in his voice as he talked about Stella, I'd urged him to put aside his own feelings and see that the

affair with Edgar Stark and all that followed had occurred because Stella was suffering from a hysterical illness. Therefore
she was not entirely culpable. Therefore she needed not punishment but care. Therefore she would get better.

Max adopted this line with Brenda. It was not a point of view
with which she had much sympathy, and in her own distinctive
idiom she argued the limits of psychiatry. Max to his credit
stood firm. He told her that Stella had suffered a nervous breakdown and that she now required patience and understanding. It
was a mark of Brenda's devotion to her son that she too agreed
to his proposal. I happen to know she was as skeptical about the
outcome as Stella was.

It was arranged then that Brenda would come to the house
for dinner. Forgotten, now, Stella's disgraceful drunken behavior; forgotten too her bloody-minded carelessness of other
people's feelings, her slovenly ways, her selfish appropriation of
the bedroom. No, what mattered now was that she cook dinner
and serve it and sustain the appearance of active membership in
a functioning if somewhat troubled family. To Max's great relief
she willingly undertook the planning and preparation of the
vital meal, she selected a menu and shopped for the ingredients,
and this alone, he tried to convince himself, suggested an
improved morale, a hint of a possibility of a gradual return to
health.

She decided to give them kidneys.

It was a fiasco. Max picked Brenda up at the hotel and brought
her to the house. She couldn't disguise her horror at how they
lived. She picked her way across the yard with an expression of
disgust on her face, for Trevor Williams had been spreading
manure for several days and the yard was running with it, the
air was thick with it. She entered the kitchen, gave Charlie a kiss
and greeted Stella in a tone of coolness inflected faintly with
sympathy, this clearly for Max's benefit, as he had continued to
work the theme of her "illness," her "breakdown." Stella was in

an old shabby dress with an apron tied around her waist. Max suggested they have a drink in the sitting room, and Brenda allowed herself to be taken upstairs.

She insisted on seeing over the whole of the house, and was shocked at their sleeping arrangements. Max had failed to prepare her for the shared bedroom. That her son, a highly qualified psychiatrist, should have to live like a schoolboy—! When Stella followed them upstairs she found Brenda perched uncomfortably on the couch as if it carried contagious disease. She gazed at Stella helplessly; Stella had never seen her at a loss for words before.

"My dear," she managed at last, "I had no idea Welsh housing was so primitive."

Stella laughed gaily. "Yes, we were very spoilt down south with all those big rooms. We have to make do like everybody else now."

"So I see."

Max was alert for toxins in the air. He intervened adroitly.

"We're not uncomfortable," he murmured; "there are many worse places we could be living."

"Oh?" said Brenda. She clearly found this difficult to believe.

"Oh yes," said Max. "The Welsh are a burrowing people, they like dark houses tucked away under hills, or deep in the woods. They like gloom. This house isn't gloomy."

An eyebrow rose a millimeter on Brenda's marble forehead. It was the index of a deepening skepticism.

"John Daniels was telling me," said Max, "that depressive illness is significantly more prevalent in this part of Wales than anywhere else in Europe. Except Scandinavia, of course."

He had just made this up, Stella could tell by the way he said it. It showed how desperate he was.

"I wasn't impressed with John Daniels," said Brenda. "Where did he learn his psychiatry?"

"Edinburgh."

"You surprise me."

They then began discussing departments of psychiatry in various British universities, and Stella left them to it. She went downstairs to see to the kidneys and refill her glass from a fresh bottle.

By the time she called them down to eat she had finished that bottle and started on another. God knows I'll need it tonight, she told herself. The problem was of course that while drink subdued anxiety it also destroyed inhibition; after three or four glasses she became what Max, she told me wryly, called "disinhibited." She was disinhibited as she served them leek-and-potato soup.

"Not what you're used to, Brenda," she said, "but needs must when the devil drives."

"Regional cuisine can be surprising, don't you think?" Brenda spread her napkin in her lap. She lifted her spoon. "Well," she said hopefully, "this looks hearty."

Stella served herself last and then sat down, untying her apron and tossing it in the general direction of the pegs on the wall by the door.

"It can," she said, "if you can afford the ingredients. Not that there's much available in these parts. Anyway, on Max's salary it's a struggle just to put food on the table."

"You're exaggerating, darling," said Max.

"Cold mutton sandwiches I give them," said Stella. "On Sundays we have cabbage. For a treat."

She looked at Charlie, and he was wriggling on his chair and grinning. He thought it was funny.

"You're being facetious, my dear," said Brenda smoothly. "But I take your point. One is often limited by the availability of local ingredients. When Max's father and I were traveling in Spain in the forties we often dined on a bowl of garlic and a loaf of bread. There was nothing else to be had."

"Fancy," said Stella. She had been trying to make the point that they were poor, and here they were talking about bowls of Spanish garlic. Max took the opportunity to tell his mother that all the good histories of Spain were written by Englishmen, and Stella couldn't tell if he was making this up as well.

"Isn't that interesting," said Brenda.

"Fill our glasses, please, Max," said Stella. "If you drink enough you won't notice what you're eating. Collect the plates, please, Charlie."

She rose and busied herself at the stove.

"I don't suppose you've ever eaten in a kitchen, have you, Brenda?" she said without turning. "It's how the other half lives."

"Charles and I were often in straitened circumstances in the early years," she said.

"Hard to imagine," said Stella, and turned with the casserole to see Brenda glance at Max and hear her quietly sigh. The dinner was not going as Max had hoped it would.

It didn't improve. There wasn't an argument as such, rather a series of snarls in the thread of the evening, small disruptions of the flow of talk Max was working so hard to promote. Stella was responsible of course, being disinhibited, and even felt disappointed by the end that she hadn't provoked Brenda to a good bitchy hiss. But the older woman wisely wanted no part of her manipulations.

"Good night, my dear," she said when Max was ready to drive her back to the Bull. "I hope you feel better soon."

With that she climbed into the car.

Max returned in a fury an hour later and found Stella further disinhibited. He stormed the length of the kitchen to the window and stood there staring out and bristling. She was still at the table among the dirty plates, drinking wine and smoking cigarettes.

"Not only are you selfish," he said, his voice low and hoarse with anger, "you are also stupid."

She put her elbows on the table and held her glass in front of her face and gazed at him over the rim and said nothing.

"Do you realize what you've done?"

"What have I done, Max?"

She expected him to tell her she had destroyed any chance of Brenda ever giving them money. But he surprised her.

"You've squandered the last of your resources." His voice had become suddenly quiet.

She did not enter into the melodramatic spirit of the moment.

"The last of my resources," she said. "What's that?"

He smirked bitterly. There was a brief silence. Then she snorted.

"What does that *mean*, Max?"

"It means you're on your own."

"I've always been on my own."

"Oh no you haven't. You've never been on your own. I'm going to bed."

"What the hell are you talking about?"

She was on her feet by this time. She didn't like all this ponderous finality. She stood by the table and seized his sleeve as he tried to get past her to the stairs. He stared at her with a fury colder than any she'd seen in him before.

"Let me go," he said.

She gripped his sleeve harder, got a bunch of material in her fist, and grinned at him.

"Let me go!"

He jerked free of her and lost his balance slightly. He stumbled and reached for the banister.

"You're disinhibited!" she shouted.

He went up the stairs.

"What sort of crap is this, Max?" she shouted. "What do you mean, I'm on my own? I've always been on my own, married to you!"

He came back down a few steps.

"Just shut up now, will you? We'll discuss the details in the morning, but I don't want you waking Charlie."

"What details?"

They stood there glaring at each other, him halfway up the stairs but half turned to face her where she stood at the bottom. She saw Charlie first, on the landing rubbing his eyes and frowning.

"Sorry, darling, did we wake you?" she said. "Daddy's just pretending to be a bloody fool."

Max darted up the stairs. "Come on, you," she heard him say, "back to bed," and the pair of them disappeared. Stella returned to the kitchen table and finished whatever she could find. When Max came back down he bluntly told her the news he had kept from her all day. He told her that Edgar Stark was in police custody. He'd been picked up that morning. In Chester.

They were holding him there.

The next couple of days felt unreal. She buried her response to the news about Edgar and channeled the affect into fury at being paraded in front of Brenda to show off her mental health so the old bag would start giving Max money again. Max was quieter than she'd ever known him. Such was the ferocity of the rows they'd been having that apparently he felt there was no longer any future for the marriage. He abandoned the psychiatric perspective, and who can blame him? He tried to talk to her about separation but she wouldn't listen, she walked out of the room.

"This won't go away," he said.

But she wasn't going to have an argument like that with him. And as he wouldn't talk about it while Charlie was in the house she was able to evade the discussion he so eagerly wanted about the details.

Not a happy household. Each time she went out she half expected to come back and find the locks changed. She talked to Trevor Williams about it and saw a queer glint come into his eye. Let him try it, he said. He told her nobody could change the locks on the house but him, which put her mind at rest to some extent. Somehow the forms of family life persisted. She didn't give up the housework and the cooking no matter how great the gulf grew, there was a sort of comfort in them that had nothing to do with anybody else, it was to do with her, to do with sustaining a structure to the day, a sense of order that she seemed to need more than ever, what else did she have? Silence and hatred, misery and futility, these things she could tolerate, not disorder. Not chaos. Not a dirty house and unplanned meals.

For she was holding on by her fingertips now. Waves of despair came without warning, and at these times she just wanted to lie down and die, but she was holding on, she wouldn't let go, she wouldn't surrender to it, not yet, though it gnawed at what small reserves of willpower she had left. And this shaky refusal to give up was what forced her through the routines of the day, making the beds and doing the laundry and cooking the dinner. It wasn't for them that she did these things, but herself. She clung to housework to save her sanity.

They sat down each evening to a silent meal and afterward Max and Charlie might go for a walk if it was dry. Stella cleared up and washed the dishes. She had another drink and sat at the window and watched the fading light, for it didn't get dark so early anymore. In three hours I will be asleep, she told herself, and another day will be over without me going mad. It was beginning to feel like an accomplishment, getting through the day without going mad. She didn't think about the future, thinking about the future only makes sense if you want something. She didn't want anything now but to get to the end of the day without going mad.

He was in Chester! *Twelve miles away.*

In police custody.

All lost. There could be no more fantasy of flight and escape. It all collapsed then, the entire structure. And it's at this point I think we can say that Stella sinks into clinical depression proper.

One night they sat at supper and Charlie was agitated. He kept glancing at Max, and Stella guessed he wanted him to say something to her.

"Well, what is it?" she said eventually. "Why don't you tell me yourself?"

He cast a stricken look at Max, who sighed and dabbed at his lips with his napkin.

"Charlie's worried you've forgotten his class outing to-morrow."

"Are you still going to come?"

She stood up and went to the sink and put her plate on the draining board and leaned against the counter with her back to them. Through the window over the sink she could just see the sky to the west, lacy islands of cloud drifting into the sinking sun and a glow of the palest orange imaginable. A few seconds went by. She felt the blackness rising in her.

"Yes, I suppose so."

11

The bus came at half past nine. Charlie was pathetically grateful that his mother was going with him. She had had a bad night and in the morning regretted agreeing to this outing, but she didn't relish the prospect of staying by herself in the house. In better days, she thought, she would have asked Max to prescribe her something, after all there has to be some advantage to living with a psychiatrist; but then in better days she wouldn't have needed it. So she drank her coffee and smoked her cigarettes and Charlie packed his satchel, telling her about the pleasures awaiting them. She reflected on the child's ability to live in the present and be so seemingly unmarked by the unhappiness around him. There she sat, hollow-eyed and silent, the black hole in the heart of the family, the one responsible for destroying the joy of his childhood, and yet in the excitement of a day out together it was all forgotten, all that mattered was that he would board the bus with his mother, and the fact that she was a bitter, depressed woman who had shown him sparse tenderness or affection for weeks, this was forgotten.

They got on the bus and her heart sank as the eyes of two dozen Welsh schoolchildren and half a dozen adults watched them make their way down to the last empty seats at the back. Hugh Griffin, sitting by the driver, made friendly noises, but his was the only voice in that silent bus which did. Stella realized then that Charlie's unhappiness had locked him out of this community as effectively as hers had, and she felt a dull sense of confirmation, she felt she might have known, this is the nature of people, they unerringly select as their victim the one who most needs their warmth. They were outsiders, Charlie and she, and they sat quietly at the back of the bus, and slowly the murmuring of the adults resumed, the babble and cries of the children, as mother and son gazed out of the window at the foreign fields.

Cledwyn Heath was a barren tract of rolling upland and their bus labored as it climbed up out of the valley and onto the plateau. For miles around a desolate landscape of moss and bracken stretched in all directions with here and there a stunted tree hardy enough to sustain its bent and twisted outline against the wind. Deep fissures came into view, sudden gulleys that plunged away steeply from the road and formed steep pockets in which stagnant water pooled, these pools overhung with clumps of weeds and low trees in whose shadow the water looked black and thick and evil. Stella hated it, there was an atmosphere of violence about this lonely moor, and she was not the only one who sensed it, the rest of them fell silent and all that could be heard for a while was the wind. Eventually they pulled off the road and parked in a sheltered spot near some woods and as the children left the bus their voices rose again, and then Hugh Griffin was organizing them into groups and arranging where and when they would meet for lunch. Charlie and Stella were part of a group that was to follow a track around the eastern rim of the heath. Apparently they would come upon a prospect a clear sixty miles to the sea. They set off, mother and son bringing up the rear of the party, and another parent, a father who had hiked in the area, leading them.

Her feeling of unease deepened as she tramped along in her Wellington boots, her raincoat tightly belted and a head scarf knotted under her chin. The track was narrow and stony and the climb was steeper than it first appeared. There was low cloud overhead and the sky threatened rain. Already the others had disappeared from view, and they seemed now the only living creatures in this bleak place where hillocks and heather spread on all sides, rising and falling, and no structure, no tree even to break the empty vista of land and lowering sky. Charlie marched on ahead of Stella, his satchel bumping up and down on his back and his head moving from side to side so as to miss nothing, turning now and then to make sure his mother was keeping up, eager pleasure in his lonely little face. She felt the blackness rising in her again and wished she'd stayed at home, this was no place for her, these empty wastes, among unfriendly strangers, pushing against the harsh damp wind. By the time they reached the prospect of the sea she was struggling hard to keep going for there were forces at work in her mind that would have her sink to the ground with her arms over her head and never rise again. The father tried to talk to her but she had no conversation for him, she was beyond that.

They tramped on and eventually found themselves at the picnic site, a sheltered spot in the lee of a hill. On a low flat outcrop of rock Hugh Griffin and the others had begun to spread their sandwiches and drinks. The children were form-ing into small noisy groups while the adults gathered around Hugh Griffin and poured hot tea from thermos flasks. There was laughter and shouting as a sudden gust of wind lifted a map from the rock and blew it away. Stella wandered a little way off by herself and a minute or two later was aware of Charlie beside her silently eating his sandwiches. He asked her if she was hungry and she shook her head. He asked her if she wanted to see what was on the other side of the hill and she said yes. Soon they were out of sight of the others. Charlie made his way down the steep slope to the pool at the bottom, where weeds grew thickly in the shallows. Stella followed him and settled herself on the ground some way back. She felt the first spots of rain. Charlie shouted that he thought there were newts. Stella let her head fall forward onto her knees and covered her face with her hands. This time it was very bad. Black waves swept through her. The ground seemed to be undulating beneath her. She lifted her head and the air was misted with a fine black dust like specks of graphite. It was starting to rain. She saw as though from a great distance and through a heavy scrim the dark pool, its surface running with little waves and splattered with raindrops, and Charlie splashing indistinctly among the dense weeds at the edge. She pulled out her cigarettes and lit one, cupping her hand around the lighter's flame. Charlie was trying to catch something in the shallows but it evaded him. She watched him mutely and passively and smoked her cigarette as he grabbed it, whatever it was, and lost his balance. The air was dark and the rain was coming harder now and the awful undulation had almost stopped and she felt the creeping numbness that always came afterward. Charlie was in deeper water now, trying to scramble upright and flailing around and shouting, and something in his shouting brought her to her feet. She stood in the gusting wind and rain with her shoulders hunched up tight and watched him for a few moments. Then she turned her head to the side and brought the cigarette to her lips. The edges of her head scarf fluttered wildly about her face; the waves were almost gone. She turned back and dimly saw a head break the surface, and an arm claw the air, then go under again, and she turned aside and again brought the cigarette to her lips. With one hand she clutched her elbow as her arm rose straight and rigid to her mouth. She turned her head to the side and again brought the cigarette to her lips and inhaled, each movement tight, separate, and controlled.

She didn't see Hugh Griffin appear at the brow of the hill behind her. She didn't hear him shout as he saw her there, smoking her cigarette, turning her head away, then back, then away again, as an indistinct figure struggled in the water. She was aware of him only when he came bounding past her through the rain and went crashing into the water, still shouting.

It was all rather confused after that. Stella stood by while Hugh Griffin came splashing out with Charlie in his arms and laid him on the ground and tried to revive him. Then the others came running over the hill and she was forgotten in all the flurry of the children being got back to the bus, and the police being called, and so on, and one of the women gave her a cup of tea and put a rug around her shoulders, and she heard her say to someone that Mrs. Raphael was in shock, and eventually, after the bus had left, the police arrived, and when they got to the police station Max was there and after more cups of tea he drove her home and gave her a pill and she went to bed and slept.

She slept through the following day and when she came downstairs Mair told her Max was with the police and would be back at lunchtime. They sat in silence at the kitchen table. It was still raining.

"What a terrible thing," Mair said at last. "Terrible."

How would she know? Stella wondered. She hasn't any children. How would she know it was terrible if one of them drowned?

When Max came home Mair left. He sat down at the table and stared at her, simply stared at her. Then he said, in a tone of utter bafflement, "But why didn't you shout?"

She found this amusing: Max was asking her why she hadn't shouted.

"You didn't make a sound," he said, in the same astonished tone. "You didn't open your mouth."

Usually they want you to keep your mouth shut, but sometimes they want you to shout, and they expect you to know the difference. This was what amused her.

"That man Griffin," he said. "He's saying it was your fault."

There was a silence.

"Well, say something for Christ's sake! Don't just sit there, say something, tell me how it happened. Oh Christ."

He calmed down.

"I don't know what I'm saying," he murmured. "Traumatic reaction, you're the same. It won't properly dawn on us for a day or two. Best to stay calm."

He rubbed his face with his hands for several moments then once more stared at her from that gaunt face he had newly acquired.

"Why didn't you *shout?*" he whispered.

"Why didn't you shout, Mrs. Raphael? When you saw the boy was in trouble?"

She was in the police station and she didn't have an answer there either.

In the days that followed their sympathy disappeared. This was as a result of Hugh Griffin's insistence on the fact that when he came over the hill Charlie was in the water screaming and his mother stood by smoking a cigarette. She didn't try to help him, he said, although the boy was clearly in serious trouble, and he also said that had she raised the alarm he might have been saved, though this was later disputed, given the distance between the top of the hill and the water. No, what horrified them was that she had made no noise and hadn't moved. When they properly understood this it all changed, because then she was a mother who'd watched her child drown and done nothing to save him. It was unnatural, they said. It was evil. They couldn't understand it; she has no feelings, they said, she isn't human, she's a monster. Or perhaps she's mad.

She was mad. How could you explain it, unless she was mad? You had to explain it, a child was dead; either she was a monster or she was mad. The first thing they were going to do was charge her with manslaughter. She was remanded. She was put in a cell once more. She was numb and empty and utterly detached from the woman who was moved from room to room, and questioned again and again, and still failed to tell them what they wanted to know. She watched herself endure the hours of those strange days, watched herself both from within, from some barricaded citadel deep in the psyche, and also from a point, so it seemed, a few feet over her head and slightly off to the side.

It was then that I came to see her. She hadn't been expecting me, and at the sight of me she felt the first faint stirring of emotion she'd known for days. I was shown into the room and did my best to communicate my sympathy and concern.

"My poor dear girl," I said, and that was enough. The tears came.

Now she was able at last to give up, she said, to abandon her grip on things and just sleep and dream and drift, because now she was getting pills and nothing was expected of her anymore. She was able to tell me what it was she'd seen in the water. I was not surprised. Nor was I surprised that since I'd seen her last she'd put on weight and her hair was lank, and her eyes were ringed with shadows, though her skin was as white and clear as ever: she was still a beautiful woman. She was also a profoundly depressed woman. My visit became the central event of her day and made all the rest of it tolerable. There were more interviews with various men; I was present. There was a court appearance; I made sure it caused her as little distress as possible. She didn't attempt to understand what was happening to her, she left it all to me. One day I asked her if she wanted me to keep on looking after her.

Of course, she said, with a flicker of alarm. Why did the question need asking? Was I saying I might leave her?

I told her what was going to happen. She was going to a hospital. She'd been sick and I wanted to treat her. Was she sure she wanted me to treat her?

"Oh yes," she said.

Then she must come to my hospital. Did she know the name of my hospital?

She told me the name of the hospital.

"That's right," I said. "You'll come to the hospital and I'll look after you there."

I was convinced I was the man best qualified to treat her. And while bringing her back to the hospital might seem unorthodox, or even, given the circumstances, positively dangerous, I was in a position now to make it happen.

Max went to see her. I had warned her that this would happen and she pleaded with me not to make her go through with it. Quietly and firmly I insisted on it. She told me I was a cruel bastard and I reminded her that if I was treating her she must trust me. I told her it was as much for Max as it was for her.

"This thing has broken him," I said. "Make peace with him."

"Peace," she said.

"For both your sakes."

So she agreed.

They met in a bare room with a wooden table in the middle and a single high window. Stella was deeply anxious when she was brought in, clutching only a packet of cigarettes and a lighter. Max was already there; he rose to his feet and they stood there facing each other as the door closed.

"Hello, Stella."

Her first impulse was to turn and walk straight out again but she didn't want to disappoint me. She sat down. He sat down. He had lost weight, and he had been a lean man before. There was a fragility to him now, as though he would shatter like fine bone china if you struck him. He offered her a cigarette. He seemed older too, not so much in how he looked as in the way he moved and held himself. He seemed to have reached the stage when men begin to think of themselves as no longer robust, and deliberately adopt the first mannerisms of age; as though his personal resources were limited and must be husbanded with care. She took the cigarette he offered. What did she look like to him? she wondered. The slut who'd ruined his life was now the pale fat witch who'd drowned his son.

"What did you want to see me about?" she said.

This surprised him. He opened his mouth and a small, coughlike laugh came out.

"Sorry," he said. "Straight to the point. I didn't think that question would need to be asked."

She waited for him to get to the point.

"I dare say you won't be interested in my thoughts about everything that's happened to us. Where the responsibility lies."

Like an accountant, she thought. Debit column and credit column. I'll take the blame for this, you take the blame for that. Then we can sleep at night.

"But I don't know anymore if it matters. Well, say something."

"It was Edgar in the water."

He nodded. "I thought it probably was."

There was silence then and she grew restless. She turned in her chair and glanced at the door. She wanted them to come and get her.

"Do you still hate me?" he said.

She thought of a dream she'd had a few nights before. She was in bed with Max and the bed was full of shit. She told him this. She saw him recoil.

"So you do," he said. He made a mild sort of snorting noise. She watched him carefully. He put his hand over his mouth and stared at her with those hollow eyes and she turned away.

"So should I hate you?" he said.

She wasn't interested in this arithmetic.

"It seems unfair to Charlie," he said.

A tug at the heart, this, presumably. But it had no visible effect. Another small silence. Maybe their time in this room wouldn't be up till he went to the door and called them. She was about to ask him to do this when he began to talk.

"Do you know what's going to happen next? The shock is going to wear off and you're going to start feeling guilty. I know what I'm talking about. It will be a truly terrible guilt. It will devastate you. You'll be carefully watched, for you may attempt suicide, that's how bad you'll feel. Eventually, with Peter Cleave's help, you'll come to terms with what you've done. And when that happens you won't hate me anymore and I hope you won't hate yourself. You'll just be terribly, terribly sad, and you won't lose that sadness for the rest of your life."

That's when she flung her lighter at him and tried to climb over the table to get her fingernails into his face. It was her screaming that brought them running in. They took her away and left Max to congratulate himself on his skill at the psychiatric interview.

The female wing of the hospital comprises two blocks each with a pleasantly spacious enclosed yard with flower beds, lawns, and benches. Its southern aspect gives onto the terraces, so the ladies with parole privileges may wander among the gardens and down the stone steps between the grassy banks just as their male counterparts do, though the sexes are separated, of course, by an internal wall. Many of my own patients are in the female wing, in fact administratively speaking the female wing has been my domain for years. I always feel a rather proprietary pride when I gaze out over its orderly, well-tended paths and yards and terraces.

Stella was driven down the next day and admitted to the hospital. She brought only three suitcases with her; she said she needed just a few essentials, though I noticed she'd packed most of her evening clothes, including the black silk dress. I didn't ask her how it felt to come up the hill in a police car, to come past her old house and into the hospital not through the Main Gate but through the gate of the female wing, and from there to the admissions room behind the front office. She stood by while the police handed over her paperwork to me, and then I went through a brief formal interview with her before taking her up to the admissions ward with a female attendant, a competent young woman called Mary Flynn. In a large communal bathroom Stella was asked to undress. She did so. She was taken into a cubicle and bathed. I gave her a thorough physical examination, then she put on a cotton shift and we escorted her down the ward to her room.

"Here we are," said Mary as she unlocked the door. There was a bed, a window with bars in it, a toilet, and a basin. There was a grate in the door, also barred. I followed her in.

"What now?" she said.

"I want you to settle down now and have a good sleep," I said. "Is there anything we can get you?"

She told me later all she could see was the bunch of keys in the hands of the woman standing in the doorway. She shook her head.

"Wait!"

We paused in the doorway. "Yes?"

She wanted to say, in a reasonable tone of voice, Please don't go, please don't shut the door, please don't lock me in! When she was on remand she'd been locked up but somehow it hadn't been like this. She'd assumed that the nightmare would be over when she got here, or that it would at least be less dreadful. But she couldn't say anything, not to what she later called our cool faces with their slightly lifted eyebrows. She shook her head.

The door banged shut and Mary locked it.

An hour later she came back. Stella was lying on the bed staring at the ceiling when she heard the key in the door. Mary had a cup of tea for her and some pills. Stella asked what they were and was told just to take them, Dr. Cleave had prescribed them.

She sat up and swallowed the pills and drank some of the tea. Mary sat at the end of the bed and watched her. She told her the superintendent was very concerned about her.

"Who is the superintendent now?" Stella said.

"You don't know?"

"It was Jack Straffen but didn't he retire?"

"Oh yes, Dr. Straffen has gone. It's Dr. Cleave now."

I thought it best if she found out like this, informally, from one of the staff. But yes: when Jack retired they came to me, for no one knows the place better than I do. Reluctantly I agreed to take over. Stella said her last thought before she drifted off to sleep was of Max, and how he used to think the job was his.

The next morning an attendant called Pam brought her her breakfast on a tray. She had slept deeply and now she couldn't properly wake up, she was bleary and sluggish from the medication. She sat there on the side of the bed nodding over the tray and it began to slide off her knees. Pam grabbed it before it fell and put it on the floor. Stella crawled back into bed and went to sleep again.

She was awakened sometime in the afternoon by the key in the lock, and this time it was me. I sat on the bed.

"How are you feeling, my dear?"

I took her hand and stroked it.

"Awful."

She rubbed her face. The blurring of consciousness produced by the drugs seemed to be wearing off a little. I apologized. I told her it was standard procedure to prescribe heavy sedation for new admissions, it gave the ward staff a chance to see what sort of state they were in.

"All they see of me," she said, "is how I sleep."

"This'll pass. We'll have you out in the dayroom in a day or two."

She yawned. "I'm so groggy," she said.

"I know." I patted her leg. "I'll come and see you tomorrow."

I rose and left her. She sank back onto her pillow and stared at the ceiling. When Mary Flynn came in with her pills that evening Stella said she didn't need so many but Mary paid no attention, and she hadn't the energy to argue with her.

The first days, then, were lost days. She lived in a sort of twilight state, never left her room, had brief woozy conversations with the attendants and a daily visit from me. I began gradually to cut back her medication and she grew more alert. On the fourth day I had clothes brought to her, not her own but hospital issue, and she emerged for the first time onto the ward. She told me later it was fortunate she was still dazed by the medication, for she didn't belong here, this was clear to her immediately. As Pam escorted her down to the dayroom she gazed with sleepy horror at the poor creatures who shuffled by her in the corridor, withdrawn women with lowered heads who inhabited worlds other than this one, hellish worlds they were unable to tear their eyes from. They ignored Pam's cheerful greetings.

They reached the dayroom. Now she had the full spectacle, the women of the admissions ward at their recreation. The uncanny first impression was again one of private hells coexisting in public space. It was a long room with sunlight streaming through large barred windows onto a polished floor with tables and chairs the length of it, and a television set at the far end with couches and armchairs grouped around it. One woman stood absolutely still, staring at the wall. Another sat picking at invisible threads on her skirt, picking with fierce concentration at nothing at all. A third sat rocking gently from side to side, smiling and murmuring to herself.

"Here we are," said Pam brightly. "Let's meet some of the girls."

The "girls" Stella met were all as broken and doped as she was. She sat at a table with Pam and two other women and they smoked. Stella looked at them and they looked at her and it was like peering across a chasm at distant peaks and acknowledging that she wasn't entirely alone, there were others in this wild region. No conversation seemed possible despite Pam's earnest efforts. The murmuring quiet of the dayroom was shattered once by a peal of strange laughter, and once by a sort of whimper, and once by a small explosion of excitement when the tea trolley was trundled in and a loud voice cried, Tea, ladies! Later, when it was time to go back to their rooms, a woman she hadn't noticed appeared at her side and quietly asked if Stella could give her a smoke. With slow fingers Stella pulled a couple out of her packet and the woman said, Thanks, love, and tucked them up the sleeve of her cardigan. They made their way down the corridor together. They brought me in with nothing, said the woman. Just the clothes I stood up in.

Stella shook her head. She wanted to say it was outrageous but all she could seem to manage was a shake of the head. Take care, love, the woman whispered. She squeezed Stella's hand and disappeared into her room.

Her life on the ward quickly fell into a pattern of meals, medication, time spent in the dayroom, and time spent locked up. I came to see her several times and told her not to worry, that we would start talking properly very soon. For the time being, I said, I just wanted to settle her down.

Settle me down. She felt like a squalling infant, she told me later.

As the days passed she began to lose the feeling that she didn't belong here, though whenever she noticed this she made a conscious effort of will to resist the idea. I do *not* belong here, she told herself, though she had no idea anymore where she did belong. But she no longer saw the other women as so very mad or strange or different from herself. She began to understand how they had ended up here, and it was often through a bizarre chain of events, not unlike the events of her own life, culminating in some sort of public humiliation. The woman who'd said she'd been brought in with just the clothes she stood up in, this woman told Stella her name was Sarah Bentley and that she'd been married to a man who beat her whenever he was drinking, which was three or four times a week. When she couldn't take any more of it she told him she'd kill him if he ever laid hands on her again. He promised he wouldn't but two months later he came home drunk and hit her and then passed out on the couch. She stabbed him in the throat with the kitchen scissors, cut him open, cut his heart out, and flushed it down the toilet. Then she went to bed. The police were at the door in the morning and when they took her away all the women who lived on the street gathered to watch her go. She said some of them cheered her and some of them jeered.

Nobody could understand why she'd flushed his heart down the toilet, she said, but it was obvious to her. She didn't want the bastard coming back.

Then she asked Stella what she'd done, and Stella had barely begun to attempt to formulate an answer when she was overwhelmed by the unutterable horror of it all. They were in the dayroom, sitting by the window, and Sarah tried to calm her down but it did no good and a few minutes later she was locked in her room, sedated but still weeping.

I went to see her the next day. I sat at the end of the bed nodding as she told me about the wave of horror that had welled up inside her. I told her this was natural, this was to be expected, she would have to go through a certain amount of grief before we could move on to anything else; it was good this process had started, I said. I told her I wasn't going to increase her medication, but that I would make sure the ward staff knew what was going on.

The next time I saw her I asked her if she was ready to tell me what had happened, from the beginning.

"What is the beginning?" she said.

"Edgar?"

Her head came up and she gazed at me with an expression I found difficult to read precisely. Pain, apprehension, even dread, all this and something else too, what I now believe to be a dawning awareness of the new nature of our relationship. Nothing was simple anymore. I was the doctor, she the patient. We were on opposite sides. She required a strategy.

But of course we had to start with Edgar. Stella had come to us because she'd stood by and watched her child drown, but the pathology there was straightforward. The literature on maternal filicide is not large but it is clear: usually an extended suicide, the removal of the child from a situation the mother finds intolerable, though in Stella's case complicated by the projection onto the child of the intense hostility she felt toward its father; a classic Medea complex. Recovery involved, first, guidance

211

through an initial intense period of suffering whose main feature would be guilt; then acceptance of the trauma; then the integration of the trauma into memory and identity. Routine psychiatry. No, from a clinical point of view her relationship with Edgar was far more intriguing, in fact it was one of the most florid and dramatic examples of morbid obsessional sexual compulsion I had encountered in many years of practice. Consider: what she had seen in the water, in extremis, was not Charlie, not even Max. It was Edgar.

Now that I had her here in the female wing I relished the prospect of stripping away her defenses and opening her up, seeing what that psyche of hers really looked like. I understood of course that she would resist me, but we had time.

I thought it a good sign when she began to worry about her appearance once more. She said that now that she was invariably dressed in the gray cardigan, blue blouse, gray skirt, gray stockings, and black laced shoes that we issued to the patients in the female wing, she was acutely aware of how smartly *I* dressed by comparison! Each time before she saw me she went down to the office at the front of the ward and asked to use the cosmetics tin. This was an old biscuit tin filled with a clutter of lipsticks and eye pencils, little vials of perfume, jars of cream and powder, all donated by members of staff and shared by the women on the ward for important occasions such as a visit from the doctor. Seated at the table in the front office with a compact mirror propped in front of her, she did the best she could with what she had, then combed her hair and mentally apologized to me for so dismally failing to meet my own high standards. She went back down to the dayroom to wait, and the other women complimented her in a sisterly way on how she looked.

There was a small conference room next to the office and that's where we had our first proper talk. I asked her how she was feeling, and then we started. I gazed at her with my fingertips pressed together and resting on my top lip. My eyes, she said later, seemed to bore into her soul like a pair of skewers.

"Peter, what are you doing? You make me feel like a specimen! God knows I don't bear scrutiny these days. Why must you dress us like nuns?"

How long it had been since she'd even tried to talk like this, flippant and smart, the way she and I used to talk all the time! For a fleeting moment she was a pale shadow of her old self, a woman at ease with an old friend.

"We have a lot to get through," I said. "It's going to be painful for you."

She busied herself getting a cigarette alight. She tried to sustain the brief flare of gaiety but I'm afraid it collapsed in the face of my gravity.

"Let's talk about Edgar. Tell me about the first time you seriously entertained the idea of having sex with him."

This was blunt, but I intended it to be so. She dropped her eyes and played with the cigarette packet, carefully aligning it with the edge of the table. Her voice was wary.

"Oh God, I don't know. The first time?"

I nodded.

"In the vegetable garden," she said quietly. I watched as the experience gradually assumed shape and definition once more.

"Go on."

In her mind's eye she relived the moment in the garden, in the sunshine, when she knew it was inevitable that they have sex because it was impossible not to. It was just not possible not to. Not thinkable. Risk was no deterrent, when the impossibility of avoiding or deferring or ignoring the necessity became apparent. She tried to explain this to me.

"It was a necessity?"

"Yes."

"And you think he shared your sense of necessity? Despite the risks?"

"Oh yes."

"Why?"

She shrugged slightly. "I could tell. I knew."

"Is it conceivable that Edgar was using you because he planned to abscond all along?"

"No."

"All right. Did it live up to your expectations?"

She tried to make a joke of it. "You want the details, Peter? The grope and fumble in the undergrowth?"

"You found a place in the garden."

"Yes, at first. The conservatory."

I ignored the distaste in her voice as she tossed me this gobbet of information.

"And then?"

"The pavilion."

"Ah, the pavilion." I sat back. "I'm sorry, my dear, I don't embarrass you for my own pleasure. Was Max really so unsatisfactory?"

"I suppose he must have been or it wouldn't have happened."

"Why not?"

"I'd have thought you could only fall in love with someone if you weren't already in love with someone else."

"You weren't in love with Max. But did you love him?"

She gazed blankly at me.

"You've never been married, have you?" she said at last.

"Were you frustrated?"

A bark of laughter. "Isn't everyone?"

I waited.

"Oh, Peter, I don't know what to tell you. I rather admired Max in the early days. I wanted us to go back to London, but that was our only real argument. I wasn't craving excitement, if that's what you mean."

"A normal marriage, then?"

"I suppose so."

"A husband, a home, a child, reasonable contentment. Yet you jeopardized it all for a sexual relationship with a patient."

"That sort of calculation didn't come into it."

"Was it exhilarating to think that your whole way of life was at risk?"

I sat now, an elbow propped on the table, projecting an expression of warm, frank curiosity.

"I'd fallen in love, that's what exhilarated me," she said.

There was a silence.

"This love," I said, "this feeling over which you had no control. What is it exactly?"

Another silence. Then, wearily: "If you don't know I can't tell you."

"There's no defining it, then? No discussion possible? It springs to life, it can't be ignored, and it tears people's lives apart. But we can't say more. It just is."

"Words," she murmured.

"Words perhaps," I said briskly, "but what else do we have? Let me ask you to consider a possibility: that this love of yours was just a blind for something else."

"What do you mean?"

"Look at the effects of it. You abandon everything. You cultivate disdain for a man you've grown used to—"

I paused; she had started quietly to cry. I gave her a handkerchief. I could see she hated herself for exhibiting feminine frailty. If I rejected her, she said later, if I despised her, if I condemned her, then she had nothing. She was nothing. I recognized all this.

"All right, that's enough," I said gently, and we talked of other things. But before I went away I asked her to think about what it meant, to love. Be rigorous, I said.

She said she would.

She told me later that our talk left her confused and anxious. She returned to the routines of the ward with great unease. She was silent and preoccupied in the dayroom. She tried to work out what I was doing. I had deliberately upset her: why? It must be a way of testing her, of seeing how strong she was. And she had done rather poorly, caving in like that. I had shown her how fragile she had become, I had held up a mirror and let her see her weakness. This was good psychiatry, she supposed: I didn't tell her to be strong, I led her instead to want to be strong.

It took her several days to work this out, she said. It occurred to her to be grateful that she was in so protected a place, that she was safe here, and in wise, healing hands. She tentatively began to think of herself in a new way. Restricted since Cledwyn to a tiny cluster of superficial selfish concerns, and numbed lest she think of Charlie, she now opened herself, just a little, to the extent that she accepted that she was damaged and needed help. She looked to me to give her that help, and when it was time to see me again she mustered as much courage as she was capable of and came in with a brave smile, apparently eager to go further but, as I immediately detected, inwardly terrified at the prospect. I came around the table and pulled out her chair.

"Don't be so anxious," I said quietly, pushing the chair in as she sat down. I put my hand on her shoulder.

My fingers rested on her shoulder for several seconds and I could feel her intense awareness of the contact, for an electricity was there. I sat down and asked her how she was doing on the ward, and she managed once more to be almost her old self, witty and ironical, and she made me smile as she described her eccentric community. The mood shifted abruptly, however, when I pressed my fingers to my lips and allowed a certain contemplative expression to steal across my features.

"Have you thought about what I asked you to?" I said.

"I don't know what to tell you, Peter."

"Describe Edgar physically."

She said she'd been afraid of this. She said that when she deliberately aroused the memory of him it felt as though a screen had been interposed between herself and his image. I reminded her that it was Edgar she'd seen struggling in the water that day on Cledwyn Heath, and I told her this strongly suggested to me that she was desperate to let him go, to bring the pain of her compulsion to an end; it is a stage we see in all such relationships, I said, craving the death of the lover. I wanted to know how far this process had advanced, to what extent the affair was really over.

We talked about him for almost an hour. After she'd made a halting description came questions that were much harder to answer, questions of feeling. She found herself telling me that for the first time in her life she'd desired someone with a physical and emotional intensity she had never experienced before, directly, but only sensed in men, coming from men. I nodded as she spoke, I encouraged her when she faltered, and somehow she found words for the chaos of feelings she had known in the few weeks she was with him. She told me how they conducted the affair on the estate, and what happened when she was in London with him. I was curious that she made no sort of moral judgment of him, not when he absconded without telling her, not even when he hit her.

"Why not?" I said.

She didn't know. She said the question seemed all wrong. In order to criticize him she would have had to see him conditionally: I love you *unless you do this.* It simply didn't arise.

"You accepted him without reserve?"

"I suppose I did."

"Even when he hit you."

"I know why he did it."

"If I told you he was in the hospital now, what would your reaction be?"

I was watching her closely. I saw something flare briefly to life in her eyes; then she shrugged. She said it hadn't occurred to her that he would have been brought back here, though once she thought about it it was obvious. Though it didn't matter now. When she said this I regarded her with what she called that rather frightening detachment that made her feel like a specimen on a slide.

"It doesn't matter?"

"It's finished, Peter. It finished when Charlie died."

She lifted her head and met my gaze squarely. I wanted to believe her, but at the same time I knew that she knew that this was what I wanted to hear her say. I tested her again.

"The question was hypothetical, Stella. He's not here."

Again that almost imperceptible flare of feeling.
"I'm glad," she said.

It takes a few weeks to tidy up someone who comes to us in as
bad shape as Stella was, but we did it. The ward reports came to
my desk every morning, and I watched her gradually taking an
interest in the world once more, narrow and circumscribed
though that world was. She was still avoiding dealing with
Charlie's death and I felt no need to rush her. I was concerned,
however, about the effect my question about Edgar might have
had on her. I was afraid I had inadvertently disrupted the transference I wanted to effect, the displacement of whatever feelings she still harbored toward Edgar, to me, her doctor. For it
was essential that she now see me as her sole source of support.
    During the next days she became noticeably more alert.
Mary Flynn, who'd seen her when she was first admitted, told
her it was grand to see her coming along so well. She was more
talkative than we'd known her so far. She became interested in
hospital gossip, she wanted to know more about this community to which she now belonged. She began to spend as much
time in the dayroom as she could, which we tend to regard as a
good sign. Her brief identification with the other women, with
Sarah Bentley in particular, she gradually abandoned. Sarah was
subversive, she liked to mock the attendants and upset ward
routines, she failed to hide her contempt for her situation and
her belief that she should not be here. I killed the bastard
because I hated him, she told Stella. He hurt me. That doesn't
make me crazy. I should be in jail. Then at least I'd know when
I was getting out.
    Sarah could talk like this all morning, and Stella saw now
that friendship with her was a liability. She tried to explain to
her that here you had to be diplomatic. You had to understand
what was expected of you. Sarah refused to see this. As far as
she was concerned they were all goons and she had no intention
of keeping quiet about it. Stella thought this a mistake. There

were times, she told her, when you should keep quiet. Sadly she saw that she and Sarah could no longer be friends.

She asked to work in the laundry.

"You?" I said, in an amused tone of voice, concealing my suspicions. "Now, why on earth would you want to work in the laundry?"

"Oh, Peter," she said, "of course I don't actually want to work in the laundry but I'm bored stiff up here. Can't you find me something to do?"

"You are coming along nicely," I said dryly. "You'd perhaps like to go downstairs."

She gave me a frank smile. "I don't really think I belong up here," she said, "do you?"

I was vague. She knew I didn't altogether trust the improvement she seemed to be showing. She could see me wondering, behind what she called my silky disquisitions, if it was a false recovery I was seeing, one that presaged collapse into a depression deeper than the first.

"Do you think about Charlie?" I said.

"Yes."

"And?"

A quiet tone of voice now. "I'm coming to terms with it."

Now the frown, the fingertips pressed together against the top lip, as I gazed at her. A silence. We were in the conference room at the end of the ward, it was April, and through the bars the branches on the chestnut tree were covered with pale buds. The day was warm, and from the corridor came all the usual sounds, keys turning in locks, a murmur of voices, the muffled cry of Rooms, ladies! The clatter of a mop in a pail. The smell of bleach. In the silent room off the front office I pondered the pale woman sitting across the table from me. Then I rose abruptly to my feet.

"Not yet, Stella," I said. "I don't think you're ready yet."

"Why not?" She gazed up at me, troubled, disappointed.

"I don't know. I'm not sure of you yet."

"I won't argue with you," she said quietly.

I nodded. Despite the fact—or because of it?—that I was, to Stella, far from the neutral figure generally considered appropriate to perform this sort of dynamic psychotherapy, I was becoming more convinced each time I saw her that the transference was occurring as I wanted it to, that she was shifting her dependence onto me. The thought gave me a peculiar and rather complicated satisfaction, which to my deep regret I failed properly to analyze at the time.

Her behavior now followed a predictable course. She began to cultivate a different attitude to time. She had to think in terms of months, if not of years. She had to find a way to manage her impatience. With her medication reduced it became a problem tolerating boredom, and she was quite well aware that a single outburst of frustration could undo weeks of painstaking self-control. Nor must the effort be visible to the attendants. A calm, good-tempered demeanor, amiable but not hysterical, composed but not depressed, this she knew was what we wanted to see, though what made the masquerade so difficult to sustain was not knowing how long was long enough, never being certain whether we noticed how well she was doing, and trying to cope with the idea that she was going to rot up here, grow old and die on the admissions ward. But she didn't have long to wait. A few days later Mary Flynn told her I was moving her to a downstairs ward.

Life was less eccentric downstairs and she quickly came to understand why. Upstairs, no sort of behavior provoked surprise because it was accepted that all were mad. Being unhappy and bitter and relentlessly derisive, as Sarah was, that was mad, just as mad as picking at threads that didn't exist or becoming agitated about a missed appointment and tasks left undone twenty-seven years ago. You ceased to be mad when you began to behave as though you weren't in a madhouse, as though you weren't locked up with no real idea when you were getting out again. Once you appeared to accept these conditions as perfectly satisfactory, then you were seen to be improving and they moved you downstairs. This of course is a patient's perspective. From our point of view, the self-control involved in making these calculations and then acting on them is a necessary first step in getting better.

The women downstairs had made that first step, that's why they were downstairs, and nobody was being mad there, at least not in front of the attendants. Being downstairs meant greater privacy and some freedom of movement, and with this came opportunities to be mad without being seen. Often this meant simply the freedom to weep for a ruined life, a fractured family, a lost spouse. A dead child. Weeping was mad, certainly a symptom of depression, therefore to be treated with drugs, and drugs were the thief of alertness and clarity, which the women craved, some of them at least.

Downstairs they were allowed to wear their own clothes. This made a difference to Stella. I remarked on it as soon as I saw her. She was in a dark skirt and an elegant cream blouse with a high neck and an attractive brooch pinned to the breast. She was slower and more deliberate in all her movements and expressions now, there was a quality of stillness to her that rather dramatically heightened the effect of her beauty, which had always tended to the stately. She thanked me warmly for having her transferred; she was aware that most patients spent far longer on the admissions ward than she had. I waved away her gratitude.

"I couldn't see that it would serve any useful purpose keeping you up there," I said.

She was watching me carefully. I had come to the ward and she'd taken me to her new room. It was larger than her room upstairs, it had no bars on the window and no grate in the door. There was a rug on the floor by the bed, a table and chair, and a cupboard for her clothes. It was the sort of room you'd give a senior girl at a boarding school.

"No photographs?" I said. "No knickknacks, nothing personal?"

"No," she said quietly. I was on the bed, she was on the chair facing me. She noticed the change in my attitude toward her, a friendliness I hadn't shown her when she was upstairs. The brisk, detached, inquiring tone had been abandoned. She felt I had made myself properly available to her again as a friend and not merely as a doctor. She didn't try to exploit it, this new warmth, not yet, for she didn't do anything spontaneously now.

"Would you like to talk about Charlie?" I said.

This was difficult now. She gazed at me silently for a moment. I felt she was telling me that she was not denying to herself how and why her child had died, but that she couldn't speak of it.

"No, Peter," she said at last, "I don't think so. Not yet."

"Why not?"

"Too painful."

I nodded. "Do you think about him much?"

A small ironic laugh. "Do I think about anything else?"

I nodded again. "We will have to talk about it soon. I want to give you time."

"I know that. Thank you."

Once more I waved away her gratitude. I stood up.

"I must go," I said. "Bloody meeting with the Ministry of Works. Administration. Drives me to distraction."

"Poor Peter," she said.

She stood in the doorway of her room and watched me make my way down the ward, an elegant, elderly man with a sheaf of files under his arm and an institution on his shoulders. I was touched by her solicitude. She was my patient, but she was also a woman of taste, a woman of my own class, and I was not blind to her qualities. In recent days I had more than once imagined her in my house, as she once so frequently had been, among my furniture, my books, my art. Oh, she had a place there, among my fine *objets*, she would be better off there than she was here.

She now enjoyed the privilege of walking on the terrace of the female wing at certain times of the day, and she took full advantage of it. Spring was here and she loved to gaze out at the countryside, her coat draped around her shoulders, for it was still cool even in the sunshine, and often windy. She was in no hurry to make friends with the women on her new ward; she thought it best to allow this to happen gradually, so she held herself somewhat aloof. It was known that she was married to Dr. Raphael, who until recently had been deputy superintendent, of course, and that Dr. Cleave was an old friend. Her whole story was known, in fact; all the more reason to try and create a little mystery about herself.

12

In the weeks that followed, her mystery eroded as she was gradually absorbed into the life of the hospital. Although she retained a certain air of detachment she did not pursue it to the point of isolation. She communicated poise and dignity, and wore as though it were a veil an air of great sorrow, rather like a heroine in a Victorian melodrama. I watched her perfect a small sad smile, and saw how both staff and patients responded with respect, even with deference. She dressed in somber shades of blue, gray, and black and always carried a book. She was a frequent visitor to the hospital library.

Seeing this, I believed that she was healing, that in the more inaccessible reaches of her being she was facing and accepting what had happened on Cledwyn Heath. I saw her a couple of times each week, and when I alluded to Charlie's death she would always give me to believe that yes, she thought of little else, she constantly pondered the horror of it, its moral gravity weighed on her soul and was effecting deep change within her.

She began to give the impression of a holy woman, a woman in a process of purification as the profound remorse following a terrible act ate like an acid at her old self and brought to life something new in its place. The hospital thus became a priory, a convent, and she a lady with a great grief whom the monks had taken in so that she might make her spiritual journey in cloistral quiet.

There was a particular bench she liked to use on the terrace, and she made a point of sitting there at the same time every afternoon, between three and four. Sometimes she was joined by another patient, or an attendant, often she was alone. There she sat, her coat around her shoulders, gazing quietly out over the countryside, smoking, and she did not go unnoticed by the patients working in the gardens on the terrace below. One of these was a fit young man with a wild mop of black hair who whenever he paused to lean on his hoe, or his spade, did not turn to the landscape but looked up the hill, to where the lonely woman in the dark clothes sat lost in thought, day after day, between three and four in the afternoon.

When this was reported to me I was concerned. I wanted no one interfering with Stella during this difficult convalescent period, and most emphatically not this particular black-haired young man, a psychopath called Rodney Mariner. He was one of mine. I immediately took him off the work party, stripped him of his parole status, and transferred him to the Refractory Block. It was a purely precautionary measure.

We seemed to be in for another hot summer. The days were clear and still, with long, warm evenings heavy with the drifting fragrance of the first blossoms. I was astonished to think that it was almost a year since Stella had walked along the terrace with Max and me after the hospital dance, it seemed a lifetime ago. I wondered how she was responding to sights and sounds that must remind her of that summer, and I watched her carefully for signs of unusual agitation. But it was becoming clearer all the time that Edgar no longer dominated her thoughts as he once had, and this seemed confirmed when I discovered that she was troubled now by a different psychic intruder. For it was during one of our conversations at around this time that she told me she was starting to have headaches at night, and that these headaches invariably followed indistinct but terrifying dreams. She was often woken by them, she said. She would suddenly sit up in the darkness with images still alive in her mind, and for a moment or two she would know utter panic at her inability to escape whatever it was that threatened her. And until the dream vanished, until it sank back into whatever chamber of her mind it had risen from, which mercifully took only a second or two, and was forgotten, leaving only a few faint traces to mark its awful passage through her sleeping brain, and a steady, throbbing pain, until that happened her head was filled with the sound of screaming.

I was not surprised to hear this, it was what I'd been waiting for. When she saw my concern, however, she immediately tried to make light of it, she said it was just a silly nightmare, all she wanted was aspirin for the headaches. She wasn't able to tell me anything more about this screaming, but I had a strong intuition that what we were seeing were the first stirrings of a guilt she had so far successfully repressed. For I believed that what she was hearing were the screams of a drowning child.

I knew then that her recovery was properly beginning, that she had let go of Edgar and allowed herself to start dealing with the death of Charlie. What remained now was to work through the guilt. I was confident that while this would be painful it would be straightforward, and relatively quick, at least in the initial, acute phase. After that there would be no point keeping her here; she could hardly be considered a danger to society. This being so, it was time for me to consider her future: to think about what was going to happen to her in a month or so when she was well enough to leave the hospital, and who was going to look after her.

.　　.　　.

A few days later I drove up to north Wales to discuss my plans with Max Raphael. Poor man, he didn't want this visit, he had no desire to have me see how he lived. He hadn't given up his job in Cledwyn, nor had he moved out of Trevor Williams's house, but I had the sense that he'd turned into something of a recluse.

I arrived at Plas Mold in the early afternoon and the house, the yard, the fields beyond, all were much as Stella had described them. The Beast was barking, the manure was thick in the nostrils and deeply unpleasant. I had hoped to catch a glimpse of Trevor Williams himself, that barnyard Lothario, but there was no sign of either him or his wife. Max shuffled out of his back door in shirtsleeves and suspenders and bedroom slippers and asked me in. He was thin as a rail. He looked utterly defeated. He led me through the spotlessly neat kitchen and up the stairs to the sitting room, which had now become his study. He offered me a glass of sherry.

The room was spartan in the extreme. No paintings, no radio, no television set, merely an armchair, a few shelves of books, and a desk at the far end looking out over the valley. As he poured me a drink I rose from the armchair and went to the window, though it was not the view that interested me, I was drawn by the cluster of framed photographs he kept on his desk. Most were of Charlie alone, a couple of Charlie with his father. I lifted one to the light. Max appeared at my elbow and gave me my sherry, and together we gazed at his son. I murmured the obvious, that there was no photograph of Stella in evidence.

He sighed. He waved me toward the armchair and turned his desk chair to face me. "No," he said, "no Stella."

I told him I saw no point in beating about the bush and said what it was that I'd come to say. He was only slightly surprised. I know what happens to psychiatrists like Max, men whose lives have gone horribly wrong and for whom their own suffering becomes a source of fascination, every provincial mental hospital has at least one. They continue to function, competently if not energetically, but they are bowed by what seems a great burden of experience, their own and their patients'. They lose all spontaneity and humor and respond to pathology with a sensitivity too acute to permit them any distance from what they see and hear on the wards every day. They blur the line between sickness and sanity and, Christ-like, suffer for all humanity. They can never again be refreshed and they begin to read philosophy, usually of a mystical stripe. This was Max. With an air of gloom and preoccupation he said he presumed Stella was getting on well in the hospital, and I briefly gave him the clinical picture.

He nodded a few times and then sank again into silent frowning reflection. "I think," he said at last, "you must be careful."

Caution acquires great importance for burnt-out cases like Max. "Careful?" I said.

"I hardly dare presume to advise you," he said, and there was a brief, leaden hint of irony in his voice. "You are her doctor, after all. I am merely"—dry cough here—"her husband."

I waited for more. It was slow in coming. It occurred to me that he didn't have long to live. I wondered if he had cancer.

"She brought him into the house, you know."

I said nothing, thinking: if this man were my patient I'd have him on antidepressants.

"She should be in prison."

"You're still very angry, of course."

"Don't patronize me, Peter. I know what I'm talking about. But I suppose"—another dry cough—"we must look after our own."

"Which is what I intend to do."

"You have my blessing. But I warn you."

Another excruciating silence.

"Of what?"

"Perfidy. Mendacity."

He sounded like a Jesuit. But I had what I wanted. I murmured something noncommittal and rose to my feet. But he hadn't finished. He took off his spectacles and began to polish them on his handkerchief. "Not that it matters," he said. "It's Stark you're after."

"They are both in my care."

He glanced up at me but said nothing more.

In the yard he stuck his hands in his pockets and shivered in the wind. He looked up at the sky and said, "One struggles with shame every day. The hardest thing is taking responsibility."

As I drove away he was still standing there, in the wind, with his hands in his pockets, looking up at the sky. I saw clearly what had happened to him. He had turned his punitive tendencies in on himself and was slowly putting himself to death. He had no real interest in Stella anymore.

When I next saw her I told her I was so pleased with her progress that I was thinking of writing to the Home Office about a release date for her; not immediately, of course, but some time in the future. She was guarded in the reaction she showed me, for her pleasure had to be tempered with grief. We talked very much like old friends now. I announced one day that we need not meet on the ward anymore, and the next afternoon she was escorted to my office in the Administration Block. There was no point in keeping her in the dark about my intentions any longer.

I greeted her at the door and told the attendant to come back in an hour. The superintendent's office is the best in the hospital, a large, high-ceilinged room that gives the impression of a chamber in a gentlemen's club, all polished wood and old leather in tones of black, brown, and oxblood. There's a conference table at one end and a big desk at the other, and behind the desk high windows with a deep view over the terraces and the countryside beyond.

Stella drifted around the room and commented on its strong air of male cultivation. The walls were paneled in dark wood and hung with paintings and prints, some the hospital's but most from my own collection. She noticed several pictures familiar to her from my house, and stood before them as though reacquainting herself with old friends.

"You remember this one," I murmured, standing close beside her and indicating a small Italian still life that she'd always loved.

"Oh yes," she said.

She wandered to the bookshelves and found alongside the standard psychiatric texts several shelves of literature. She pulled out a volume of poetry and was leafing through it when she heard a familiar sound, one she had sorely missed in the last weeks, the clink of bottle and glass. She turned and saw me setting a bottle of gin and a couple of glasses on my desk.

"Would you like a drink?"

She stood there with the book in her hands and I could see her rolling the question around in her mind as though it were wine of a good vintage. It was a question to be savored without haste. She smiled.

"Gin and tonic?" I said. "I always have one around this time."

"I should love a gin and tonic, Peter."

"Good."

Nothing was said about the wisdom of giving alcohol to a patient, we behaved as though it were the most natural thing in the world, two civilized people having a drink together in the middle of the afternoon.

"Sit down," I said, waving at the chairs ranged in a semicircle around my desk. She settled into a comfortable wing chair upholstered in maroon leather and I sat beside her, and together we gazed out across the terraces at the large sky with its rags and pillows of driven white cloud. Barely were we settled than the phone rang, and I rather irritably agreed to see someone in an hour. I sat back frowning.

"I shouldn't have taken the job," I said. "Running this place is most definitely not my sort of thing at all."

"I wouldn't have thought it was," she said.

"I'm frankly not very good at it."

"Oh, I'm sure you're perfectly competent," she said, "but

with all the administration you don't do enough psychiatry. You should, you know."

"All the same, I think I might retire."

"Peter!"

"Does that surprise you? I don't see why. I'm not so decrepit that I can't still write. And decide what to do about my garden, which is starting to look positively Russian. Why not?"

"But you must have wanted the job when you applied for it."

She had begun to sense that all this was leading up to something, some kind of dramatic revelation.

"Oh, I think everyone understood that I was merely a stopgap. They all assumed that when Jack went Max would take over. He was the obvious choice."

A pause; she said nothing.

"But no, it was not to be," I said briskly, "so they asked me to look after the place until they could find someone for the long term. I think I've given them enough time. If I stay much longer my anxiety will become chronic. Have you been thinking at all about Max?"

She was willing to talk about Max. She said she wished he could have been direct with her, after Edgar, and told her what he felt. Not behaved in bad faith. Perhaps they could have cleared the air, found a way of living together. Perhaps then Charlie—

Pause here. Drop the head. Lapse into silence. From me, a sort of sympathetic grunt. It was a lovely spring day, sunny and mild, and there was a cool breeze through the open window. A group of patients tramped along the terrace in yellow corduroys and work boots, their jackets slung over their shoulders. Their voices drifted faintly into the room. On the wall my clock ticked. I was being passive, receptive.

"Go on," I murmured.

"Oh, I don't know what I feel now. I wish he'd never met me. Have you talked to Brenda?"

"Yes."

"And?"

"Still deeply distressed, as you can imagine. She's under the care of her own doctor."

"How she must hate me."

"I don't think so. She'll survive, as you will. Tragedy isn't as rare a feature of life as we sometimes imagine."

She managed a small smile. "I'm glad the outlook isn't too bleak."

That small smile told me that now was the moment. I am past sixty. I shall retire soon. I have fifteen good years left, with luck, and I do not want to spend them alone. It had occurred to me some days earlier that after she left the hospital Stella should come and live with me. There were many advantages to such an arrangement, from my point of view. She was a cultured, beautiful woman. She understood how I lived and would find such an existence agreeable. Art, travel, gardening, and books, these were the interests we shared. She would bring light and grace into my quiet house and my measured life. I could see her in those elegant rooms. I felt I could share them with her. We would talk, I would come to know her. Understand her affair with Edgar.

She, in turn, would find comfort with me. Safety. Asylum. I said this to her.

"Asylum?"

She was astonished. She stood up and walked to the far end of the room, leaned against the wall and looked at me as I sat there still gazing out of the window with my back to her. One thing emerged clearly enough from the turmoil and she said it.

"But I'm still married to Max!"

Now I turned in my chair.

"I've been to see Max," I said. "He'll let you go."

"Oh, he will."

I nodded.

Suddenly she found it all hilarious. A romantic proposition from the medical superintendent, with her husband's complicity, what an afternoon she was having. She felt like a consignment of damaged but retrievable womanhood, in the process of being transferred from old owner to new, after being stored for a while in a warehouse. She put her hand over her mouth and stared at me as the laughter silently swept through her and made her shoulders shake. She didn't stop until I led her back to her chair, where she clutched my jacket and pressed her face into my shoulder. After a moment or two she brought herself under control. She let go of my jacket and made use of a handkerchief I produced from my breast pocket. She patted her hair then reached for her drink.

"I must look a sight. Please don't sedate me."

"You don't want anything?"

"I don't need it."

She was working with her compact and lipstick, repairing the damage.

"I must say," she murmured, peering at her face in the little mirror, "you've an unusual way of delivering bad news."

"This is bad news?"

"I mean Max. Letting me go."

She pronounced the words with heavy irony.

"I know you don't love me," I said, "but I think you need me, you do at the moment anyway. I'd be prepared to gamble on that changing. Your affection for me deepening."

Another silence.

I sensed her pity then. The poor man, I imagined her thinking. She smiled slightly. She wasn't taking me altogether seriously. But she behaved herself. She turned her glass in her fingers and gazed at it from lowered eyes as the sun caught the crystal facets and threw off tiny splinters of light. She lifted her eyebrows. She knew I was watching her.

"Are you a very passionate man, Peter?" she murmured.

"I think perhaps that's something we would have to discover," I said gently. I put a faint stress on the "we." I was telling her there would be nothing she didn't choose. She became aware that I was still talking.

"What?"

"You can imagine it, then?" I said.

She wandered down to the bookcase and ran a finger along the spines. I am the woman of sorrows, said her back, I am deep water, I am grief, my soul is torn and bleeding, will you touch the wound? A small silence. He won't do it, she told herself, he won't tear me open; and I didn't. I let the silence continue as she returned to her chair. At last she spoke.

"You'd be taking on rather an injured bird, you know."

"I'm good with injured birds."

"If I married you—"

Oh, and my face, she said, was suddenly suffused with tenderness! What a delightful sight it was, and what good it did her, to see that tenderness! She smiled and put her hand on mine where it lay on the desk. Her eyes searched my face, absorbing every last flickering ember of feeling she had aroused in me.

"When would we do it?"

"July."

"I won't be here?"

I shook my head.

"It would be quiet, wouldn't it?"

"Yes, it would be quiet."

Now she gazed at me with a look that said, If only it were so simple. I read the thought.

"It's perfectly easy."

She pressed my hand.

"Dear Peter," she said, though I suspect she was still thinking, Poor Peter. She sank back into her chair.

"I think," she said, "I'd like to go back to the ward now."

"Of course."

The woman of sorrows followed her routines and kept to herself her astonishing proposal from the medical superintendent. It occurred to her to tell the ladies on the ward, just to see their reaction, but she could guess what they'd say. Marrying the superintendent? Of course you are, dear. And I'm the bride of Christ. My proposal had amused her at first, but I knew she would soon make a complicated calculation of self-interest, and I was confident she would see marriage to me as her best course. I was placing a heavy burden on her, given everything else she was having to deal with, but I believed she was strong enough now to bear it. She was still reluctant to tell me about her dreams but I drew her out without too much difficulty. I knew that just talking them through would bring about the discharge of that first painful freight of guilty feelings.

The screaming child of course was Charlie. When at last she talked about him she said she was aware of forces at work in her that tried to defend her from him, but he was too strong, he came through despite everything. She would sit up in bed with her hands clasped to her face and her mind clearing, but not fast enough to prevent her seeing his fading image, and in one particular recurring dream he gazed back at her and said in a voice she knew so well, his serious voice, the voice that had always been accompanied by a funny little frown, that voice clearly saying, *Mummy, can't you see I'm drowning?*

Those words! They lingered on into the morning, as she followed the fixed routines of ward life, as she washed and dressed and walked down corridors with the other women to the dining room. It was the hardest time of the day, she said, those first hours, when she had to maintain an outward poise and a pretense of serenity as inwardly she reeled from that small, serious voice. Mummy, can't you see I'm drowning? Of course, my precious darling, of course I can see it, I'm coming to help you, don't panic, darling love, Mummy will help you, Mummy won't let you drown! But who did she cry this out to, who could hear her? Nobody; her voice echoed as though trapped in a vault full of shadows, and no answering presence, no warm familiar companion emerging from the darkness to take her hands and comfort her, tell her it was all right, it was only a dream. She may have been awake but it wasn't all right because it wasn't only a dream. Charlie was dead but he lived on in her, crying out in his panicky failure to understand why she wasn't helping him.

She became deeply upset, telling me this, and I comforted her. I have met this before, I told her. Charlie *is* dead, I said, and we can't bring him back, but I can help you. I can relieve this suffering. You are not alone anymore. She said she dreaded going to sleep now, she felt as though she were about to descend a ladder into a cellar where she would meet only horror. This was what the night began to mean to her, a passage into horror. Its shadow lengthened, it clung on longer and longer in the morning, filling the first hours of the day with its foul psychic aftertaste—

Oh, it was a subtle game she played with me. She never saw me in the morning, that was when I attended to my many administrative duties. It wasn't until after lunch that I saw patients, and she freely admitted to me that by that time the voice had faded and her composure was far less precarious. So we talked more calmly about Charlie, and she played down how bad it was, and allowed me to see that she was playing it down, before we moved on to more pleasant discussions about our marriage. Our marriage. It was an idea that clearly still amused her, she smiled whenever I mentioned it, as though I'd made a particularly good joke. Our friendship, at least before all this, had often involved the making of good jokes. This was the best joke of all, though I seemed to be in earnest. I know she had always assumed I was homosexual. Now she must have thought, Perhaps he is, and what he's proposing is more a domestic arrangement with therapeutic implications than a marriage as such. She pictured my house and my garden and I think that even without intending to she began to yearn for it, for it meant peace and sophistication and comfort, and what else did she want? Suddenly she wanted the life I was offering her.

My only concern now was that she not change her mind! I became for the first time in many years troubled with a mild insecurity. I imagined her thinking, Peter every day. Peter at breakfast, lunch, and dinner, every day. Under the same roof, sharing the same rooms, every day. But then I reassured myself, and imagined her realizing that I would surely make daily life a cultivated, amusing affair, for she knew she need not fear some ghastly revelation of grubby habits, petty cruelties, unforeseen rigidities; she knew I was in no sense a shabby man. No, she could live with me. She was less sure about sleeping with me. In that department one was invariably surprised, and rarely pleasantly—

She led me to believe that she could fulfill my expectations of marriage. She led me to believe she could make me happy, and in the process provide herself at least a modicum of contentment, it would not be difficult given the kind of man I was and what I possessed. Comfort makes for decency, she said. She and I both knew what happened to love in squalid surroundings: that love had burned, but oh, with what a ragged, restless flame! Love like that could never be contained by the sort of life she and I contemplated, it was an inferno compared to the small mild lick of civilized warmth she and I intended to nurse. But I thought we were in tacit agreement by now that those large emotions by their very nature tend to blaze freely and then die, having destroyed everything that fed them. In any case it was over now, all that. Or so she led me to believe.

She asked me to increase her nightly medication and I saw how appalled she was when I suggested that she might be better off without any sedation at all, that by suppressing her dreaming she was blocking unconscious material that could usefully be exploited as she came to terms with Charlie's death. I saw the effort it cost her to bite back the exclamation, Nothing is suppressed! Instead she said that her memories were so much with her during the day, she could at least be allowed to forget while she slept.

"As you wish," I said. I did not pursue it, I did not force her. I was not too worried, although of course in retrospect I should have been. But I didn't see just what a difficult performance she was sustaining, in the teeth of an intense and unremitting pain the precise nature of which I had not guessed at; all I saw was guilt. I decided not to increase her nightly medication. I told her she was on quite a high enough dosage as it was.

.   .   .

I didn't see her for several days. July, I had told her; it was now late May. Five or six weeks. She followed her routines, dressing carefully in the morning, visiting the hospital library, taking her book down to the dayroom and reading there by the window unless one of the women wanted to talk to her. She remained composed, distant, courteous, sad.

There is a certain special way people behave toward a patient who is soon to leave the hospital. It's as though she's become something between a patient and a free woman, neither the one thing nor the other. There's an air of quiet celebration, for a patient released is a credit to the staff and cause for hope for other patients. Stella had been in the hospital only a short time but she had diligently maintained her poise and earned general respect. People wished her well and asked her what her plans were. She said she would be living in London with her sister's family. They must have wondered why none of her sister's family had ever come to visit her but nobody said anything. She didn't ask me if I'd told the people at the Home Office about this impending marriage.

Meanwhile she was escorted to my office every afternoon, and for an hour in that large comfortable room she and I would discuss our plans, which soon evolved from the extremely quiet wedding to the honeymoon in Italy, where I intended to show her Florence, which I know well, and Venice, which I know less well. We would travel in late September, we decided, when the weather was mellow and the tourists had gone home. Then we would come back and settle down to a life of civilized companionship. I told her one afternoon that marriage was held to be the answer to the problem of sex, but that I rather thought that marriage, at least as we conceived it, would instead be the answer to the problem of conversation.

And did the prospect of this companionable marriage make her happy, did it promise to answer for her too the problem of conversation? I thought it did, I thought that was what was going on as she sat on the bench overlooking the terraces, wearing her somber clothes and her air of melancholy resignation, and making her heart's calculations.

I continued to look after the hospital, chairing meetings and dealing with paperwork in the morning, attending to my case-load after lunch. Contemplating the prospect of imminent retirement, I began to prepare my patients for my departure. Only one gave me real cause for concern, and this was Edgar. For of course he was in the hospital, I'd seen to that, where else could he go? He'd come to us soon after being picked up in Chester, on his way to Stella, though whether to carry her off or murder her I had not yet been able to establish. I was holding him in a room on the top ward of the Refractory Block, by himself, which may seem punitive but was not.

We have some details of his movements after Stella left Horsey Street, not many, though I hope soon to have more. He returned to the loft and stayed on for three days by himself, working without rest on the head. On the fourth day someone apparently came to see him, we don't know who, and told him that the police were on their way. He fled with a few clothes and books stuffed into a duffel bag, and ironically it was only a few minutes after he had gone, and the police had arrived, that Stella made her appearance. All the contents of the studio were impounded, and I was later invited to come and see if any of it could shed light on the whereabouts of my patient. What most intrigued me was the art he'd made while Stella was there, the batch of drawings and the head itself, all of which he'd left behind.

He then disappears, absorbed, we think, by an underground network of artists and criminals who sheltered and fed him in the following weeks. We believe he moved constantly, from studio to studio, flat to flat, and I have a mental picture of this big, bearded man in a workman's jacket with the collar turned up and his cap pulled low, appearing at people's doors in the middle of the night and being made welcome; though I imagine the wives were uneasy. One report had him in Cornwall, living in a remote cottage near the sea, but my own hunch is that he stayed in London, where he knew his way around. Until, that is, he decided to go north and look for Stella. As for Nick, he was taken in for questioning and then let go with a caution. His father was a judge.

It was April when Edgar was readmitted to the hospital, and since then he had consistently refused to speak to me. I had no wish to leave him languishing in the Refractory Block, but he gave me no choice. It was frankly a nuisance. I needed to give him a thorough psychiatric evaluation and recommend a treatment strategy before passing him on to a new man. I knew he would come around eventually, I'd waited for tougher characters than Edgar, and they'd all softened in the end; but now I didn't have time. So I told him of my engagement to Stella, and I did not employ delicacy. I was blunt, and I was aggressive. I wanted to force a reaction.

We were in a side room off the office at the front of the ward, a bare cell with walls painted green, a single barred window, a heavy, battered table, and a pair of wooden chairs. He was bent over the table, idly fingering a cigarette, rolling it back and forth. He was wearing a hospital shirt and hospital trousers, no belt, no shoelaces. His hair was cropped and the beard had gone. He had lost weight, and he had lost confidence too. He looked young, and oddly vulnerable, like a big unhappy child. I watched him closely. I wanted him not only to start talking to me again, but to give me an indication of his present feelings toward Stella, for I wasn't yet certain why precisely he'd tracked her to Chester. He slowly sat up, and I saw the emotion shift across his features like wind on water, bitterness, amusement, skepticism.

"You?"

It was the first thing he'd said to me since his return.

I nodded. But he would not rise to the bait.

"What do you feel about that?"

He shrugged, shaking his head slightly. I sensed the struggle in him.

"I heard what happened," he said.

I allowed a small silence. Then: "I think she deserves a little happiness, given what she's been through," I said, "don't you?"

There was a sardonic twist to his lips.

"Answer the question, Edgar."

Now he bit.

"You answer the question, *Peter*. The question is, What would she want with an old queen like you?"

I concealed my satisfaction.

"You resent it, then? The idea she could love someone else."

"She wants to get out of here."

I paused. Naturally it had occurred to me too.

"So you still love her."

"She's an animal."

This I had not been expecting.

"How so?" I murmured.

"You don't know her at all, do you?"

"You do?"

He didn't answer. He'd hunched over the table again, not meeting my eye, gazing at the unlit cigarette as he rolled it about.

"Should I remind you what you do to women when you think you know them?"

I sat across from this murderer as he straightened up in his chair and left the cigarette alone. There was an attendant just outside the door, in case he went for me.

He had cut Ruth Stark's head off and stuck it on his sculpture stand. Then he'd worked it with his tools as though it were a lump of damp clay. The eyes went first. One of the policemen told me it was like something out of a butcher's shop. You wouldn't know what it was, but for the teeth, and a few clumps of matted hair.

It could have been Stella. It very nearly was.

That evening I returned to my office when the hospital was quiet to ponder our talk. He had expressed only cynicism and contempt toward Stella, but I was not convinced. Edgar was a complicated man, and he was more than usually adept at concealing his true state of mind. I considered it quite possible for him to call Stella an animal but think her a goddess: he had no reason to be honest with me, considering I not only controlled his fate but was about to marry the woman he had once loved and quite possibly still did; after his fashion. But if he did still love her, would he tell me she was an animal?

If he wanted to shatter the image I had of her, and replace it with one of his own making, yes.

I went back the following afternoon. I had a word with the attendants before he was brought down from the ward, and to my surprise he'd had a quiet night. I'd expected to hear that he'd smashed up his room, or gone for someone on the corridor, but he'd done nothing out of the ordinary, and for a second I wondered if he genuinely didn't care what Stella did. But no, all my instincts told me that he cared very deeply indeed. It is of course a clinical commonplace that love and hate closely coexist in the psychic economy. What I wanted to know was to which pole Edgar was gravitating, and to what extent his feelings were pathological.

They brought him up to the front of the ward, and he was dressed as before in hospital grays. He'd been shaved, though not very expertly, there was a nick on his leathery cheek crusted with dried blood. His attitude was as detached as before. When we were alone I offered him a cigarette, which he tucked behind his ear. I came straight to the point.

"Why is she an animal?"

"What made her an animal, or how do I know?"

"How do you know?"

He gazed straight at me. Behind his eyes I saw the seething turmoil of sick thoughts and sane ones. A sick thought emerged.

"I could smell it."

This I had not heard before.

"What could you smell?"

"Rutting. They were always at it. She was the same with me out there in the garden. Always in heat."

"Who was always at it?"

"Nick and her."

"Nick!"

She had been candid with me about Nick. She had allowed him into her bed only once, and that was in the hotel. Edgar was watching me now with an expression of gloating disgust. Was I seeing it again, that spontaneous reorganization of experience to make it conform to a subsequent delusional production? Wasn't this precisely what he'd done to his memories of Ruth Stark, hadn't he inferred a pattern of promiscuity in her, too, that didn't exist? We regarded each other carefully.

"Wasn't that what you said about Ruth?"

"She was a whore. Stella, she'll do it with anyone for nothing."

I couldn't help thinking, with a pang of unease, about Trevor Williams. I covered my mouth with my hand and watched him for a few seconds. He hated her, all right. He hated her and he was as sick as ever, and I felt desperately sorry for him, sorry that everything he felt and thought about Stella was contaminated by this foul falseness.

As I left the room I heard him quietly humming. Then, just as the door closed, he cried: "Cleave!"

I came back in and waited with my hand on the door.

"Well?"

He stood up and I thought he might be about to attack me. But it was gone, the insolence, the bitterness. Now just a desperate sincerity as in a low hoarse voice and in a tone of utter reasonableness he made his plea.

"Let me see her."

I was astonished.

"What harm can it do? Just for five minutes."

He had almost succeeded in making me believe he hated her. But he couldn't sustain it. I regarded the poor sick doubled creature before me and felt a great surge of protective tenderness for him. Whatever it was that Stella had given him, he was far too fragile now to live without it.

"No."

.   .   .

She began to hear talk on the ward of the dance. She was asked if she would be going. Her first reaction was to recoil from the suggestion. For weeks she had struggled to sustain an image of herself, despite the humiliation of her change of status from doctor's wife to patient, and it had not been easy; she was frequently aware of veiled contempt from both patients and staff, particularly as she obviously enjoyed special favor with the superintendent. No one had insulted her directly, a tribute, she thought, to her successful incarnation as the woman of sorrows; but to play the woman of sorrows at the hospital dance, this was a performance she did not relish. For she was not at all confident of her ability to behave with serenity in the Central Hall, it would be just too brutally exposed, the fissure in her life. The unavoidable conclusion, the glaring moral of the story, would be that this was just another fallen woman, and a pathetic creature at that. She didn't want that.

But then the familiar dilemma arose, the murmuring inner voice that reminded her of the delicate politics of her situation. Would it matter to me? I was still her psychiatrist. Dare she risk an act of nonconformity? Dare she stay away? There was no knowing, and it made her anxious having to think it through. Oh, but a woman planning her honeymoon in Italy does not quail before the prospect of a hospital dance! And it occurred to her then that this might be the last real challenge she faced in her short career as a mental patient. Well then, face it she would, she would give a last performance as the woman of sorrows.

So she steeled herself for the ordeal and began to consider her wardrobe, her makeup, her hair. She would not be seen as the fallen woman even if the eyes of the entire hospital were on her.

By my calculation it would have been that night or the next that instead of swallowing her medication she held the pills in her palm, and later hid them, probably at the back of her cupboard, perhaps tucked into the lining of a brassiere. Parole patients are trusted and we do not expect them to hoard their medication, which is why they are permitted a degree of privacy. At dawn I imagine her standing in her nightgown staring out of the window at the courtyard below and watching the first light bringing up the tones and textures of the bricks. It must have somehow become clear to her that nothing would ever change, that neither psychiatry nor the passage of time would obliterate what she'd seen that morning on Cledwyn Heath, the head breaking the surface, the clawing arm.

But whose head? Whose clawing arm?

Shadows shifted in the courtyard. The sun was rising.

I immediately knew something was wrong and I was concerned. She had been brought across from the female wing as usual, and no sooner was she in my office and the door closed behind her than I was peering at her closely.

"What's happened?" I said, taking her arm and leading her to a chair. I sat down beside her.

She didn't want me to suspect anything out of the ordinary.

"Nothing's happened. What could have happened?"

She managed to get some humor into this, as if to say, We both know how eventful life can be in the female wing. Still I frowned at her. I was being the doctor now.

"I don't like the look of you. Are you dreaming again?"

She had told me a few days before that the dreams were far less vivid now, and far less frequent.

"I wake early and then I can't get back to sleep."

"I don't want to increase your medication," I said. "I don't think you want that either, do you? You don't want to be in a stupor all day."

"The medication's fine, Peter, really it is. I always wake up early in the summertime. I don't suppose there's been anything from the Home Office?"

I shuffled through the papers on my desk. It didn't escape

me that she was attempting to steer the conversation away from herself. "Apparently we'll hear something by the end of the week." I looked up. "Is it an awful strain, my darling?"

"One can't help feeling anxious."

"Please don't worry. They'd tell me if there was a problem. Are you looking forward to your new life?"

She put her hand on my arm. "Of course I am," she said.

I regarded this sad, beautiful woman and thought of Max, broken Max, solemnly intoning, Perfidy, mendacity. No, it was absurd, and I dismissed the thought.

She never caused the night staff any concern. She dared not, for any disturbance would alert them to the fact that she was unmedicated. Her sleeping body never betrayed her. She was never shaken awake by an attendant, so she had to assume she appeared to be sleeping soundly. By day the woman of sorrows, by night the dreamless sleeper; in these last days, as she would have started thinking of them, the days before the dance, she was performing all the time, hers was a total performance, with no chance ever to peel off the mask and unfasten the costume, let it fall to the floor and step out of it.

The women around her grew daily more excitable. The dance was of vital importance to the patients of the female wing. What bustle there was! She made small jokes about it. I of course had attended more hospital dances than I cared to remember and smiled as I thought of the tide of suppressed hysteria that swept the female wing in the days before the great event.

"And it's a full moon," I said.

"Oh dear," she said, "that's very bad."

"Actually it's not. What is bad is the morning after. Such an anticlimax. A lot of you ladies are rather depressed the day after a dance."

"I shall have to be on my guard."

"Oh, I don't think I'm worried about you. In fact you don't

have to go if you'd rather not. I'd understand perfectly if you didn't."

"I wouldn't hear of it," she said. "Not go to the dance? How very antisocial."

"You'll be much looked at and commented on. You know that, don't you?"

"Yes I do," she said.

As she was being escorted back along the terrace to the ward she must have realized that her worries were needless after all. But having decided for diplomatic reasons to attend the dance, she had begun in an odd way to look forward to it. For she had decided, I believe, to let what happened there determine her fate.

The female patients were all in their places in the Central Hall before the men were brought in. For the last few hours the atmosphere on the ward had grown steadily more feverish till it reached a pitch of anticipation that could only end in disappointment. Frantic women in all states of undress roamed the corridor in search of hairpins, perfume, underwear, makeup. A squabble over a cheap brooch would have come to scratches but for the intervention of an attendant. There were screams, there were tears, there was much silly chatter from the younger women about boyfriends and love affairs. The more mature women tried to stay calm but it was difficult to ignore the mood sweeping the ward and growing steadily more frenzied as seven o'clock approached.

Stella stayed in her room and dressed carefully. The smart clothes she had brought with her from Wales were too tight on her now; not precisely woman-of-sorrows, they suggested sin, rather, but then how was a woman to come by her sorrows if she knew nothing of sin? She again counted her pills. She was calm now. She had, she thought, enough.

When she left her room and joined the other women on the ward her appearance had a dramatic effect. They realized immediately that she was by far the loveliest among them. They were proud of her, and intended to enjoy a reflected glory when they entered the Hall, or rather, when the men came in. They left the ward rather quietly, given the cacophony of a few minutes ago. The awful majesty of the evening was brought home to every woman there.

Escorted by their attendants they made their way across the courtyard and along the passage to the gate that gave onto the terrace. The evening was warm and the light was just beginning to thicken in the scented air. Women whispered to one another, the last anxieties were voiced, as a slowly swelling pride in their collective womanhood and their one true flower of beauty grew in all hearts. Stella was their flower of beauty, as she moved calmly among them with a loose black shawl thrown over her bare arms and shoulders against the evening air. The woman of sorrows, among her handmaidens, was making her farewell appearance.

The Central Hall was as she remembered it. Chairs were placed around the walls, the big bay windows were thrown open to the evening, and the band was tuning up on the stage. A few attendants were waiting for the women, and as they entered I came in from the terrace with the chaplain. I acknowledged her immediately with a bow, and then I saw what she was wearing. I stood there, as did the chaplain, and we gazed at her with astonishment. Then, as it dawned on me what she'd done, and what it must have cost her, I slowly nodded. For under the shawl it was the same dress, the same black evening dress of coarse ribbed silk, cut low at the front to reveal the curve of her breast, that she'd worn to the dance a year ago. The effect of it was more dramatic than it had been even then: not only did the dress complement her extraordinary physical beauty, but the very wearing of it, here, tonight, was the gesture of a spirit unbroken by shame. I felt proud of her.

She settled down and watched the bustle around her, the attendants moving back and forth, conferring with one another, and the more restless of the young women already over at the table for their soft drinks; and the senior staff talking and laughing with exaggerated ease like the aristocracy they were. It was all a sham. Not one of them could think of anything but that she had been one of their number just a year ago, and the covert glances cast her way were numerous. That she should choose to wear that dress—! I had no recourse to covert glances. I made it clear that I was watching over her with affection and solicitude. My calm eye oversaw everything and missed nothing, and Stella was not disturbed. The propriety and order of the event were a direct effect of my presence, my quiet authority, and the deference I enjoyed from patients and staff alike.

Time passed, and beneath her composure she grew tense. She saw the men coming in and felt the atmosphere change, felt it grow charged and slightly dangerous. The aristocrats were less languid now, the attendants more attentive. As for the women of the female wing, they grew very alert indeed. The band had already gone into its first number as the last of the men's wards were escorted into the Hall. They filed in and took their places, and Edgar was not among them.

No, Edgar was not among them, he was in no condition to attend a dance.

She danced several times over the course of the evening and although the eyes of the entire Hall were upon her not once did the mask slip. She didn't dance with me; I danced with no one; but she caught my eye each time she did dance, and I understood that her demure, inscrutable smile was directed at me, that in a way it was with me that she danced. The chaplain alone of all the senior staff asked her out onto the floor. He danced well and allowed her to move with ease and grace in his arms. The glimpses she had of my face, the fleeting instants when our eyes met, all reassured her that she was carrying it off beautifully, that she appeared exactly as I wished her to appear. Poor Peter, she must have thought.

Toward the end of the evening I went onto the stage and stood at the microphone and said a few benign words and made

a joke or two, as was customary. I am a popular medical superintendent, and the blessing I bestowed was warmly received.
Stella watched me, not listening to my words, just absorbing the
presence I conveyed that night, my patrician ease, my warm,
wise humor. I believe she genuinely hated the prospect of caus-
ing me pain.

She sat out the last dance and joined the other women when
it was time to go back. They made their way in the moonlight
along the terrace to the female wing. There was some excited
chatter but mostly they were quiet, and a sort of tired satisfaction seemed to be the mood. All agreed it had been a good
dance, perhaps the best for years, and while some romances had
been cruelly crushed out others had sprung to life. On the ward
they fondly said good night to one another and went to their
rooms.

Stella prepared for bed. The lights were turned out and the
ward was silent. A little later she quietly got out of bed and
turned on the cold tap and let the water run into the basin.
Then she opened her cupboard and reached in.

I was sitting in my office writing. Outside my window the terrace and the gardens and the marsh beyond were bathed in
moonlight. I paused and looked up, frowning. Something had
been nagging at me since I'd seen Stella in the Central Hall, a
vaguely disquieting feeling I'd suppressed until now, something
connected to her wearing the dress she'd worn the night Edgar
had taken her in his arms and pressed his penis into her groin.
Absurd to think she could still be in love with him! And then I
thought: but what if I'm right? And that's when I saw it. That's
when it all became clear, and at last I knew that it was not dead,
that it was far from dead, and I understood why she had worn
the black silk dress.

Now I was alarmed. I capped my pen and reached for the
telephone. I dialed an internal number and a telephone rang in
the front office of a downstairs ward in the female wing. Oh, I
had been blind! It was not for us, that dress, it was not a gesture

of pride, or defiance, thrown in the face of the hospital community, it was for *him*, she'd worn it for *him*, it was her wedding dress, she'd worn it the night she became wedded to him, and as I waited for the phone to be picked up I at last realized the full extent to which I'd deluded myself: I had allowed my judgment to be clouded by private concerns, and in the process lost my objectivity. Classic countertransference—

The attendant on duty spoke to me briefly. Without replacing the receiver she left the office and went along the corridor to Stella's room. She opened it a crack and saw that the bed was occupied and its occupant asleep and breathing deeply. She closed the door and returned to the office and told me what she'd seen. I thanked her and replaced the receiver. I did not resume writing, however, instead I stood gazing out of the window, still profoundly uneasy.

Rapidly I reviewed the events of the last weeks. I remembered the flare of feeling I'd seen in her eyes the day I'd suggested he was here in the hospital. I imagined how it might have affected her, this fragile kindling of hope, and realized that when I'd then said that it was hypothetical, that he wasn't here, the feeling wouldn't have been extinguished, that once aroused it was too strong to be snuffed out with a word. I imagined her returning to her room and breathing on that small flame of hope, keeping it burning.

She had kept it burning ever since. Oh, she would have quickly worked out why I should first tell her the truth, that is, that Edgar *was* here, and then regret telling her, and contradict myself, and she'd have realized too that for me a measure of her mental health would be her indifference to the mention of the name Edgar Stark. She'd have known then that she must pretend not to care. Everything that followed—asking for a job in the laundry, sitting alone on her bench—*even the dreams of a screaming child*—all a performance, a distraction, invented to keep me from the truth. And the truth was that her suffering these last weeks was not remorse for the death of her child, the truth was that she was still obsessed with Edgar Stark, to the virtual exclusion of everything else.

Yes, even the dreams of a screaming child, for it was not her child who disturbed her nights, it was him, it was Edgar! And her engagement to me, that too a masquerade, the desperate duplicity of a woman still passionately in love with another man and frantic to conceal it—

I found I was pacing the floor, my mind ablaze with this new truth, and with an effort I brought myself under control and sat down at my desk. And then I thought, If she believed he was here, and she wore the dress for him, and he didn't appear, how would she react to that? And I knew then what my psychiatric intuition was telling me, and why I'd been feeling so uneasy. If she couldn't have Edgar then she might as well be dead. Life was no longer tolerable without him. Better to die than suffer this way. This response is rare, but it happens. It is the last stage of all.

A few minutes later I was moving along the terrace in the direction of the female wing. My pace quickened and soon I was striding with some urgency through the shadowy cloisters and moonlit courtyards of the sleeping hospital.

Through the long hours of the night we fought to save her, but Stella had been among psychiatrists quite long enough to gauge with precision a fatal dose of sedatives. She didn't regain consciousness and shortly before dawn she died. As she relaxed, as she let go all effort of deception and repression, her face changed, her beauty became even more remarkable, and once again she was as pale and lovely as when we'd first known her. Everyone was distressed. I reminded them that those who wish to die will always find the means, sooner or later, but it was no real comfort to those of us who had been looking after her and had come in our own ways to love her. We buried her in the hospital cemetery three days later, outside the Wall, behind the female wing, and the chaplain conducted the service. There were not many mourners present, apart from staff. It was a hot, bright day and we were all uncomfortable in black.

The Straffens sent their regrets, apparently Jack's health is not good, but Max came, and so did Brenda. Max had changed dramatically even in the few weeks since I'd seen him in Cledwyn. He was more than ever like an old man, thin, stooped, with skin like paper. He clung to his mother for support. She was strong, as I'd expected she would be; Brenda is good at tragedy. Afterward I gave them a glass of sherry in my office. If Max was conscious of the poignancy and irony of his presence in my office, the superintendent's office, that day, he didn't show it. Brenda surprised me by resorting to unctuous platitudes. She murmured that she hoped that Stella was at peace now. I nodded and turned away, slightly disgusted at her vulgarity. Max clearly had not told her of our marriage plans.

I have not retired as I planned to. I still have work to do. Edgar remains on the top ward in the Refractory Block. No appreciable improvement in his attitude yet, he remains hostile and uncooperative, but that will change, already I sense him weakening; he must know that I am all he has now. I have not told him that Stella is dead, for I am eager to hear his side of the story first. There are many questions still to be answered. Max, for one, is still convinced that his clothes were not stolen on impulse, as Stella said, but that she gave them to Edgar, in other words that she was acting against us even then, and knew he intended to escape.

On reflection, Edgar will hear of her death whatever I do; if he hasn't already. This is a large institution, and people talk. His suffering will be acute, and we will have to be vigilant. Like me, like all of us who knew her, he responded strongly to Stella's beauty, but he went deeper than the rest of us, he idealized her and then had to struggle against the chaos of his own passions when the image he'd created could no longer be sustained. I think perhaps it's what he was unconsciously trying to get at in his last sculpture, despite his claim to be engaged in an attempt to overthrow habit and convention in seeing, to be working against certainty. I feel for those two poor disordered souls, trapped here these last weeks, twisting in their private hells, each aching for the other. I have known more than a few of these destructive affairs, and they all come to this, or something like this, in the end.

I have resumed my habit of returning to the office in the evening. The police were most accommodating, and I now possess all the drawings he made of her in the studio, and also the sketch done in the vegetable garden. They are curiously tentative in outline and feature, and as a result have a sort of softness to the eye, what the Italians call *morbidezza*. I also have the head. I have had it fired and cast in black bronze. I keep it in a drawer in my desk. He worked so obsessively at it, those last days before he left Horsey Street, and he so worked it *down*, that it became slender and tiny in the end. It is a thin, beautiful, tiny, anguished head now, no bigger than my hand; but it is her. I often take it out, over the course of the day, and admire it. So you see, I do have my Stella after all.

And I still, of course, have him.

ABOUT THE AUTHOR

PATRICK MCGRATH was born in London and grew up near Broadmoor Hospital, where for many years his father was medical superintendent. He has lived in various parts of North America and spent several years on a remote island in the North Pacific. He moved to New York City in 1981. He is the author of *Blood and Water and Other Tales*, *The Grotesque*, *Spider*, and *Dr. Haggard's Disease*, and is coeditor, with Bradford Morrow, of *The New Gothic*. He now lives in New York and London and is married to the actress Maria Aitken.

ABOUT THE TYPE

This book was set in Berling. Designed in 1951 by Karl Erik Forsberg for the Typefoundry Berlingska Stilgjuteri AB in Lund, Sweden, it was released the same year in foundry type by H. Berthold AG. A classic old-face design, its generous proportions and inclined serifs make it highly legible.